FIRETRAP

ALSO BY OTHO ESKIN

The Reflecting Pool

Head Shot

FIRETRAP

A MARKO ZORN NOVEL

OTHO ESKIN

OCEANVIEW PUBLISHING
SARASOTA, FLORIDA

ISBN 978-1-60809-570-4

Published in the United States of America by Oceanview Publishing

Sarasota, Florida

www.oceanviewpub.com

10 9 8 7 6 5 4 3 2 1

ACKNOWLEDGEMENTS

I would like to thank my literary agent, Judith Ehrlich, for her constant support, superb literary advice, and invaluable creative guidance. Thanks also to Meg Gilbert, my multitalented assistant; Sean Dugan for his expert help with marketing and promotion; Ludovica Villar-Hauser, for her steadfast encouragement; and my publishers, Pat and Bob Gussin and the rest of the Oceanview team for their ongoing enthusiasm and fine support of my literary endeavors. Additional appreciation goes to Laura Apgar for her skilled and insightful editorial input, and to Erica Ferguson for her careful copyediting. Finally, my deepest gratitude to Therese, who has always been my biggest fan.

FIRETRAP

CHAPTER ONE

THE CAR, ONCE a Ford Explorer, is a roaring inferno.

I park my MG convertible in a No Parking zone, put my Police placard on the windshield, and get out to investigate. First responders, in full firefighting gear, are covering the burning car with white foam. I feel chilly. It's cold for an April day in Washington, and there's a slight breeze. I push my hands into my pockets to keep my fingers warm. Three DC fire trucks and a rescue vehicle form barricades at both ends of the block to keep curious onlookers away. A sudden gust of wind swirls the smoke into my face, heavy with the acrid smell of gas and burning rubber. My eyes sting. In the distance, more fire trucks are racing toward the fire, sirens wailing.

Watching the inferno is a woman I've met before—a DC fire department captain named Claudia Collins.

I show her my badge. "Marko Zorn. DC Police. We got a call from you folks saying you had a homicide. This looks more like a car fire to me."

"Wait till you see what's inside."

I follow Captain Collins so we're both looking through the driver's-side window, staying far from the scorching flames. Even at this distance, the heat is intense. Captain Collins's face is pale and drawn. In my experience, firefighters are stoic and have nerves of steel. But today, this woman has seen something so awful it's beyond imagining.

"What am I looking at?" I ask.

Collins points at the car. "There. In the front seat, you can see a man in there—on fire. Or, at least, I think it's a man. Maybe it's a woman. Who knows? Anyway, it's on fire."

I peer through the flames, smoke, and the air that pulses with heat to make out the form of what I think was once a human being. The corpse is turning black before my eyes.

"We got multiple calls this morning reporting a car fire," Captain Collins tells me. "When my crew and I arrived at the scene, the vehicle and victim were already engulfed in flames. There was nothing we could do."

I scan the crowd bunched at the far ends of the block. They're all staring at the burning car with fascinated horror. Except one man, tall and muscular, with a stiff, military posture and spiky white-blond hair. He's not looking at the burning car. He's looking at me. When he sees me observe him, he turns quickly away and disappears into the crowd. There's something about him that bothers me, but I can't put my finger on what. Why is he not looking at the burning car like everyone else? He's gone now. No use worrying about it.

"Did you try to get the victim out?" I ask the fire captain.

"Of course! We couldn't manage it. The doors are all locked, probably by one of those electric keys. We tried to break through the windows. Even though we have tools for that sort of thing, it was impossible. We didn't have time. In situations like this, the gas tank can explode."

A large truck pulls up, and half a dozen more men, dressed in heavy protective gear and face coverings, pile out of the truck and unload thick, black hoses.

"How long will it take for you to put out the fire?" I ask. "My people will need to examine the body."

"We'll suppress the fire in a couple of minutes," the chief tells me. "But you won't be able to get into the car for at least another half hour. The vehicle will be too hot to touch. You got to give it time to cool down. Then this mess is all yours, Detective. You'll have to share it with our arson team."

"You think it's arson?"

"I know it's arson."

I have a major crime on my hands now. This is going to ruin my weekend. I call headquarters and direct that the medical examiner and forensics teams come to the crime scene.

We're on a residential street of single-family, redbrick row houses with tin roofs and wooden shutters. The buildings are probably around fifty to one hundred years old. Some are derelict with broken windows, doors covered by sheets of plywood, shutters missing or hanging loose, and front yards full of weeds and trash. Other buildings have been well maintained, their front lawns cared for—some even have small flower beds.

I don't know this street. Washington is two cities. One, the city of grand monuments and museums, broad boulevards, and majestic government buildings. The other, the city of crime and fear. The dome of the United States Capitol building gleams in the morning sunlight over the rooftops just a few blocks away from where I'm standing. We're in one of the poorer, more dangerous, and desperate parts of Washington. It's often the site of drug dealing, gang warfare, and shootings. This is not a part of town I visit unless I'm on official police business. Then it's always bad news.

This burning car is not gang warfare, though. I'm sure of that. This is something worse.

I call my partner, Tyrone Clifford, and ask him to check Robbery to see if a black two-door Ford Explorer has been reported stolen or missing. Then I tell him to come to the crime scene. I'm a little reluctant to bring Tyrone into the investigation, but it's a mess and I'm going to need help. And, despite everything, Tyrone is very good at police work.

The fire captain and I stand silently and watch while the firefighters cover the Explorer with more white foam, making the wreck look like a gigantic cream pastry.

"Did you ever see anything like this?"

She shakes her head. "Never. And I hope never to see anything like it again. That's a single car in flames, and that's not supposed to happen. The interior's on fire—not just the exterior. That couldn't be unless somebody drenched the victim with gas and then ignited it. And the victim . . ." She's having a hard time speaking.

I know how she feels. I've seen a lot of violent deaths in my time as a homicide detective, but it's usually death by gun or knife or baseball bat. Burning a man to death is a new one for me.

"Did you get a look at the victim's face at all?" I ask. "White? Black? Young? Old?"

"What face?" Collins demands. "By the time we got here, there was no face left. It had melted away."

"Are you Detective Marko Zorn?" a voice from immediately behind me asks in a deep, rumbling baritone.

A question like that might be a prelude to asking where the nearest grocery store is located. Or it might be a prelude to a man drawing a six-inch knife and driving it into my chest. In this part of Washington, all bets are off.

Someone once told me that when you're face-to-face with a possible assailant, just look into their eyes and you can tell whether he means to kill you. I've never found that to be helpful advice. People who say things like that have never been in a knife fight.

The baritone voice asking me the question belongs to a large Black man who must be six three and weigh in at around two hundred and fifty pounds of muscle. He wears a brown felt porkpie hat. His arms are covered by old razor scars. Next to his right eye is a tattoo with five silver dots: four making a square pattern, the fifth inside the square. His neck and his throat are covered with other tattoos, some of which I recognize as gang and prison tags. The man is about fifty and looks like someone who was once a serious brawler. His tone of voice is courteous, though, and soft-spoken. He doesn't look like he intends to kill me. Can you really tell by looking into a man's eyes? I'll take my chances.

"Sure. I'm Marko Zorn. What can I do for you?"

"Sister Grace wants to talk to you."

Now that comes as a shock. I know I'm in that part of Washington that belongs to Sister Grace, and I wonder for a moment if she had anything to do with the car burning behind me. I dismiss the idea. It's not her style.

"I'm involved in an investigation just now." I point toward the heap that was once a car and is now a Viking funeral. "Can Sister Grace wait until tomorrow?"

"Sorry. Gotta be now. This is a serious emergency. It can't wait. She impatient, know what I mean?"

The big man shoots me a cheerful, ingratiating smile. It's the smile of a man who shares a silent bond with me. We both know how Sister Grace is.

"She says it'll take only a few minutes to tell you what you gotta do. Unless you try to argue with her, which I don' recommend at all."

"How did you know I was in the neighborhood?" I ask.

"Sister Grace knows ever'thing that happens in her territory."

"What's your name?"

"My name is Stryker."

"Good to meet you, Stryker. Take me to Sister Grace."

CHAPTER TWO

STRYKER AND I go through a room where Sister Grace's security is stationed. I'm normally checked by her enforcers for weapons or a wire, but not today. There's no time for that. Everybody's in a hurry to get me in to see Sister Grace. And everybody is nervous. I really don't like to be surrounded by a group of nervous, heavily armed men. Stryker leads me immediately into the parlor, a room I know too well.

It's a cozy space furnished with worn, somewhat faded 1950s furniture. There's a floral chintz-covered sofa, several large, over-stuffed armchairs with poofy cushions embroidered with images of cats, and two side tables each decorated with a vase filled with African violets.

A faint smell of lavender mixed with Marlboro cigarette smoke lingers in the air. There are no windows—the only light comes from two floor lamps placed on either end of the sofa. A picture on one wall shows Jesus Christ surrounded by adoring children. The room is furnished to be welcoming. I never feel welcome. Or safe. I feel trapped, with a strong desire to be somewhere else. Anywhere else.

This room is the most dangerous place in Washington, DC. And home to the most dangerous woman in Washington. That's saying a lot.

A tiny Black woman sitting on the sofa summons for me to approach. "Good morning, Detective Zorn," she croaks. "We need to talk."

I look around for the mangy cat she usually holds in her lap but see no sign of him, or her, assuming the thing has a gender. I suppose it's gone to its final reward, like so many of Sister Grace's associates.

Stryker stands watching me carefully, his back to the door, his porkpie hat clutched in his left fist. He's bareheaded to show respect for the lady. His presence is unusual. Normally, Sister Grace insists exchanges between us be strictly private. This isn't the only change in our meeting today. The security outside Sister Grace's building is the highest I've ever seen. She always has gunmen in and around her building, but today there's double the usual number. Cars are parked around the block filled with armed men. More men are patrolling the rooftop. All of them carry walkie-talkies. Sister Grace's people are seriously spooked. Something bad is going down.

"Take a seat, Detective," the old woman directs.

I sit in one of the armchairs across from her. She seems smaller and even more dried up than the last time I saw her. She wears, as always, a cotton ankle-length housedress with a delicate white-lace collar at her throat. Her white hair is cut short. She looks worried. That's not like her.

Sister Grace picks up a crumpled pack of Marlboro cigarettes, and I lean forward to offer her a light with the cigarette lighter I always carry with me. She takes it from my hand, flicks it, and lights her cigarette. Then she examines the lighter, turning it slowly in her fingers.

She coughs. "It's very pretty." She reads the inscription. "As I recall, this has some sentimental value for you."

She's always been curious about that lighter, but I don't talk about it with strangers. And, in matters concerning my private life, Sister Grace is very much a stranger.

"You always use this when you smoke?" she asks.

"I've given up smoking."

"Why you carry this around, then?" She passes the lighter back to me. "I want you to do somethin' for me, Detective Zorn."

Her voice is husky. Age, I wonder, or fear?

"I'm havin' serious trouble. I want you to fix it."

For as long as I can remember, Sister Grace has ruled this part of Washington with an iron fist. This is her territory, and she's never faced trouble she couldn't handle. Except, of course, for the time she had to call me in for help. But that was a family affair. I fixed the problem, although not in the way she expected. Had I refused, I would have ended up roadkill. You do not argue with Sister Grace.

She drags on her cigarette and silently studies the burning end for a long minute. I wonder whether she's getting senile and has forgotten why she sent for me. I glance at Stryker, but he seems unconcerned by Sister Grace's silence.

"It's drugs, Detective," she says at long last.

I was not expecting *that* at all. Her organization has been dealing drugs in the Washington area for decades. She's never shown any qualms about drugs before.

"You mean you have competition?" I ask.

"I always have competition. I can take care of anybody who gets in my way."

"What's different this time?"

"Speedball."

"Come again?"

"You heard me correct, Detective. 'Speedball.' A new drug is in town. Some call it 'Greenies.' Some call it 'Jellybeans.' Most call it 'Speedball.' I want you to stop it."

"What's different about Speedball from the other drugs circulating in the city?"

"I'll tell you what's different—this is the most powerful damn drug I ever seen. You take it an' you stop breathin'. That a fact, Stryker?"

"Yes, Sister Grace. Worse'n anything I ever seen, even in the joint."

"What do you expect me to do?" I ask.

"Stop Speedball! Stop the dealers. It's killing my people. And sooner or later, your people, too."

"That's not my job."

"Why, bless your heart, Detective, it's your job if I say it's your job."

"You have muscle on your payroll who can do that. They can run the dealers out of town. You do it all the time."

"These are new people. Not the usual thugs. They're organized. And heavily armed. And mean as hell."

"I've never seen a group you couldn't handle."

"Don't think I haven't tried. Tell him, Stryker."

"We've sent some of our best men to close down this Speedball market. Want to know what happened to them? They ended up dead. The dealers have heavy protection. Some kind of international security organization with trained operatives. They don't allow anybody to interfere in their business. Includin' Sister Grace. And they ain't shy about killin' people. I talked to the local dealer myself. Tol' him to leave town. I thought I was gonna die that day."

"It rubs me the wrong way to ask a cop to take care of my problem," Sister Grace says, stubbing out her cigarette. "It don't sit right one bit. I been tryin' for weeks to take care of this mess myself. Now they after me. It's personal. I'm in trouble. That's what you do, Detective—you take care of trouble. You think I'm exaggeratin'. But I'm dead serious," she says. "Stryker, you tell this policeman about Muffin."

I wonder for a moment whether "Muffin" is one of Sister Grace's enforcers. I doubt it.

"Three days ago, Muffin got out of the building," Stryker tells me. "We searched ever'where. Muffin was gone all day and night. Sister Grace made us all pray for Muffin. I was on my knees for that damn cat."

"Watch your language, Stryker," Sister Grace snaps.

"Then yesterday, some kid delivers a box. It was wrapped in brown paper, and somebody wrote the name 'Sister Grace' on the outside. An' the word 'Personal.'"

Sister Grace's hands are clenched as she listens.

"Muffin was cut into little pieces," Stryker says. "Head. Paws. Legs. It was disgustin'."

"Muffin was my life companion," Sister Grace says. "She was my best friend."

That settles the gender question.

"There was a note with what was left of Muffin," Stryker goes on. "'Tell the bitch to stay out of our business or she'll end up like the cat.' That's no way to treat a lady."

Muffin and I never liked each other, but some words of sympathy seem called for, so I say, "Sorry for your loss, Sister Grace."

She gives me a sour look.

"I'll contact the drug division in the police department," I offer. "I'll report this new drug infestation."

"Don' bother. Your drug cops know all about Speedball. They either too scared or too bent to do anythin'."

I never argue with Sister Grace about something like this. She knows more about police corruption than I do.

"I'll inform the Drug Enforcement Administration . . ."

"They already know about what's goin' on. We seen their guys in the neighborhood askin' 'round. They done nothin'. That's why I sent for you. You have special ways to deal with scum. Ways regular cops can't."

"You want me to kill the man distributing these drugs? You know I don't do that."

"Do whatever you gotta do. Just get this poison outta my community. Understand, Detective, this ain't just my problem. This gonna be your problem real soon. Ain't just Black folks gettin' sick and dyin' from Speedball. It startin' in the clubs on U Street. Now it's spreadin' to the bars on Fourteenth Street and around Dupont Circle. You know, the fancy parts of town. They already sellin' Speedball to them nice young kids in Georgetown an' Spring Valley and pretty soon they gonna die, too."

"You mentioned a dealer."

"He used to work out of Philadelphia. Goes by the name of Dr. Love."

"Have you talked to this Dr. Love?"

"Two weeks ago, I spoke with the man. Told him real nice to get out of town. He didn't say nothin'. He just looked at me funny. Two blocks away I was jumped by a bunch of white guys. Left me for dead."

"Stryker spent a week in the hospital," Sister Grace says. "The doctors say he was hurt real bad."

"Where can I find this Dr. Love?" I ask.

"On Sundays and Wednesdays, he usually hangs out at a bodega near the corner of Orange Street, just off Malcolm X Avenue. Can't miss him. He always draws a big crowd."

"I'll talk to him."

"Do more 'n talk," Sister Grace says. "Stop him. You'll get your usual fee."

"That won't be necessary this time, Sister Grace. I want to see this poison taken off the streets as much as you do. Washington is my town, too."

"The dealers are a real rough bunch. You'll need backup."

"I don't need protection. I can take care of myself."

"I say you need protection. I'm makin' Stryker your partner for this job."

"I already have a partner."

"Your other partner is a cop. No cop can operate in this neighborhood. Stryker your partner now. Understood?"

She takes a drag on her cigarette. "You gonna do this thing for me, Detective? You gonna get Speedball off the streets?"

"I'll do what I can. That's a promise, Sister Grace."

CHAPTER THREE

By the time I get back to the crime scene, fire trucks, ambulances, and police vehicles fill the street, parked helter-skelter on sidewalks and on people's front yards. I look for the man with the spiky white-blond hair but don't see him. He's vanished. Tyrone Clifford, my new police partner, stands next to the foam-covered wreck of the Ford Explorer looking with horror at what's left of the figure inside. Two men and a woman in fire gear move carefully around the car, checking that all flames have been extinguished.

Tyrone Clifford is a good-looking young Black man who graduated with honors from Howard University and has been with the Metropolitan Police for five years. He was assigned to me just over six weeks ago right after my former partner, Lucy, was promoted and reassigned to a better job. She was also rewarded, according to the fancy citation presented to her during the ceremony, for her role in foiling the assassination of the visiting prime minister of Montenegro. Tyrone spent three years in Internal Affairs before being assigned to Homicide. I suspect that Tyrone was made my partner to keep an eye on me. To report to someone what I'm doing. He denies it but I'm pretty sure.

"Do we have any identification on the victim?" I ask Tyrone.

"Nothing yet. We haven't been able to get in the vehicle to do a search."

One of the members of our police team circles the burned-out car, taking photographs. "The firefighters say we can check out the victim now," Hanna Forbes, our forensic team leader, calls from a distance.

No one jumps to be the first.

I'm thinking, as ranking officer on the scene, it should fall to me to do the job, but then Celia, the assistant medical examiner, saves me. She squares her shoulders and walks to the car. She wipes foam from the window before she peers in. And recoils. She tries to open the driver's-side door, but it won't budge.

"It's locked tight," one of the firefighters says.

"Probably fused shut from heat," somebody else adds.

One of the firefighters brings a large device that looks like a gigantic pair of pliers, which, I think, is called the jaws of life. One of the firefighters carefully inserts the device between the car's post and the edge of the door and slowly opens a gap until the door pops out and falls to the street with a thud.

The photographer approaches and takes flash photographs of the interior. Then, very cautiously, Celia crawls partway into the car. From where we stand, we can't see what she sees. After about three minutes, she emerges, her protective gear and her face mask smeared black with something I can't identify.

"Dead, of course," she mutters.

"Male or female?" I ask.

"Who knows? I'll tell you when I get it to the lab." Celia takes a deep breath. "I think I'm going to be sick."

Hanna and one of the firefighters lead her away from the wreck. Celia removes her face covering and stands silently, eyes closed, her face covered with sweat, heaving great gulps of air. Then she goes back to the car and removes the charred remains and places them in a body bag.

A large police flatbed truck is backing up to the wreck, making beeping noises, and we all move out of its way. The truck crew attaches hooks and heavy chains to the Ford Explorer and hauls it up the inclined ramp onto the flatbed.

"I'm taking the car in for examination," Hanna tells me. "I'll give you my report later this afternoon. Due to the intensity of the fire, I doubt I'll find anything of use. I hope Celia has better luck when she examines the body."

My cell phone rings and it's Frank Townsend, chief of Homicide, and my boss. "Tyrone Clifford tells me you've got a burning car."

"And someone inside it, Frank."

"Dead?"

"Very."

"Turn over the investigation to Tyrone. Get back here now. There's someone you need to see."

"I have a murder here, Frank."

"Let Tyrone handle it."

"Is this more important than a murder investigation?"

"Definitely. Come back to headquarters. Now."

CHAPTER FOUR

Frank Townsend looks more gloomy than usual when I step into his office.

"How's your car wreck investigation coming?" Frank asks. He sits at his cluttered desk. A half-empty mug of coffee stands on a pile of what I suspect are unread police reports. He's in his shirtsleeves, his feet resting, as usual, in an open desk drawer.

When Frank took over as chief of detectives we had a rough patch for a few weeks while we got use to each other. There are a lot of forms detectives are supposed to fill out explaining what they did during their shift. Somehow, I kept forgetting to fill mine out. At first that bothered Frank a lot. Eventually he decided he didn't really want to know. We get along just fine now.

"It's not a car wreck. It's a homicide. What's so important I had to come back immediately?"

"The chief wants to meet you. In person."

My heart sinks. Here we go, I think. The new chief of police wants to meet me. Nothing good can come of this. She's been on the job three weeks, and she's spoken with all department heads. Now she's reaching down into the rank and file. I expect I'm about as rank as she'll find.

"Why does she want to meet me?"

"You know why." Frank takes a deep breath and stares moodily into his coffee mug. "I just came from her office. We had a long talk about you. She wants to make her own personal assessment of you before she takes any action."

"What kind of action is she thinking of?"

"You'll be the first to know."

"I'll try to behave."

"Try real hard. It's your ass on the line. I know how you feel about management. You think senior officers just get in your way. My advice is keep your opinions to yourself. Don't argue with the lady. And don't ever be sarcastic. She has no sense of humor."

"This does not sound good."

"It isn't good, Marko. Try to work with her. She's come up through the ranks and has headed several police departments. She runs a very tight ship. She cleaned house in Cleveland and later in San Diego. She's already had two senior officers and three sergeants here busted. I told her you have the best arrest and conviction record in Homicide, but she knows your reputation. Be nice, Marko. Your job depends on it."

That's going to be a challenge. I'm not good at being nice.

Sitting outside the office of the chief of police is Gladys. She has been executive secretary for the last three police chiefs and is extremely efficient and a lovely person. "Good luck, Detective Zorn," she whispers.

"Come in," Captain Kelly Flynn tells me when I knock on her door.

I've not met the new chief of the DC Metropolitan Police in person before. I'd seen her being interviewed on television and I attended a police convocation when she was sworn in.

I'll admit Chief Flynn does have an impressive record. She cleaned out several corrupt police departments. She single-handedly faced down a crazed gunman in a liquor store and took down three armed carjackers. All without firing her weapon.

I knew she'd be trouble.

And here I am face-to-face with it.

I remember her from the convocation only as a woman in her early forties wearing the formal uniform of the chief of police: starched white blouse, blue pants, and regulation dark blue jacket with a gold badge and a bunch of gold stars on her shoulder. I was too far away to count the number. She had reddish-blond hair, cut short. Onstage with the new chief was a young woman, maybe sixteen or seventeen, who was introduced as Chief Flynn's daughter. There was no mention of a Mr. Flynn.

Standing before me now the chief looks almost human—almost. She's in her police uniform but without the jacket and the stars. Her blouse is starched and blinding white, her pants crisply pleated. Her face is pale, her complexion almost translucent.

From a distance I'd seen her as a woman approaching middle age. That's okay with me, but she is management—a class I normally don't approve of, or get along with. Up close, I find she has an enigmatic attraction. Her figure is lithe and slim. Beyond that, I know nothing about the lady. According to rumors circulating in the squad room, she supposedly enjoys playing pick-up basketball in her free time. She's also said to be a big fan of Washington's professional basketball team. Although she's been in town for only a few weeks, she's already been seen at several Washington Wizards basketball games—court side.

She wears no makeup, not even a touch of lipstick. She has no jewelry. I see no wedding ring. I detect no hint of perfume. The chief has obviously gone to some trouble to minimize any feminine appearance. All signs of softness and vulnerability have been scrubbed. Her androgynous uniform, the lack of makeup, the haircut, her entire deportment and posture says: I am no frail female and don't dare treat me like one.

I get the message.

At this moment, she's stone-faced, her expression hard and determined, intended to intimidate. But . . . am I just imagining it? Or are there laugh lines around her eyes? That's probably just wishful thinking on my part, but I can't help wondering what she looks like if she smiles. I'd like to see her laugh.

She takes a seat in an office chair. I sit opposite her.

"Detective Zorn, you and I have to come to an understanding."

"Of course."

"I've studied your record. And I've had several conversations about you with your supervisor, Captain Townsend. He speaks very highly of you, and I respect his judgment. Fortunately for you."

I don't like the way this interview is starting out.

She doesn't take her eyes off me, which is disconcerting. She has large green eyes that seem to see through me. Her speech is calm. I'm not fooled.

"I'm supervising almost four thousand police officers. I wonder why your name keeps coming up."

"Beats me."

"Among other things, it's because you've been associated with some very unorthodox investigations. You consort with dangerous people, people in the criminal world who should, by all rights, be in prison, but are counted among your friends."

"I'm not sure 'consort' is the right word. And they're certainly not my friends. As a homicide detective, I'm obliged to deal with all kinds of people, not all of them nice."

"I believe you have trouble with authority."

"Maybe just a little."

"That may be admirable in a shepherd or a hermit. But it's not admirable in a police officer. Washington is a city that reveres power and hierarchy. You do not seem to be able to tolerate power. Why is that, do you suppose?"

"Because DC is run by a bunch of hacks. Present company excluded, of course."

She studies me to determine whether I'm mocking her. Then she goes on. "Also, people connected to your investigations often end up dead."

"Only the evildoers."

"I've known people like you," she continues. "I know your type. You're vigilantes at best and psychos at worst. There's always one in every police department. Men—and they're always men—who think they're above the law. You have a personal code of honor. That does not work in my organization. You're not above the law, Detective. You *are* the law, and don't you ever forget it."

"I'll try not to."

"Try really hard. Do you want to know what happens to those who forget that?"

I don't want to know, but I'm sure Chief Flynn is going to tell me anyway.

"The better ones are sent to traffic enforcement. The others I fire and are probably working night-shift security at some Walmart. In my last command, I was known, behind my back, of course, as the Wicked Witch of the West. There was a reason for that."

"Point taken."

"You've pissed off a lot of important people in this town. How did you manage to do that?"

"Just lucky, I guess."

"If I hear from one person in a high position complaining about you, you're finished."

"Yes, ma'am."

"I understand you're currently investigating an incident involving a burning car."

"Yes, ma'am."

"I'm not the queen of England, Detective, so stop calling me ma'am. You may refer to me as Captain Flynn."

"Yes, Captain."

"You investigated the scene yourself?"

"Yes, Captain."

"Were you armed while you carried out your investigation?"

"No."

"Why not?"

"I don't like guns."

"I don't much like guns myself, but you're a police officer and are required to be armed when you're on duty. Is that clear?"

"I am familiar with police regulations."

"Why don't you carry a gun? You're a homicide detective. That means you must deal with some very dangerous people. You must be properly prepared."

"I am prepared."

"You're making no sense."

"In my experience, if I'm faced with a dangerous opponent who is threatening me, it makes sense to talk them down. I'll offer him or her a deal. That's far better than drawing a gun and shooting someone. Guns make negotiations impossible. Most people would rather talk than die."

"Not everyone. Some prefer to kill, then talk. Aren't you ever afraid?"

"Not normally."

"That's foolish."

"The only person I'm afraid of is me."

The chief studies my face carefully. "That makes no sense. What do you mean?"

"It's complicated."

"I'm sure it is."

I don't even try to explain. Anything I say at this point would just annoy the chief more and get me in deeper.

"I understand you have a replacement partner." I'm relieved the chief has changed the subject.

I nod. I think she means Tyrone Clifford, not Stryker.

"Captain Townsend tells me there is some friction between you and Detective Clifford."

"We get along."

"You better. I don't want personalities to interfere with police work. Cooperate with your partner."

So, the chief knows about Tyrone Clifford—my partner and my minder. She probably knows about his background in Internal Affairs. And she almost certainly approves of him snooping on me. I don't say anything.

"Detective Zorn, did you hear me? I want your partner to be closely involved in your investigations. Tyrone Clifford is an outstanding officer. Work with him."

"Of course. Every step of the way."

The chief sits back in her chair. I hope this means she's going to throw me out of her office. No such luck.

"What kind of car do you drive, Detective Zorn?"

There's no way I can duck that question. I'm sure she has all that information spelled out in her file on me sitting on her desk. Probably even photographs.

"Right now, I drive a 1968 MG."

"Is it a convertible?"

"It's a roadster, yes. Soft top."

"What color?"

"Racing Green."

"Isn't that rather ostentatious for a police officer to be driving around?"

"These days I don't drive it that much. I don't like to park it on the street, know what I mean? It'll probably get stolen."

"What do you use instead to get to and from work?"

"When I'm on duty, I usually use an unmarked police vehicle. This morning, I drove the MG because I went to the crime scene directly from home."

"And when you're off duty?"

"I use the MG. And, in good weather, my motorcycle."

The chief is for a moment speechless. "You ride a motorcycle? Why?"

"Because it's fun."

"You drive around the city of Washington on a hog?"

I can tell she's trying to think of reasons why that's against police department regulations. She almost smiles. But not quite.

"When I first took over this position, I looked at your record. My first instinct was to fire you on the spot, Detective. Or at least demote you to patrol duty. But I have, for the moment at least, made no final decision about you or your fate. I know you've had success in many difficult cases. I understand you were recently instrumental in preventing the assassination of the president. I've met several times with the head of the FBI Criminal Investigative Division, a Ms. Carla Lowry, whom, I believe, is a friend of yours."

"Sometimes we work together."

"Interagency cooperation is good. It's even essential in some cases. But there are channels for such cooperation. Observe them. Ms. Lowry told me you are a dedicated and very resourceful police officer who gets the job done."

"That was very kind of her."

"She also said not to trust you for one minute."

"Did she really say that?" I must have a word with Carla.

"Initiative is fine as long as it's done by the book and according to department rules. We have rules for a reason. No organization can exist without them. Otherwise, it's anarchy. I will not tolerate anyone in my organization breaking the rules. Is that clear? And if you get in trouble, don't expect any help. You have enemies in high places."

She bites her lower lip. She clearly has something else on her mind but is hesitant to bring it up. Whatever *it* is.

"I'm told you earn extra income by taking jobs on the side," she says at last. "Side hustles that are only marginally legal—if that. Listen to me very carefully now. There are to be no more questionable side hustles. That's an order. Do I make myself entirely clear?"

"Very clear."

"I'm told you're often seen at expensive restaurants, the theater, and art-show openings with beautiful women hanging on your arm. How can you afford that lifestyle on a police officer's salary?"

"I save coupons."

"Do you take your lady friends for rides on your motorcycle?"

"The lucky ones, yes."

"And while I'm on the subject of your private life—the women I've talked to here at headquarters find you, for reasons I cannot begin to fathom, irresistible and charming. My secretary referred to you as 'delicious.' You leave my secretary alone, Detective. Gladys is close to fifty, happily married with three children. And don't think you can try your charms on me. They won't work."

"Have there been any complaints about me?" I ask. "Do any of these women you've talked with think I've stepped out of line?"

"No, but if you screw up, I'll see to it you never work in law enforcement. I hope we don't have to repeat this conversation. If we do, it will be the last one and you'll be out on the street. I guarantee it. Dismissed."

As I leave, Gladys looks up at me and smiles. "Are you in trouble?"

"Probably."

"Please be careful."

"That's just it. I don't know how to be careful."

CHAPTER FIVE

POWERFUL LIGHTS FLOOD the burned-out wreck and half a dozen white-suited technicians crawl in and around its hulk. The doors have been removed, the windows are blown out, and the tires are flat from the intense heat. The seats, or what's left of them, have been stacked in front of the wreck, their fabric gone, leaving only scorched metal springs. Bits and pieces of the Explorer, all neatly labeled, are in piles on the floor nearby. The Ford's exterior is blackened by the flames. Inside, the trim and molding have been reduced to molten plastic. The steering wheel is the shape of a pretzel.

"This is one holy mess," Hanna says. "Gutted. There's nothing left here to find. Nothing flammable survived the fire."

"We're going through everything, but it looks hopeless," Tyrone Clifford says. "They torched the car and the driver on a street in broad daylight. They were taking a real risk. They could have been seen by anybody on the street."

"Maybe they wore masks," Hanna suggests.

"And head coverings." I think of the man with the white-blond hair I saw watching me. "Anything to cover identifiable features. I'm pretty sure any such disguises would have been disposed of far from the crime scene. Have you located the car keys?"

"No sign," Tyrone answers. "That means the doors were locked from the outside."

"And the victim was trapped inside. That means we're definitely looking at murder."

I search through the interior of the car, not really expecting to find anything.

"How did your meeting with the chief go?" Tyrone asks. His tone is pleasant and nonchalant, but I wonder how he knew about my session with Kelly Flynn. Is he the source of the stories, the one who told the chief about what she referred to as my side hustles? Is he the informant?

"It went fine." I'm not about to share the details with Tyrone.

I stop to examine bits and pieces of scrap metal on the concrete floor not far from the car. I kick away a piece of twisted metal.

"This is a license plate," I observe. "It's been embossed."

I pass the plate to Tyrone who moves his fingers over the surface. "There seem to be six numbers and maybe a letter of some kind. I think I feel a nine, and a seven."

"Try the top of the plate. See which jurisdiction issued the tag."

Tyrone shuts his eyes to concentrate and slides his fingers back and forth over the surface. "I think there's a name. It's in italics." He stops, holds his breath. "Maryland. The plates were issued by the state of Maryland."

"Can you read the numbers?"

"Give me time. I'll get them."

"Get the plate numbers and call them in to the Maryland Motor Vehicle Administration. We can find out who this car was issued to."

"What can the fire department's arson people tell us?" I ask Hanna. She points to a man peering into the trunk of the Ford. "This is Gordon Ashe, head of the DCFD arson investigation unit."

"What have you got?"

"Definitely arson. There's no way this could have been a spon-taneous combustion. Even if the gas tank had ruptured—which it didn't—that could not have led to this fire. It was started inside the vehicle while the victim was in the driver's seat. You've seen the victim?" He grimaces as he speaks. "He was soaked in fuel and then ignited. This was no accident."

*   *   *

An hour later, Celia, the assistant medical examiner, is waiting for me in the lab. The victim is lying on an autopsy table covered with a heavy cloth. For which I am hugely grateful. I don't want to see what lies beneath.

"Can't tell you much," Celia tells me. "We don't have a lot to work with. We're still examining the victim, but I don't expect to learn more considering the condition of the body. I'm pretty sure the victim was male. Judging from the bone condition, probably about seventy. Maybe older. About five eleven in height."

"Race?"

"More than likely white."

"Fingerprints?"

"Are you kidding? There's no skin left on the hands. There are no hands left."

"Teeth?"

"Badly damaged. Lower jaw mangled. Partial upper dentures. Mostly melted."

"Was the victim alive when he was set on fire?"

It's not often I see Celia flinch in the face of violent death. "It looks like it. I know he was breathing. The interior of his mouth and trachea are scorched."

"That means that whoever did this wanted his victim to suffer horribly before he died."

"It's no way to die."

"Tell me what is."

My cell phone rings.

"I've got a lead on the car," Tyrone Clifford tells me. "The vehicle was registered to a rental agency in Bethesda, Maryland. It was rented this morning. They were not happy when I told them what became of their car."

"Who rented the car?"

"A Dr. Harvey Young."

"Address?"

"Young gave his address as the Holiday Inn on Wisconsin Avenue in Bethesda."

I call the number of the Holiday Inn. "Do you have a guest by the name of Harvey Young?" I ask when someone answers the phone. "Can I speak with him?"

"I'll connect you to his room."

A telephone rings.

"Yes?" a woman's voice asks cautiously.

"May I speak with Dr. Young? My name is Detective Marko Zorn. I'm with the DC police."

"Oh, shit," the woman murmurs.

"Ma'am?"

"My husband's not here at the moment. He's out on a business appointment. Can I help you?"

"Are you Mrs. Young?"

"I am. What do you want?"

"I'd like to speak with you as soon as possible. Could we meet at my office at the Metropolitan Police Department in downtown DC?"

"Does your police department have a bar?"

"Alas, no. If you'd prefer, we can meet where you're staying. Would that be more convenient for you?"

Long pause. "Sure. There's a coffee shop just off the lobby here. I'll be the sweet, little, white-haired old lady drinking her breakfast from the miniature vodka bottles we got on the flight to DC yesterday. With any luck, I'll be incoherent by the time you get here."

CHAPTER SIX

MRS. YOUNG SITS at a small table in the corner of the coffee shop, gripping a porcelain mug. She wears a simple linen dress with an onyx intaglio brooch on her breast. Her hair is gray, tied in a bun at the back of her head, and a few loose strands straggle at the side of her face. Her eyes are red. She looks to be about sixty. She forces an anxious smile as I approach.

"I'm Marko Zorn." I produce my police badge, which she waves away impatiently. "Are you Mrs. Harvey Young?"

She nods. "What happened to Harvey?"

"We believe Mr. Young may have been involved in an accident." There is no need at this stage to introduce the word "murder." The woman is already under enough stress. I don't want to add to her pain. Not yet anyway. And I sure don't want her to go to pieces on me. I hate it when women go to pieces on me while I'm conducting an interview.

"He's dead, isn't he? Of course, he's dead." She covers her eyes with her hands.

"A man was found in a burning car this morning," I tell her. "It's possible it may have been your husband. We haven't been able to make any definitive identification yet."

"It's Harvey. I know it's Harvey."

"Why do you think it's your husband?"

"Because Harvey's an idiot. I'm so mad at him I could spit. We were planning a safari trip next month for our fortieth wedding anniversary. We'd been looking forward to this for years." She touches the brooch at her breast lightly. "This was so stupid. He should never have got involved with those people. He should have left it all alone."

"Left what alone?"

"Whatever damn thing he was doing. I knew—I just knew this was going to end badly. I told him—again and again—Harvey, this is trouble. And now the son of a bitch has gone and left me. Damn him!"

"You don't seem surprised your husband is dead."

"Not really. He was asking for it, wasn't he?"

"I assume you don't live around here."

She shakes her head sadly. "Our home is in Indianapolis."

"What brought you and your husband to Washington?" I ask.

"Harvey had a meeting." She scoops three spoonfuls of sugar into her coffee mug and stirs angrily. "Would you care for some coffee?" she asks.

"Who was your husband seeing at this business meeting?"

"I have no idea."

"He never told you?"

"He said what I don't know won't hurt me."

"What did he mean by that?"

She shrugs. "'Stay out of my business,' I guess."

"What *was* your husband's business?"

"He's a scientist. Was—a biochemist. Right out of grad school he taught organic chemistry at Purdue. Then he and a friend formed a company of their own. They called it Altavista. And they created a new drug. They named it Zemlon."

"What did Zemlon do?"

"Zemlon made people happy. Harvey and his partner did well. Until the Poole brothers came into our lives."

I'm lost here. I'm thinking maybe Mrs. Young has gotten to the miniature vodka bottles after all. "Who are the Poole brothers?"

"That's Maximilian and Sabastian Poole."

"I've never heard of them."

"That's because they're invisible. The Poole brothers now own Altavista, which produces Zemlon. Zemlon earns them tens of millions of dollars a year. Maybe hundreds of millions. Not that Harvey gets any of it. Colin saw to that."

"Who is Colin?"

"Colin Stone. My husband's partner from many years ago. He handled the business side of things. Harvey was the real brains."

"Is this Colin Stone a friend of your husband?"

"Colin was once a friend. He's still an in-law."

"Colin Stone is an in-law?"

"He's my brother."

"Did your husband come to Washington to meet with this Colin Stone?"

"No, they've hardly spoken in years. They had a bitter fight long ago."

"About what?"

"About the Poole brothers. About the brothers' plans for Altavista. Colin wanted to sell out. Harvey was against it. Harvey was the strong one. Colin is weak. He was always weak."

"Did your husband come to Washington in connection with this drug Zemlon?"

"I can't be sure. I know Zemlon was Harvey's life."

"When did you last see your husband?"

"A little after eight this morning. We had breakfast right here." She waves her hand around at the coffee shop. "He said he was going to pick up a rental car and see some people."

"What people?"

She shakes her head.

"It's very important, Mrs. Young."

She struggles for a moment, and I think she may burst into tears. Finally, she gets control of herself. "It might have been somebody called Alsop. He had a thick manila envelope he brought with us from Indianapolis and he took with him when he left to pick up the rental car. He'd written the name 'Alsop' on the outside of the envelope, I think. And I know he talked to this Alsop woman on the phone in recent days, including last night."

"Do you know who Alsop is?"

"No clue. Sorry."

"Maybe an old friend of your husband? Someone from his past?"

She looks at me pityingly. "I'm his past. Me and his research. All I can say is when Harvey spoke to Alsop, he would shut himself in his office. When he came out, he always looked upset. He would never tell me why. Then yesterday he said he had to go to Washington. I insisted I come with him. I was worried."

"Do you know how I can reach this Alsop?"

Mrs. Young is silent for a moment. "I can give you a telephone number." She rummages through a capacious handbag and withdraws a cell phone. "I wrote it down once. Like I said, I was worried." She passes me her phone and I copy the number.

"Whatever he was here for, Harvey said it was a matter of life or death." She finally bursts into tears. I imagine she's been holding them back for hours. They roll down her cheeks, smearing her mascara. She makes no attempt to wipe them away.

"His death. That bastard's left me." She gulps. "What do I do now for the rest of my life?"

*   *   *

I stop in the hotel lobby and make a call. The phone rings seven times and I'm about to give up, when a voice answers cautiously. "Hello. Who is this?"

It's a woman's voice, low-pitched, probably middle-aged. It sounds cultured and educated.

"Is this Mrs. Alsop?"

"Who's calling?" the voice asks suspiciously.

"My name is Marko Zorn. I'm with the Washington, DC police. I would like to speak with Mrs. Alsop about Harvey Young."

There is a long silence at the other end. I think I've lost her.

"I don't want to speak with you. About Dr. Young or anything else. Goodbye."

I sense the woman is on the verge of panic and is about to hang up on me.

"You and Mr. Young have been speaking recently. I know that."

There is a long silence. "What do you want?"

"I need to know why you've been in contact with Mr. Young."

"It's Dr. Young. And I can't tell you anything. I really can't help you. I'm sorry."

"This is official police business. I'm afraid I must insist."

"Tell me again who you are."

"I'm a police officer with the Washington, DC Metropolitan Police. My name is Marko Zorn. I'm investigating the murder of Harvey Young."

"Did you say murder?"

There is no point in softening the news. I need to get her attention.

"That's what I said. He was murdered."

"When did this happen?"

"This morning. Sometime around nine."

"Oh, my God. Oh, dear God." There's a long silence.

I think I've lost her again when her voice comes back on the line. It's stronger now and in control.

"Very well, I'll speak with you. I can't today. I'm very busy. I don't think I can help you. I've never even met Dr. Young. Can we meet on Monday?"

"The matter is urgent," I say. "I can come to your home now, if possible."

"I'm extremely busy. If you insist, we can meet tomorrow."

"Tomorrow is Sunday."

"Some of us have to work Sundays," she tells me with asperity.

"I'd prefer to speak with you today."

"Not possible." It's almost a shout.

The woman is adamant. I see no way to talk her into seeing me today. If I was with her, face-to-face, I think I could win her over by using my charm offensive, which often works with middle-aged women. An engaging, boyish smile often melts women's hearts. But on the phone, I don't have a chance. "Very well, tomorrow."

"Tomorrow, then. At three thirty. I have a few minutes free at that time. Here at my lab."

"Where's your lab?"

"At the offices of the Food and Drug Administration." She gives me directions on how to reach her lab in Rockville, Maryland, just outside of Washington. "Please bring your police identification with picture ID when you come. Don't be late."

Who else is she expecting? I wonder.

CHAPTER SEVEN

THE MAN I'M looking for is standing under the portico of the main entrance to the Orlando L. Fisher Memorial Hospital in Anacostia, across the river from downtown DC. What little hair he has left is rumpled by the fresh breeze, which blows across the river. In fact, his whole appearance is rumpled: tie hanging loose, top button of his shirt unbuttoned, trousers that long ago lost any memory of a pleat. He looks distressed and anxious. He always does. He has a rumpled soul, and with good reason.

I've worked with Harlon Vine for years despite the fact that he's a senior bureaucrat in the federal government, a species I normally avoid. Harlon is an official at the Drug Enforcement Administration, but we get along fine.

Harlon grabs my arm and leads me into the hospital.

"Why did you want to meet here, Harlon? I need to ask you about a new drug on the market. We could have done that in your office."

"Speedball. You told me." He punches a button to call for an elevator. "If you want to know about drugs, don't visit us bureaucrats in our nice, clean, well-maintained offices. Visit a jail or a hospital. That's where you'll learn the truth about drugs."

We step into the elevator along with two men in scrubs and go silent as we rise to an upper floor. Once the doors open, I follow Harlon down a crowded corridor.

"What's your interest in Speedball?" Harlon asks.

"Somebody asked me to look into it. It seems like it's the new drug in town."

"That's right. It's appeared in just the last six weeks. But not just here. It's everywhere. New York, Detroit, Houston. It's even showing up in other countries. It will be only a matter of time before it can be bought anywhere, from the Arctic Circle to North Africa. In just a few weeks the sales of Speedball have gone from nothing to priority one for the DEA."

"What's so special about Speedball? You've got a tsunami of drugs flooding the cities—crack, heroin, not to mention fentanyl."

"Speedball is one of the most powerful drugs we've dealt with on the illicit market. It's many times more powerful than other opioid analgesics and even stronger than fentanyl."

He pushes open a wide double door, and we're in a clinic. There are beds from wall to wall, each with an occupant. Many are on respirators.

"We're running out of beds to put the victims in. It's the same throughout the city and in Baltimore and Philadelphia. The hospitals can't keep up."

"Speedball does this?"

"And it's lethal."

"Can't you close the lab down?"

"We would, if we could find it."

"I've seen enough. I hate hospitals."

Harlon leads me out of the room and we stand together in the corridor.

"What makes Speedball so powerful?"

"Opioids are derived from, or mimic, natural substances found in the opium poppy plant," Harlon says. "Chemically, Speedball is based on a commercially available semisynthetic opioid analgesic. This one, we believe, is probably one called Zemlon marketed by a company called Altavista. But our chemists believe the Zemlon formula has been laced with sufentanil."

Altavista is the company my murder victim, Dr. Young, worked for. Could Speedball have something to do with his death? That's something I'd better find out.

"What's sufentanil?" I ask.

"Sufentanil is an analog of fentanyl, a synthetic opioid. Both are easy and cheap to make. That's led to their production in countries like Mexico for illegal use. Sufentanil is five to ten times as powerful as fentanyl and many times as powerful as all the other opioid analgesics."

Sounds like some horrific stuff.

"Where does sufentanil come from?"

"Sufentanil was introduced in Belgium around 1974 by a company called Janssen, which is owned by Johnson & Johnson."

"Why have I never heard of sufentanil? I'd think it would be a great drug for those suffering from severe pain."

"Its medical applications are very restricted in the U.S."

"Is it a pill?"

"Not in this country. The FDA has approved it as an injectable and, more recently, for sublingual use under the tongue. It's available only with medical supervision and not through pharmacy retail sales. It's a very controversial drug. Because it's so powerful, it is hard to control its abuse and it can easily lead to addiction and death."

"I guess I'll stick with baby aspirin."

"We suspect that Altavista may be the original source of Speed-ball. But we can't prove it. Speedball is certainly not produced in any of Altavista's US plants. Probably in one of their offshore operations. All we know is that whoever is making Speedball is well financed and well organized and has a worldwide distribution network and sophisticated production plants. Speedball is not something you can cook up in your kitchen."

He runs his fingers through his sparse hair. "I've been in this business for twenty years. It gets worse every day. It was bad enough when I joined DEA. It's far worse today. There are more drugs, and more powerful drugs. We're losing the war, Marko. Hell, we lost the war during the Nixon administration. Sometimes I just want to give up. At least once a day I decide to retire from the DEA. Maybe go back to Michigan, where I grew up. Maybe look for a job teaching high school."

"Why don't you, Harlon?"

He glances back at the door we just came out of. "Because of them. I see the victims and I just can't turn my back on them."

CHAPTER EIGHT

"THAT'S DR. LOVE right there," Stryker tells me, pointing at a tall, dapper white man wearing a checkered sports jacket.

A crowd of men and women mill around the man on the sidewalk in front of a small bodega. Among them are five or six kids, some as young as nine or ten, mostly boys.

"This is as far as you go, Stryker."

Across the street is parked a black SUV with four men inside. They're watching the bodega and the crowd outside. And us.

"I'm your partner. Sister Grace said so. I'm supposed to look after you. Don't go near that man. Not by yourself. He's dangerous." Stryker pulls his porkpie hat down firmly over his head, as if getting ready for action. He points to the black SUV. "And he has backup."

"I believe you and Dr. Love have a history."

"He tried to have me killed."

"I want to make a deal with this Dr. Love. I don't want any personal history between you and Dr. Love to get in the way. This is a meeting I have to take alone."

Stryker starts to argue with me then shrugs. "Be careful."

"Are you looking for me, Detective Zorn?" the tall man in the checkered sports jacket asks when I stop in front of him.

"How do you know my name? We've never met."

"I know who you are. I know what you are. And I know why you're here."

"If you're the person who goes by the name of Dr. Love then I'm looking for you." I use a neutral voice. We're not at the threat level. Not yet. I try to impersonate a "good cop / bad cop" persona. That's always hard to do when you're one person. Up close, I can see that Dr. Love's face is disfigured by old scars, probably from acne from when he was a child. He speaks with a slight Caribbean accent.

"I'm the one and the only Dr. Love."

"You don't look like you belong in this neighborhood."

"I belong wherever the good times roll." He indicates the entrance to the bodega. "I've been expecting you. Join me in my office." The man leads me into the bodega. An elderly Black man standing at the counter scratching a lottery card looks up as we enter and quickly leaves without a word. The other person present is a scared-looking Korean man. Dr. Love makes a small flicking motion with his fingers, and the Korean man disappears through a door into what I assume is the back storage room.

"Did Sister Grace send you, Detective? Are you her errand boy today?"

"I've come to give you a message. Stop selling Speedball in this neighborhood. Or anywhere in Washington. You're not welcome here." I speak softly. I forget whether I'm supposed to be a good cop or a bad cop at this point.

The man grins at me. "Seems to me I got that message once before. Know what happened to the messenger boys who came last time?"

"I heard."

"Then you should know better than to threaten me."

"I'd like this exchange to be civil and reasonable. I'm making a polite request. Just a friendly warning. No more Speedball."

"Who's going to stop me?"

"Me."

He outright laughs. "You don't scare me none."

"Now that's a serious error in judgment."

"You don't seem to be getting my drift, Detective Zorn. If you stick your nose in my business, I will have to hurt you."

That's rude, I think.

"Up to now, this has been a civil exchange. One professional to another. Now you're threatening violence. That makes it personal. That's your second big mistake. And the day is still young."

"I hate to see our friendship end on such a bad note," Dr. Love tells me. "Stay out of my way and you'll live. Otherwise . . ." He leaves his sentence unfinished. Instead, he walks to the door and nods for me to leave.

I'm a block away from the bodega, heading back to Sister Grace's building, when I see a man approaching me. It's not unusual to see an armed man in this neighborhood, but this one stands out. He's short and stocky and wears a black leather jacket. He's carrying a weapon of some kind hidden in a shoulder holster under the jacket. He wears expensive reflective sunglasses. And he's white.

He stops directly in front of me, blocking my way. "Going somewhere, buddy?"

The thing about reflective sunglasses is they reflect. I can see a second man approaching me from behind. I have company. They're going to tag-team me.

"You're blocking my way," I say to the man standing in front of me. I speak in a friendly tone of voice. "Please step to one side."

The man looks me up and down slowly. "I'm not impressed," he says.

"Prepare to be impressed."

I hit him just under the rib cage. Hard. The man doubles over, and I give him two rapid kidney punches. I spin around before he hits the ground to face the second man, who's rushing at me holding a straight-edge razor. I swing my left arm hard and push away the razor, which flies into the air and lands on the sidewalk six feet away.

With my right hand, I crush the man's nose so blood spurts everywhere. I can feel the cartilage in the man's nose crumple under the force from the heel of my hand. I give my assailant a quick kick in the groin. The man drops to his knees. He's obviously unsure whether to hold his bleeding face or his groin. He decides on his face and holds his hands to his nose, whimpering, gouts of blood seeping through his clenched fingers.

I turn back to my first assailant, who is trying to get to his knees. I reach out and grab the man's gun from his holster and hit him with it upside his head. He goes down again.

Standing in front of me is Stryker. "I warned you to be careful."

"Have you been following me?" I try to catch my breath.

"Sister Grace said to keep an eye on you."

Normally I resent people interfering in my activities. As if I couldn't take care of myself. But there doesn't seem to be any point in arguing.

"How come you didn't help me sooner?"

"You seemed to be handling the situation jus' fine."

A few people on the street have stopped to watch the events, but they don't seem overly concerned. I guess they figure a fight among some white guys is none of their business.

The man who I flattened watches me warily, then gets slowly and painfully to his feet. He stumbles off down the street, looking back at me once or twice to be sure I'm not following him. The other man is sitting up and trying to stop the bleeding from his nose.

"Let's get out of here," I say. "These guys will probably have backup, and I don't want to be here when they show up."

"Aren't you gonna arrest them?" Stryker asks hopefully. "They assaulted a police officer."

I know if I arrest them it would lead to no end of trouble, not to mention paperwork. The new chief would want to know what I was doing. And I certainly am not about to tell her. There is no way I could explain Sister Grace to Chief Flynn.

"Not worth it," I say. "These guys are bottom feeders. We've got to get to somebody higher up the food chain if we want to stop Speedball. Let's go. I faint at the sight of blood."

We walk away quickly. Nobody is following us, and I see no reinforcements coming.

After walking two blocks, Stryker stops me. "There's something you need to know."

"Okay. What do I need to know?"

"I done time. Hard time."

"I already figured that out."

"I want you to know what I was in for."

"I don't need to know that."

I've had to work with a lot of people with dubious backgrounds. They often want to tell me about their lives, criminal and otherwise. I don't want to hear any of it. They want to be friends and buddies. I don't.

"We partners. No secrets between partners."

"We're not partners, Stryker."

"Sister Grace say we partners. I killed a man once. Two men, actually."

"I don't want to know."

"When I got out of the service, I worked the offshore oil and gas rigs in the Gulf of Mexico for about five years. For the first year or so, I was a roustabout on Chevron rigs. Then I was promoted to the drilling crew, where I was a tool pusher for three years. I was clean. I don' smoke or drink or gamble or do drugs. In those days, I didn't have no record. Then I killed a man, and it all ended for me."

"I don't need the details."

"If I'm your partner, you need to know what kind of man I am."

"I think I know what kind of man you are."

"His name was Swede. He was a derrick man. We was buddies, Swede an' me, but one day we had a disagreement. We got into a fight, and I killed Swede."

"What weapon did you use?" It's always good to know what weapon a man prefers.

Stryker raises his right hand, curled into a fist.

"That's it?" I ask. "Just one hand?"

"They called in the Coast Guard, an' I was took back to shore. I served three years on a manslaughter charge in Coleman Penitentiary."

"You said you killed two men. If we're going to have no secrets, you better tell me about the other one, too."

"That was at Coleman." Stryker shrugs as if the incident were unimportant. "A man tried to disrespect me. I had to take him down. That don't count. Not like Swede."

We walk two more blocks in silence. We're passing a small, scruffy park when Stryker grabs my arm and pulls me to one side where we stand behind a delivery van.

"We don't want to go down this street," Stryker says urgently.

"Why not?"

"They's trouble here."

The street looks peaceful to me—better than many of the surrounding streets. The homes are well maintained, and there are even some trees in tree boxes. At the end of the block, there's a large redbrick church. A dozen black limousines are parked in front—some double parked, almost blocking the street. It's Sunday, so that makes sense.

"This street looks safe."

"Not to me it don't."

I move ahead. I have an appointment with a man for lunch. I don't want to be late. And it's on the other side of town.

"It can be dangerous on this street," Stryker says anxiously, keeping up with my pace.

"You mean they're bad dudes here?"

"Worse. There are good people here. God-fearing, honest, hardworkin' people. You gotta be careful with them. They can be big trouble."

We are almost abreast of the church and passing a kiosk with a large, illuminated sign announcing, "The Holy Tabernacle of the True Church," followed by the name "Prophet Marvin Divine." This, in turn, is followed by the times of various church services, the title of today's Sunday sermon— "Blessed are the merciful for they shall obtain mercy"—and something about Bible classes and day care.

At this very moment, the doors to the church swing open and people stream out. They're all Black, mostly elderly and mostly women.

"Let's get out of here." Stryker tugs at my arm to keep me moving, but we're too late.

"Yo! Stryker, my man. You can't hide from me. No more'n you can hide from your sins."

The speaker is a big Black man, probably in his sixties, wearing an ankle-length black robe with a large cross in gold embroidered on the breast. He has long black hair. His voice is loud and rich—it could easily fill a church.

The man strides down the church steps, weaving in and out among the congregants, smiling a cheerful smile, waving a friendly hand at members of his flock. Stryker snatches his porkpie hat from his head in a sign, I guess, of respect.

"Stryker, I haven't seen you in church lately." He stops in front of us, looking intently at Stryker. "How come you not here today to pay respects to Albert Morgan? We had a spirited service. Today is Sunday. You should have been here for services, Stryker." He glances briefly at me, then back at Stryker. "Up to no good, are you?"

Stryker fumbles nervously with his hat. "I'll try to make it next Sunday," he says without conviction.

"Glory, glory, hallelujah." The big man, who I assume is Prophet Divine himself, says. "Join us next Saturday for choir practice. We need your baritone. There will be great hymn singing. I remember you like hymn singing, Stryker. And my sermon next Sunday—'The meek shall inherit the earth.' You don't want to miss that. You might get a chance to meet some nice widow lady looking for companionship. It's your chance to receive the spirit."

"I'll see."

Prophet Divine turns to me and fixes me with a hard look. "You know this man Stryker here? Is he a friend of yours?"

I hold out my hand, and we shake. "My name is Marko Zorn. I'm a police officer with the DC Metropolitan Police."

I speak in a friendly, nonthreatening manner. Like I want to be friends. "I'm not here on police business. Just passing through your neighborhood, Reverend. I know what people in this part of the city think of cops, particularly white cops. I can't say as I blame them. There's a lot of history here." This prophet looks like a decent sort. I figure it always pays to be on good terms with God's legions.

The prophet's immense hand envelops mine in a warm and friendly grip. "Welcome to our neighborhood, Officer. Although you are not a member of our community, all God's children are welcome here. You got blood on your shirt. Did you know that?" He looks at Stryker. "What are you doing with Stryker here? He's a gangster and reprobate."

"Do you have any evidence of that, sir?" I ask.

The prophet smiles broadly. "God has revealed Stryker's sins to me personally."

"You know that won't hold up in court."

"So much the worse for your court."

"He's here to assist Sister Grace," Stryker says, trying to be helpful.

Prophet Divine's face suddenly hardens, his friendly smile gone. "Sister Grace! That Jezebel." Divine looks directly at me. "Are you a friend and associate of Sister Grace? If so, I pray for your soul."

"Come, let us reason together," I say. "'Though your sins be as scarlet, they shall be as white as snow.'"

The prophet studies my face for a long moment, then bursts out laughing. A loud, warm laughter. "Don't you quote Scripture to me, son. I will beat you at that game."

"Detective Zorn is trying to stop the sale of Speedball in our community," Stryker intercedes before my exchange with the prophet gets out of hand.

"That drug is a great tribulation and an abomination, to be sure," Divine replies. "Our people suffer from this infernal plague." He looks at me intently in the eye. "You know Sister Grace to be a great sinner: the greatest sinner on God's green earth. I warn you, young man, have nothing to do with that wicked woman."

There are loud shouts from the people surrounding the black limousines, urging the prophet to join them.

"I'm coming," Divine calls out. "There be no hurry. Albert ain't goin' nowhere." The prophet turns to me. "I must go now. See you in church, Stryker."

"Maybe."

"Amen." Divine turns and joins his congregants.

"I told you to keep off this street," Stryker tells me, putting his porkpie hat firmly on his head again. "Now I've warned you."

CHAPTER NINE

THE MAN WAITING for me at a table at the Four Seasons restaurant in Georgetown is short and stout with a graying beard. He wears a polka-dot bow tie and a tattersall vest. He's working on a large platter of eggs Benedict with several rashers of bacon on the side, along with an extra helping of English muffins. A martini glass with a twist of lemon sits within easy reach.

"You've got blood on your shirt collar, Marko," the man says as I take my seat opposite him.

"It's been an eventful morning." I use one of the linen napkins laid at my place and rub at my collar.

"It's your other collar. The left one."

The dining room is full this morning, crowded with those out to enjoy Sunday brunch. I recognize several members of Congress, a couple of members of the president's cabinet, and a famous reporter. He must have come directly from the studio. There are some wives and girlfriends. And the lobbyists paying for all this.

A phantom waiter materializes at my side, clutching a massive menu.

"A beverage, sir?"

"A Bloody Mary and a pot of coffee. Both as strong as possible."

"Very good, sir," he murmurs humbly, and vanishes.

"What are you after?" my companion asks, amiably. "It's Sunday. It's supposed to be a day of rest."

"Not for the wicked, it isn't. I want to know about a company called Altavista."

He stabs at a piece of thick-cut bacon. "Big Pharma."

I meet Leland Taylor, a senior finance writer for the *Washington Post*, for lunch or dinner from time to time, always at expensive places of his choosing and always on my tab. Leland provides me with information and gossip about any commercial enterprise or financial institution I want to know about. He also tries to extract any intelligence I have that might be of interest to his colleagues on the staff of the *Washington Post*.

"Why are you interested in Altavista?" Leland digs into his eggs Benedict enthusiastically.

"It may relate to a case I'm working on."

He studies me carefully, wondering what kind of case this might be if Altavista piques the interest of a DC homicide detective. He knows better than to ask. He knows I'll just lie.

"Altavista is a large pharmaceutical corporation," he announces after taking a drink of his martini. "It produces and sells Zemlon."

"Tell me about Zemlon."

"The most popular painkiller on the market. 'The Drug You Can Live With' according to their publicity department. You've probably seen their ads on TV. They're everywhere."

"Altavista must be doing well if Zemlon is so popular."

"Not quite. Zemlon is a huge moneymaker, but Altavista has a problem. Its patent on Zemlon expires this month and Altavista is about to lose its exclusive marketing rights. Within six months, the market will be flooded with generic copies of Zemlon, mostly made abroad and sold at a much cheaper price. And Altavista will lose its biggest moneymaker."

"Is Zemlon Altavista's only product?"

"Not at all. Altavista produces scores of medical products: anti-biotics, sleep aids, cold remedies, antacids, and contraception pills. A whole range of 'lifestyle' products."

Leland looks around the room for our waiter. "If there is no disease for one of their products, they'll invent one. Medications are a gold mine in this country. And Altavista is only one of several integrated companies owned by an outfit called Magma Capital Management."

"What else does Magma Capital own?"

"They have interests in mining, transportation, commercial real estate, oil, and gas exploration. Even security. But Zemlon is a major profit maker."

"Magma owns a security company?" That's odd, I think. "What's security got to do with selling medications?"

"They use Coldcreek Security to protect themselves from people who get nosy about their business practices. People like you and me."

"What can you tell me about Magma Capital Management?"

"It's a hedge fund owned by two men. Two brothers named Sabastian and Maximilian Poole."

Bingo! The names Martha Young, the widow of my murder victim, told me about.

"I'd like to know more about these Poole brothers."

"So would I. They're reclusive and never speak with outsiders."

A waiter materializes and places a Bloody Mary in front of me with a foot-long celery stalk sticking over the top. A second waiter sets a silver coffeepot next to my Bloody Mary. Leland Taylor orders a second martini.

"Where does the brothers' money come from?"

"They inherited a small fortune from their father, who was in mining somewhere out west. One of those states with mountains.

He struck it rich, and the family moved here to Washington many years ago. He had class and status ambitions. The father bought an old mansion on Sixteenth Street. The two brothers have lived there all their lives. They and their sister inherited a fortune. One of the brothers, I think it's Maximilian, is said to be a financial genius. He invested the inheritance and created a huge financial empire."

"Are there any children?"

"None. The brothers are confirmed bachelors. As far as I know, the only people they have ever been intimate with are their bookkeepers."

"What about the sister?"

"She died years ago. She had one daughter, Rebecca. She's involved with Magma Capital Management in some minor capacity."

"I'd like to meet these Poole brothers."

"Why would you want to do that?"

"I have a proposition I'd like to make."

"Not a chance. They never see anybody. The old mansion they live in is surrounded by a goddamned army. It's impregnable."

"Nothing is impregnable. Who else should I speak to in the Magma Capital Management organization to make my proposal?" I ask.

"Duncan Forest is CEO. Magma Capital Investments has a local office here in DC you could try. It's staffed by lobbyists and pit bull lawyers. You'll get nothing from them. Forest is in Washington this week. He's testifying before some congressional committee explaining why the American taxpayer should subsidize pharmaceutical companies. He makes most of the day-to-day decisions for the company. You could try him, but you won't get far."

"What's his background?"

"The Poole brothers recruited him when he was fired from a huge Internet company in San Francisco."

"Why was he fired?"

"Too unscrupulous. Just right for the Poole brothers, though."

"Who runs the pharmaceutical side of things?"

"A man named Colin Stone."

Interesting, I think. The brother-in-law and former partner of my murder victim. Am I beginning to see a pattern here? Or am I just imagining things? Maybe it's the Bloody Mary.

"How do I find this Colin Stone?"

"His office is in Indianapolis, where Altavista's headquarters are located. I've spoken with him a few times, but he wasn't forthcoming. I believe he was genuinely afraid to talk to me. Actually, that's common in Magma Capital Management. I think they're all afraid of the brothers."

"What about this niece you mentioned?"

"Rebecca Poole. She works out of the company's government relations office here in DC. She's nice, but I don't think she knows much about the inner workings of Magma Capital Management and wouldn't have the authority to make any deals with you. Mostly she handles the Poole brothers' charity activities. She gives money to worthy causes. Mostly, worthy congressmen."

"What kind of charity causes do they support?"

"Anything that will get a good notice in the public media and enhance their reputation as do-gooders. As a prime example, you should know, the brothers have offered to give their art collection to the United States government. Which will enhance their influence greatly. Rebecca Poole is the point person negotiating the deal."

"The brothers are art collectors?" I ask.

"From what I hear, they've been collecting art for years and assembled one of the finest collections in private hands. The US government is desperate to have it. And keep it from the Metropolitan Museum in New York or the Art Institute of Chicago. Art is not my beat. But I've heard they are demanding the US government build a separate museum to house their collection. I assume this gift is intended to compensate for a life of crime. I sure hope the collection is as good as they claim. They have a lot to compensate for. And they want it placed on the National Mall. They're running into a lot of pushback on that, as you can imagine." Leland stops to sip his martini.

"If you want a contact within Magma Capital Management, I'd start with Rebecca Poole. She lives right here in the Washington area and is approachable. As it happens, she's hosting a fundraising reception at the National Gallery of Art tomorrow afternoon. My wife's been invited. She's a big supporter of art stuff. Maybe you can use her invitation and get in and schmooze with the lady. You're experienced at that sort of thing."

"You said Altavista is losing its exclusive rights to Zemlon. Does that mean the company is in financial trouble?"

"I believe Magma Capital may be in a serious financial bind. The lending banks are making trouble. I've heard the brothers' massive spending on art may be driving the whole operation into bankruptcy."

"You're breaking my heart." Somehow, I can't get upset when a Big Pharma company is forced to charge reasonable prices for its products rather than acting like a mafia crime syndicate.

"But Zemlon isn't the problem," Leland is going on. "Altavista has a new product in the pipeline to replace Zemlon. It's called Neuropromine. The word on the street is that Neuropromine may be the next billion-dollar drug. The FDA won't allow Altavista to market Neuropromine as more effective than Zemlon since they haven't done clinical trials to prove that. Neuropromine just has to have some advantage over Zemlon. Such as a new delivery system. So they plan to sell it in an easy-to-swallow gel cap form. But the whispers are that Neuropromine will be a major advance on Zemlon. Bottom line: Neuropromine can be on the market in a matter of weeks once it gets FDA approval and may save Magma Capital and the brothers."

At this point, a cop I know from way back crosses through the restaurant, looking carefully from right to left. He's in plain clothes, but I can see he's packing heat. His name is Mort something. He studies me closely, nods, then passes on. Cops don't normally hang out at the Four Seasons restaurant. It's far too pricey for a cop's salary. So, Mort must be here on duty. He's at the Four Seasons to provide security for some VIP. I soon see who.

Striding behind Mort by about ten paces is a woman accompanied by a teenage girl. The woman is Chief of Police Kelly Flynn. I assume the girl is the daughter I saw at the convocation.

As she passes, the diners pause in their conversations and briefly turn their heads to look at Flynn. She's the kind of woman people stop to look at. Some may recognize who she is. Most just see a striking woman. Maybe it's her poise and grace that captures their attention. She exudes authority and people instinctively recognize power in this town. Maybe it's something about her face. The men look at her with furtive lust. The women? Perhaps it's a combination of envy and admiration.

I try to hide nonchalantly behind the celery stalk inserted in my Bloody Mary, but I'm too late. Chief Flynn has already spotted me. She misses nothing. She swerves from her intended path and stops at our table, examining my Bloody Mary. Is she also looking at the bloodstain on my collar? Her daughter stands aside, holding three large shopping bags from smart Georgetown boutiques. The chief has obviously spent Sunday shopping with her daughter.

Chief Flynn's not in her police uniform. Instead, she's wearing an Eileen Fisher linen pants suit. Nothing high fashion but still flattering. Something with style that shows off her figure. Despite a stern face, which looks at me disapprovingly, she is, I think, very lovely.

The young woman standing with her looks to be about sixteen or seventeen. She has her mother's lithe figure, and I can see something of her mother in her face. She is pretty with a smooth, youthful complexion. Her hair is light brown and tied up in a ponytail. She has her mother's large green eyes and wide, generous mouth. While the daughter's face is smooth and unlined, the mother's face shows a lifetime of experience and wisdom. It gives her a beauty the daughter has yet to earn.

"Good afternoon, Officer Zorn," Chief Flynn says to me.

I'm struggling to stand up without knocking over our table and spilling my Bloody Mary. She waves at me to sit down. "I'm not staying. We're joining friends."

She surveys the table and gives Leland Taylor a hard look, presumably trying to remember whether she's seen him on the FBI's Most Wanted list.

"Have a good day." She takes three strides away, stops, and turns back to me. "Take care, Detective. Stay out of trouble." Is she looking at the blood on my collar?

"Is that your new boss lady?" Leland asks once she's gone. "I hear she's a bear—a real ball-breaker. Alan on the Metro Desk hears she's going to dismantle your entire police department and reconstruct it from the ground up. Has she hassled you yet?"

"Why should she hassle me?"

"She will, my friend. She will."

I take a deep drink of my Bloody Mary. "Tell me about the Poole brothers."

"They're twins, although nobody's actually seen them in public in years, so that may just be an urban legend."

"They must be pretty old. Are they still fully functional?"

"They keep tight control over their businesses. Although, according to rumor, one of them is ill. That's Sabastian. And the other is almost blind. That would be Maximilian."

"Is their security detail staffed by Coldcreek Security?"

"Very much so. Coldcreek is a dangerous crowd. They recruit from Special Forces—both US and foreign—and they're not too particular about who they hire. Made to order for the brothers."

"Would you care for another, sir?" my phantom waiter murmurs from over my shoulder solicitously.

I wave him away. Where does he come from?

Leland drains his martini, dabs his lips with a thick linen napkin, which he drops on the table to signal he's leaving. Suddenly Leland looks seriously worried. "Are you really going to try to see the Poole brothers in person? Take my advice. Don't. They're dangerous men. They are surrounded by dangerous men. Professional killers. The Poole brothers are ruthless. They destroy anyone who gets in their way. People who challenge the brothers tend to die. Don't say I didn't warn you."

CHAPTER TEN

WITH THE HELP of two security guards and a groundskeeper, I find the building where Dr. Alsop's lab is located. It's a traditional government structure designed to be functional and not offend anybody, which means it has no style at all. I wander through empty corridors until I encounter a young woman in a lab coat who directs me to a sign that reads "The Center for Drug Evaluation and Research."

A woman in her sixties is waiting for me at her office door. She has short, graying hair and wears a white lab coat and bright blue Hoka running shoes, scuffed and stained green. She has a gold necklace around her neck and a man's Rolex watch with a steel expansion bracelet on her left wrist. A plastic ID card hangs by a thin lanyard from around her neck. It shows her photograph and name, and the words in bright red: "Margot Alsop, FDA."

We stand at her office door, me in the hallway, she in the doorway, ready to close the door on me if necessary. I show her my police identification. She puts on a pair of horn-rimmed glasses and examines my ID carefully, glancing twice between my face and the photo on my police ID, then returns them to me.

"Come in," she says grudgingly.

I follow her through a laboratory with three workbenches, and into a small, cluttered office, where she sits behind a desk piled high with books and folders. I take the single empty chair in the room.

"What happened to Dr. Young?" she asks. "You said he was murdered."

"He was found dead in a burning car. We're at an early stage in the investigation."

"Are you certain the man you found was Dr. Young?" Alsop demands.

"We haven't made a conclusive identification. The body was badly damaged in the fire. But we're fairly confident the victim was Harvey Young. We believe he was murdered."

"Of course, he was murdered. How did you find me?"

"Mrs. Young gave me your name."

"You spoke to Dr. Young's wife? How is she taking it?"

"As badly as you would expect."

"Poor woman."

"I told her we couldn't make a definitive identification."

She grimaces. "It's Dr. Young, all right. I'm sure of it. He called me yesterday morning and told me he was on his way to meet me here at the lab. He never arrived."

"What time did he call?"

"A little before nine, I think."

"What makes you so sure he was murdered?"

"It's just a bad feeling."

"Were you and Harvey Young close?"

"I told you, we never met."

"But you've recently been in contact."

"That's right—by phone. He came to Washington so we could consult in person. He had some material he wanted me to see."

"Do you know whether he was carrying this material with him this morning?"

"I assume he must have. That was the point of our visit. He was going to show me what he'd found."

"You said he came to Washington to consult with you. What was that about?"

She fidgets nervously with the necklace around her neck. It is made up of Hebrew letters that spell out "Margot." She looks away from me and studies a pile of papers on her desk.

"Why did Harvey Young come to Washington?" I ask.

"I can't talk about that."

"Why not?"

"It's confidential. It was in connection with an ongoing FDA investigation. And I'm not sure Dr. Young would want me to say anything about it. It's highly sensitive. He asked me not to tell anybody about his visit to the FDA."

"Dr. Young is dead. He has nothing to say about it anymore. Was it about Zemlon?"

"I'm not free to speak about Zemlon."

At that moment, the door to the office opens and a young man wearing a lab coat sticks his head in the door. He starts to say something to Dr. Alsop, then registers my presence. "Sorry, Dr. Alsop, I didn't know you had a visitor."

"Detective, this is my assistant, Dr. Malik. Harry, this is Detective Zorn. He's with the DC police. Homicide."

Dr. Malik's eyes widen. He's a young man of slight build and wears a plastic ID hanging from a chain around his neck, just like the one Alsop wears. He looks at me anxiously, as people do when they learn I'm from Homicide.

"I'm sorry to interrupt," Dr. Malik says. "Is this about Dr. Young?"

"Yes, Harry. I'm afraid it is."

The young man looks at me intently and leaves, shutting the door quietly behind him.

"This is a murder investigation. You can't withhold pertinent information."

"I'm not authorized to share that information with you."

"Dr. Young was murdered. I'm sure you'd want the police to find out who was responsible for his death."

"Of course. I'm pretty sure I already know."

After a long pause, she takes a deep breath. "I'll tell you what I'll do. As soon as I get into the lab tomorrow morning, I'll speak to the Commissioner himself and ask for authority to share information with you about why Dr. Young was in Washington. If he gives me the okay, I'll call you and tell you all I know."

"Why not speak with the Commissioner now?"

"He's out of town and not available."

I'm getting impatient with this woman. I need to know why Dr. Young was in Washington. I've already lost a day. Now she wants me to wait another day. But I don't think a boyish grin is going to work on this woman. She is made of tough stuff.

"When can I expect your call?" I ask.

"First thing tomorrow morning. I go for a run around six thirty, then come directly here to the lab. I'll speak with the Commissioner then. I'll call you as soon as I have the answer."

She takes my card and studies it carefully then places it in the middle of her desk, pushing away a copy of the *New England Journal of Medicine* to make room.

We shake hands and I leave. I have a very uncomfortable feeling as I go. I should have stayed, and insisted she tell me what's going on, with or without the Commissioner's approval. On the way to my car, I almost stop and turn back to insist she answer my questions but decide against it. I try to reassure myself with the thought that it's only a matter of less than twenty-four hours. What could go wrong?

CHAPTER ELEVEN

I'M AT THE corner of Sixteenth and K Streets in northwest Washington in the business district of DC. I sometimes think of this corner as the "heart and soul" of Washington. Except, of course, Washington has no heart. Sometimes I doubt it has a soul. But this area is, no question, the dynamo of the city. It keeps the city moving and provides its energy and drive. And the money.

As I look up K Street, I see blocks and blocks of featureless buildings, the offices of lawyers and lobbyists. These are the men and women who make this city run. Washington is not its government buildings, its grand parks, or its statues and its monuments. It's not the Capitol or the Supreme Court. It's not even the White House, which I can see at the other end of Sixteenth Street. The White House looks tiny in comparison with these shiny new office buildings, sheathed in glass and metal. The White House looks like a dwarf among them, a doll's house.

I make my way up K Street until I reach the Washington headquarters of Magma Capital Management. Outside, it looks no different than any of the dozens of large corporate offices sheathed in gray limestone.

At the far end of a reception area is a long counter with a marble top. Behind it stand four uniformed men. They do not look welcoming. Each man wears a white uniform with a shoulder patch that reads "Coldcreek Security". Behind them is a bank of elevators.

"Can I assist you?" one of them asks me.

"I'm here to speak with Mr. Forest."

"Mr. Forest's offices are in Chicago."

"Mr. Forest is in Washington today," I say. "He's testifying before a congressional committee."

"Mr. Forest is not available."

"I'm afraid you're going to have to make him available."

I show the uniformed security guy my police ID. "Tell Mr. Forest that Marko Zorn is here to see him. Metropolitan Police. Homicide."

"I'll connect you with one of his assistants."

"An assistant won't do. I'm here in connection with a murder investigation, and I only deal with principals."

That information doesn't seem to impress the guard. "Mr. Forest is in conference and cannot be disturbed."

"Really? Where is this conference? Perhaps I'll join him there."

The guard's face freezes, and I swear he turns pale.

"Where is the conference taking place?" I repeat.

The guards must have some secret messaging system because, at that moment, the other three guards converge on me. Not in a nice way.

"I'm afraid I must insist," I announce loudly. I pat the breast pocket of my jacket as if I had something important tucked away there, other than a bus ticket. "I have a court order directing Mr. Forest to answer questions about his role in distributing illegal drugs. Please don't force me to call in a SWAT team."

At this point, three women pass by and make for the bank of elevators behind the front counter. They look to be quite young. They don't look like they could put up much of a fight. One is holding a shopping bag filled with wrapping paper and colorful boxes.

"Hold the elevator," one of the girls shouts as the doors of the nearest elevator begin to close. The girls run to catch it.

"Excuse me," I say to the cluster of guards. "We'll talk later." I sprint around the end of the reception desk and join the girls, who are giggling breathlessly. I catch a glimpse of the guards as they rush and try to stop the elevator. They're too late.

"Do you girls work for Mr. Forest?" I ask, giving them all a broad smile. It's supposed to be ingratiating and reassuring. With girls this young it usually works.

They giggle. They've obviously come from a late lunch. With probably a few extra old fashioneds.

"Let me guess. Birthday? Or promotion?"

"Annie just got promoted."

"Which one of you is the lucky girl?"

The girls all giggle. "That's Annie." They point to a pretty young blond.

"About time, Annie. Congratulations. Do you all work for Mr. Forest?"

"No," they say in unison.

"We're in Accounting," a petite redhead says.

"Mr. Forest's loss." More giggles. "Where do you think I might find Mr. Forest? I suppose his conference room is on the top floor."

"Sure," one of the soberer ones says.

The elevator stops and the doors slide silently open. We're on the fifth floor and the girls stumble out. I punch the button for the eleventh floor, the top floor. I hope there's no posse of armed guards waiting for me.

Two men carrying briefcases join me on the ninth floor and we ride together to the eleventh.

"I hope we're not too late for the conference," I say pleasantly.

"It's not scheduled to start for another hour. We're okay," one says.

The doors slide open. I politely gesture for my companions to go ahead. Might as well let them take the bullets in case there is an angry reception committee waiting for me.

No one is waiting. "Which way to the conference room?" I ask. "This is my first time here."

"Straight ahead," one says and they disappear into an office.

I have no trouble locating the conference room. In front of me are broad double doors and beyond the doors I hear loud, angry voices. Or, to be more exact, I hear one loud, angry voice. I stride to the doors and swing them both open at once. It is much more dramatic to open two such doors at the same time.

I'm afraid my dramatic entrance is lost on the those in the room. Before me is a long, polished mahogany conference table. On the far side are clustered seven men and women. One man dominates the room.

He is of average size, maybe just under six feet. About fifty. He wears a white shirt with green stripes and red suspenders. His jacket has been tossed on a nearby chair. His hair is gray, and his face deeply tanned. He must have spent a long time in California. You don't get that kind of tan in Chicago. He holds a batch of documents in one hand and a cell phone in the other, into which he is yelling. While I watch, he paces back and forth. The person at the other end of the line doesn't seem to be talking much.

One of his minions keeps trying to get the man's attention to let him know somebody, a stranger—me—has entered the room.

The gray-haired man finally stops, turns, and stares at me. He flings the papers onto the table and presses the cell phone to his chest to mute it. "Who the fuck are you? Who let you in here?"

I sense the doors behind me being pushed open. I know there is a crowd of uniformed armed guards descending on me. I do not turn to look. That would be a sign of weakness.

"My name is Marko Zorn." I want everyone in the room to hear me. "I'm a police officer from the DC Metropolitan Police. I'm investigating the murder of Harvey Young. If you're Duncan Forest, I need to discuss a business proposition with you."

"How'd you get in here?" Forest holds up his hand to hold off the security guards. "Answer my question."

"Which one should I answer? You asked three questions. I'm investigating the sale of a lethal drug known as Speedball, which, I believe, is manufactured and distributed by a Magma Capital subsidiary. Is the name Speedball familiar to you?"

Forest turns in fury on the trembling assistants surrounding him. I can see by their reaction at least some of them have heard the name Speedball. "Which one of you fucking clowns has been talking to this bozo?" Forest does not wait for an answer. He turns on me. "I have nothing to say to you. Get out!"

"Talk to me about Magma's role in the sale of Speedball," I say.

"Out now!"

"You can't throw me out. I'm a police officer. You haven't heard my business proposition."

"I don't care if you're the goddamn Pope. Out!"

I sense the security troops move in on me. One of them touches the sleeve of my jacket.

"If any one of your goons touches me," I announce loudly, "he'll need a new arm." The man behind me snatches his hand away.

"Get him out of my sight!" Forest screams.

The next thing I know, I'm back in the elevator surrounded by five very upset bruisers. Then I'm on the street in front of the Magma building. Maybe not my finest hour. A little undignified, perhaps. But I got the message to Duncan Forest. I know what you're doing and where to find you.

CHAPTER TWELVE

AFTER A TROUBLED night dreaming of Duncan Forest and his red suspenders and an elevator full of giggling girls, I'm awakened at seven in the morning by the phone at my bedside.

"Is this Detective Zorn?" the caller asks.

"I'm Marko Zorn. Who is this?"

"This is Harry Malik. We met in Dr. Alsop's lab."

It comes back to me through the fog of sleep—Dr. Alsop's young lab assistant. I'm not at my best this early. Not before I've had several cups of very strong coffee. "Yes, Dr. Malik. What is it?"

"Dr. Alsop is dead."

I take a deep breath to clear my head. "What happened?"

"I got a call from somebody in the National Park Service," Malik tells me. "They found Dr. Alsop's body in the canal."

"Canal? What canal?"

"You know, the Chesapeake and Ohio Canal."

"Where are you now?"

"I'm at the lab. I don't know what to do."

"Go home," I say. "Now. Don't stay in the lab. Go home and lock your door."

"Is that really necessary? Shouldn't I inform human resources about Dr. Alsop?"

"Leave that to me. Don't talk to anyone except me."

"If you say so . . ."

"I say so. Where on the canal was Dr. Alsop's body found?"

"It was near the Great Falls Visitors Center."

"Thank you, Dr. Malik. I'll take it from here."

"Am I in danger?"

"You may be in danger, Dr. Malik. You may be in great danger."

*   *   *

I park my MG in Georgetown on M Street as close to the terminus of the Chesapeake and Ohio Canal as I can get. At this early hour there are plenty of parking spaces, and the streets are nearly empty. The kids from Georgetown University are probably still in bed, sleeping off last night's parties. The stores aren't open yet, and the tourists visiting old Georgetown with its federal buildings won't arrive for another few hours. The shoppers will come later.

The rest of my trip will have to be on foot. I find my way to the beginning of the canal at the bottom of a steep street and head along the towpath that was long ago used by horses to haul barges along the canal from Cumberland, Maryland, to Georgetown in Washington. For people who like to hike and get in touch with nature, this is a great place—or so I'm told. I'm not an outdoors person and I don't have much use for nature, so I'm a stranger to the rustic charms of the canal.

For me, it's just a long ditch. I seem to remember there are eighty-some locks along the almost two hundred miles of canal. I remember that because I've seen a good deal of it over the years. There have been occasions when I was seeing a woman who believed in vigorous exercise and good health and I was obliged to accompany her on excursions through the bucolic countryside, including hiking the canal—usually very early in the morning. Those relation-ships did not last long.

I walk briskly along the towpath, passing a few early-morning joggers, bicyclists, and an elderly couple walking a dog. When I see yellow police tape closing off the path, I know I'm close.

A uniformed Park Police officer examines my ID and waves me through the temporary barrier the Park Police have put up. A few hundred feet farther on, a cluster of men and women stand around a shape lying on the ground, covered by a tarpaulin. They all wear Park Police uniforms and, judging from the chevrons on their sleeves, they're all junior officers.

I join the group and look down at the shape at their feet. The face and body are covered, but the shoes stick out from beneath the tarpaulin. They are bright blue Hoka running shoes, scuffed and stained green.

One of the officers partially pulls the tarpaulin from the body. This is Margot Alsop. The gold necklace spelling out the name "Margot" is twisted tight around her neck. The expensive Rolex is still on her wrist.

A jolt of fury races through my body. My heart pounds, and my skin prickles with rage. "You idiot. You stupid, stupid idiot."

Two Park Police officers standing nearby look at me anxiously. "Are you all right, sir?" one asks.

I realize I'm speaking aloud. I let this woman talk me into waiting before she told me why Dr. Harvey Young came to Washington. I should have insisted Alsop tell me everything the first time. I should have insisted she be given police protection. I sensed she was in danger and now she's dead. I let her down.

My anger subsides. I breathe normally again. I'm back in control of my emotions. "That's Dr. Margot Alsop. Where was she found?"

The officer points at the canal a few yards away. "A jogger passed along the towpath and saw the body in the water. We figure she must have stumbled and fallen into the canal and drowned," one of the Park Police officers says hopefully.

"Do your park visitors often fall into the canal?" I ask.

Several of the Park Police officers shake their heads.

"How deep is the water?"

"Along this stretch, two feet or so."

"Are there any witnesses?"

"There aren't many people in this area at this hour. We've interviewed some people using the towpath closer to Georgetown, but no one saw the lady fall."

This is murder. It has all the signs of being planned carefully in advance. A single woman. Alone. Early in the morning. People don't just fall into canals. It's first-degree, premeditated murder. Probably a professional hit.

I call Tyrone and tell him about the discovery of Dr. Alsop's body in the canal and ask him to bring forensic and medical teams.

Without touching the body, I make a quick visual examination. I see a bloody wound at the base of her skull. It could have come from the fall, but I doubt it. I'll leave that to the medical examiner's team to determine. I can make out red bruises on Alsop's neck and throat where somebody tried, and failed, to pull her necklace off.

My cell phone rings. "Detective Zorn? My name is Dexter Phillips. The Commissioner must speak with you urgently."

"What does your Commissioner commission and why must he speak with me so urgently?"

"I am speaking on behalf of the Commissioner of the Food and Drug Administration. Please come to his office immediately."

"I'm taking charge of this investigation," I announce to the Park Police team when I end my call. "My partner and the medical and forensic teams are on their way. See that no unauthorized person is allowed in this area."

"Why do we need to do that?" one of the Park Police officers complains. "It was an accident. Wasn't it?"

"The death of this woman was no accident. She was murdered. The victim was healthy and athletic. It is very unlikely she tripped and fell into the canal and drowned. Not in two feet of water. The Chesapeake and Ohio Canal is now a crime scene."

CHAPTER THIRTEEN

NORMAN FOLSOM, the Commissioner of the Food and Drug Administration, waves me peremptorily into his large, sunny office. He's heavyset with blond hair and wears a seersucker suit and brown oxford shoes. He's accompanied by two young people, a man and a woman, both wearing government-regulation, junior-bureaucrat outfits. I remember to turn off my cell phone so as not to disturb the great man. This is no time to get a phone call from some credit card company offering me fabulous interest rates.

"What is your report on the death of Dr. Alsop?" Folsom demands before I'm more than a few steps into his office.

How in hell did this guy know about Dr. Alsop? She must have been killed somewhere around seven. Less than two hours ago. Who told him about the incident? Someone in the Park Police? That doesn't seem likely. It has to be someone in the DC Metropolitan Police. But at this point very few people would have heard anything about Alsop's death. Except Tyrone. I don't want to think about that possibility. Not now. I'll have to deal with this problem later.

"I don't have a report, Commissioner. I've just come from the crime scene. Our team is investigating the area as we speak."

"When will you have my report, Officer?"

"When it is concluded."

"You don't seem to realize the death of one of our researchers is important."

"I'm sure it is."

"And urgent."

"You'll get a report when I have something to report. And only through proper channels."

"I'm not sure I like your attitude, Officer. Do you know who you're talking to? I've already spoken with your chief of police, Chief Flynn."

Oh, great, I think. That's all I need. Why does this man feel he must speak directly to my boss? Normal people don't do that. Not before they've even spoken to me. After they've met me, for sure. But not before. This guy is seriously on edge and worried about something.

"Chief Flynn," Commissioner Folsom goes on, "assured me the police will be fully cooperative with the FDA. Fully. She offered to make that clear to you personally, if necessary."

I'll bet she did.

"So, I repeat my question. What happened to Dr. Alsop?"

"The body of a woman was found in the C and O Canal early this morning. We haven't made a positive identification yet, but we think it's Dr. Alsop. The circumstances of the death are suspicious."

"What circumstances?"

"I can't go into details. We're at an early stage of our investigation. My partner is at the scene now."

If I were at the scene, what would I be doing? The team will be there by now. They know what they're doing. Including Tyrone. For better or worse. I'd probably be in the way.

"Was Dr. Alsop murdered?" the Commissioner asks.

"What makes you think she was murdered?"

"You're deliberately avoiding my questions. Dr. Alsop was an esteemed member of our FDA team." He looks at the two supporting actors standing behind him. They nod vigorously in assent. "Dr. Alsop was also a very dear, very close friend. I have every right to know the details of her death."

"What was Dr. Alsop's first name?" I ask.

"What's the relevance of that question?"

"Dr. Alsop's first name is Margot, in case you were wondering."

"Detective, I don't like your attitude."

"Join the crowd."

"Will you force me to contact Chief Flynn once more to report your insubordination?"

"While we're asking each other questions. Can you tell me what project Dr. Alsop was working on?"

"That is none of your business."

"That very much *is* my business. What was she working on?"

"She was engaged on many projects. Dr. Alsop was a senior FDA researcher. She would naturally be supervising numerous projects." He glances at his lackeys for confirmation, but they just look baffled and stay silent.

This exchange seems to distract Folsom from me, and he turns his attention to the two assistants or whatever they are.

"Has Dr. Alsop submitted her recommendations?"

"Not yet, sir," the young man answers.

"She told me yesterday," the girl bureaucrat chimes in, "that she expected to have it completed last week, but something unexpected came up she had to look into further."

"What came up?"

"I don't know, sir. She wouldn't tell me."

"Wouldn't tell you? Did you not explain that you were speaking on my behalf?"

"I did, sir. She still refused to tell me."

"That woman has been working on this project for months now. My office has been getting a lot of heat to complete this process. Not just from Altavista but from Congress as well. I want her recommendations on my desk by close of business today. I'm afraid that Dr. Alsop viewed her role and that of the FDA as 'gatekeepers'. We're not 'gatekeepers' here. We're 'facilitators'. Our job is to see that precious medications get to the public as soon as possible. Not to create unnecessary obstructions. In Dr. Alsop's absence, get someone else to sign off on her report."

"Yes, sir," the two assistants say simultaneously.

"Who's in charge of the project now that Alsop's out of the picture?"

"Nobody," the young woman says. "She handled all the details of that investigation herself."

"Does she have an assistant?"

"There's a postdoc lab assistant, but he doesn't have the authority to sign off on anything."

"Damn it, get me the report and I'll sign off on it myself."

"I'm not sure that would be a good idea, sir," the young man murmurs hesitatingly.

Folsom remembers I'm still in the room, listening intently.

"Have you heard of a Harvey Young?" I ask.

Folsom looks blank. "Who's Harvey Young?" Folsom demands of his young assistants. "Does he have anything to do with the project?"

"He was the biochemist who originally developed the drug Zemlon," I answer for them.

"What's that got to do with Alsop's death?"

"I don't know. But Harvey Young was also murdered."

"So?"

"I just thought you might want to know."

"I don't care."

"What was the project Dr. Alsop was working on?" I ask again. "The one you plan to sign off on at close of business today."

"That's confidential information I'm not at liberty to share. Good day, Officer."

"I'm looking at two separate murders in just a few days. They are almost certainly connected."

"I'm not going to waste my time speculating. I warn you, Officer, I will report you to Chief Flynn. We're finished here. Douglas, escort this man to the main entrance and instruct security not to let him in again."

"Yes, sir," the young man I now know is called Douglas says. First name? Last name? Who knows.

Douglas approaches me tentatively until I give him my Klingon death stare and he backs off quickly.

CHAPTER FOURTEEN

I REMEMBER TO switch on my phone as I leave the FDA headquarters building and I'm disheartened to find numerous text messages and calls have come in and gone to voice mail while I was with the Commissioner. All but one is administrative crap. I decide to take care of those later. One text message is different and I know I must deal with it immediately. It's from Harry Malik, Dr. Alsop's lab assistant. The text reads: *I must talk to you. Urgently. Please call.*

I type: *Vietnam Veterans Memorial. Two this afternoon.* I hit SEND.

At that moment, I have something even more immediate to deal with. When I leave the FDA parking lot, a maroon Chevy Camaro with Virginia plates pulls right up behind me. As I drive toward downtown DC, the Camaro drops back four or five car lengths. My green MG is easy to spot, even in heavy traffic, and therefore easy to follow. When I reach Georgia Avenue, I floor the accelerator, taking the speed up to over seventy, and employ some mildly evasive tactics.

The speed limit here is probably around twenty-five. I hope no Maryland trooper is in the area. I don't think he'd be impressed by my DC police badge. It would probably just annoy him. My shadow keeps up with me. I turn off onto a side street, and the

Camaro turns with me. We drive through a residential area with nice houses—kids' bikes are on well-manicured lawns and basketball hoops are attached to garage doors. I creep along, keeping my speed well under twenty. The driver following me stays at my slow speed. I know for sure the driver of the Camaro is following me and is a professional—just not a very good professional.

At that point, my partner, Tyrone, calls. "I'm back from the crime scene on the canal. The victim's been taken to the medical examiner's lab."

"Cause of death?"

"Preliminary assessment is drowning. But the victim was severely hit on the head. Probably knocked unconscious, then pitched into the canal. This is all subject to confirmation by the ME, of course." There's an awkward silence. Then he says, "The watch commander has called you several times. He says you're not answering your cell phone. He wants you to report to Chief Flynn's office ASAP."

"I don't expect to be back at headquarters any time soon. I'm kind of in the middle of something just now."

"The watch commander said it's extremely urgent."

"The watch commander always says that. Tell the watch commander to breathe deeply."

"I've reported to Chief Flynn about the body in the canal," Tyrone tells me. "I hope that's okay. I thought the chief should be kept informed. And I couldn't reach you."

"That's fine, Tyrone. Keep the lady informed. In the meantime, I want you to check a Virginia license plate for me." I give him the plate number of the Chevy Camaro following me. "As soon as you have a hit, text me the details."

"What about Chief Flynn? She's expecting you."

"Tell her to be patient."

I drive until I reach Wisconsin Avenue and spot an upscale mall. I pull in and park in the lot behind a large department store. When I leave my car, I move slowly to give my shadow plenty of time to park his car and keep me in sight. I enter the store, pay my parking fee with one of my credit cards, and stroll past a cosmetics counter with stacks of lipsticks.

"Can you tell me where the restrooms are located?" I ask the girl at the counter.

"Second floor. The elevators are just to your left."

I walk slowly to the elevator bank, wait a couple of minutes, and then catch an empty elevator going up. The man who's following me sprints through the store and steps into the elevator just as the doors are beginning to close. He stands with his back to me. He has a serious dandruff problem. Even from a quick glance, I see he's carrying a weapon in a shoulder holster beneath his leather jacket. He looks vaguely familiar, but I can't quite place him. The leather jacket looks familiar, as well.

When the elevator stops at the second floor, the man remains stationary, careful to make no eye contact with me. I cross through the men's furnishing department, stop at a display of men's ties, spot a sign directing me to the restrooms, and head in that direction. I sense, rather than see, that my shadow is right behind me.

When I enter the men's room there's a man standing at one of the urinals, his back to me. The place is otherwise deserted. I immediately step behind the door I just entered, pressing myself against the wall, and wait. I feel like some kind of pervert.

A moment later, my shadow enters the restroom, stops, and looks around. He's perplexed and unsure what to do next. He thinks I should be standing in front of him. My guy's wondering where I've got to. I won't keep him in suspense for long.

He checks the stall doors, thinking I might be hiding in one of them. As he looks, he unbuttons his leather jacket, I assume to give him easy access to whatever weapon he's carrying. His back is to me as he opens the last remaining stall door. He steps inside for a closer look.

I move silently behind him, grab him by the back of his collar, and smash his head into the white tile wall over the toilet. He staggers, dazed, and tries to turn to see who's attacked him, groping clumsily for his weapon. This happens in silence. The man standing at the urinal is undisturbed. I sort of recognize the man whose head I just slammed against the wall now—he's one of the two men who jumped me on the street.

To be on the safe side, I slam his head into the wall a second time. His knees give way, and he drops into a kind of kneeling position on the floor. He grabs hold of the toilet seat to keep his balance and sways to one side. I grab him to keep him from sprawling onto the floor and I snatch a Taurus Magnum revolver from his shoulder holster.

The man at the urinal has finished his business, turns, and stares at us through the open door of the toilet stall. He's seeing one man kneeling on the floor, while I'm holding a gun to his head.

"Don't let us bother you," I say genially to the man at the urinal. "We're having a business meeting. Go right ahead and wash your hands."

The man takes one more look at my guy, kneeling on the floor as if in prayer, then rushes from the men's room without looking back. He doesn't wash his hands. I break open the Taurus revolver and dump the rounds into the toilet bowl, then slip the gun into my pocket and face my would-be assailant.

He's beginning to clear his head as he struggles to his feet and stands, wobbly, leaning with one hand pressed against the wall of the toilet stall. He gropes for his gun, realizes it's gone, and stares at me sullenly.

"Who are you? Why are you following me?"

He shakes his head.

"Who do you work for?"

"None of your damn business."

"I'm making it my damn business. I can hit your head against the wall as many times as you want."

"Just try. I'll be ready for you this time."

I step toward him, and he tenses, ready to defend himself. I slam my fist onto his hand that's still pressed against the wall. He screams and clutches his injured hand.

"Fuck, fuck. Shit, shit. You broke my fucking hand." His face twists in pain.

"Tell me who sent you," I say. "If you don't give me an answer I like, I'll break your other hand."

He holds both hands under his armpits as if that would help and twists his mouth into strange shapes. I can't tell whether he's trying to talk to me or just whimpering.

"You're wasting my time," I say. "Were you the one who set fire to the Ford Explorer?"

He shakes his head vigorously. "Why did you have to hurt Clyde like that?" I suppose Clyde is the other dude I left bleeding all over the sidewalk, whose blood ruined my silk shirt. "You had no call to break his face. He's in the hospital now. He's having trouble breathing proper."

"Is Coldcreek Security paying his hospital bills?"

"They usually cover medical."

"What's your name?" I can see he's about to argue, and I move toward him menacingly.

He flinches, pressing himself against the wall of the stall to stay as far away from me as he can. It isn't very far.

"Don't hurt me again," he gasps.

"Tell me your name."

"Spencer," he answers promptly. I don't believe Spencer is his name for one minute. He's too quick and eager to provide the name. Besides, he doesn't look like a Spencer. I'll find his name some other way.

"Isn't this so much better, Spencer, you and me having a civilized conversation like this in a toilet? Tell me, Spencer, did someone order you to kill me? Is that why you've been following me?"

He shakes his head. "Nothing like that. I was just supposed to hurt you a little. You know, get your attention."

"You got my attention. Do you work for Dr. Love?"

"No way. I'm paid to provide security for him and the local dealers when they're delivering the product."

"Where does this product come from?"

The man tries to shrug, then realizes it hurts too much to move and gives up.

"Who provides Dr. Love with Speedball?"

"I don't have any part of that. All I know is once a week there's a delivery of Speedball for Dr. Love. There are deliveries to other parts of Washington on other days."

"Who makes the deliveries?"

"I don't know anybody's name. Just some guys."

"Do they work for Coldcreek Security?"

"I don't ask. It don't pay to ask."

"How are the deliveries made?"

"Some guys come by on delivery days and pass the Speedball to Dr. Love's helpers. Then they disappear."

"What time do they come?"

"Pretty close to eight in the morning. There are always three guys—the driver and two for muscle. They're the ones who handle the actual product and cash payments."

"What kind of car do they drive?"

"I don't remember."

"Try harder, Spencer. Try real hard."

"It's always the same car. A late-model Datsun SUV."

"Color?"

"Light gray."

"Where do you pick up the product?"

He swallows hard. "An outfit called Bismarck Moving and Storage."

"And this moving company pays your salary?"

He nods. "Can I have my gun back?"

I go to the door. Stop. "Let me give you a friendly word of advice, Spencer."

The man squints suspiciously.

"Go into another line of work. You're not very good at this, you know."

"Fuck you."

"Have you considered knitting?"

I leave Spencer, or whatever his name is, in the men's room, feeling sorry for himself. The department store manager, with the encouragement of a one-hundred-dollar bill, checks the credit card used to pay for parking the car that followed me into the store's lot. The name on the card is Frederick Tyson. And there's a card number. That's a good beginning.

Now all I have to do is find out who Frederick's account is charged to.

CHAPTER FIFTEEN

As soon as I retrieve my car from the department store lot, I check my cell phone. The dozen text and voice messages still waiting for me range in tone from imploring to threatening. Most tell me to return to police headquarters at once and see the chief. Immediately!

Three are from the watch commander. Five are from Frank Townsend, the chief of Homicide and my immediate boss, and four are from my partner—my other partner, Tyrone. These messages are increasingly hysterical and peremptory in character.

First, I call Tyrone. "There's something I need you to do."

"What about Chief Flynn? She says she must talk to you right away."

"All in good time, my friend. All in good time."

"The chief says it's urgent. She's getting impatient."

"I'll talk to her as soon as I'm free. Have you got anything on that Virginia license plate?"

"It's registered to a company called Bismarck Moving and Storage in Herndon, Virginia."

"Great. Now I need you to check a credit card for me. It's issued in the name of Frederick Tyson." I read off the credit card number, expiration date, and security code. "Who's paying for the charges on this account?"

"What should I tell the chief about you seeing her?"

"Tell her to be patient." I cut off the call before Tyrone can argue with me further.

I arrive at the Vietnam Veterans Memorial half an hour early so I can reconnoiter the area. It's a warm afternoon and the sky is clear and sunny. The morning chill has gone. There's a small crowd at the memorial. Some are tourist families, the children bored and demanding hot dogs and ice cream from the concession trucks parked not far away on Constitution Avenue. There are individual visitors, most standing silently at the wall, looking for names, searching for old friends or maybe long-lost family members. No one looks suspicious. These are mostly elderly men. I wonder how many more years they'll be coming here. What will the memorial be like in ten or twenty years when this generation passes? Who will mourn the fifty-eight thousand dead then? Who will remember them? Or remember that war? There have been so many since.

I spot Harry Malik standing at the base of the monument and join him at the apex where the two stone walls meet at an angle. We stand side by side looking at the engraved names neither of us knows. Malik doesn't turn to look at me because we can see each other in the reflections in the polished black granite.

"This is the first time I've ever been here," Malik tells me, still staring at the names. "I guess this wasn't my war."

"Why did you want to see me?"

He turns to face me. "What happened to Dr. Alsop?" His voice trembles. "The Park Police told me she was drowned in the C and O Canal. I can't believe she would just fall into the canal like that. The Park Police said it might have been a mugging."

"I'm sorry to have to tell you this, but Dr. Alsop was almost certainly murdered."

I don't like being so blunt. But it's necessary. He must understand how serious the situation is.

Malik shudders, holding his arms tight around his body. "Did she suffer at the end?"

"I don't think so. She probably never felt a thing."

"That's some relief, I guess. But not much."

"Was Dr. Alsop carrying anything important with her this morning, do you know? Like papers of some kind?"

"I doubt it. She was very careful about taking work home, particularly anything involving a sensitive investigation like the one she's been involved in."

Her attackers wouldn't have known that, I think.

"Whoever did this tried to pull off her gold necklace," I say. "The one with her name in Hebrew letters."

"She always wore that necklace."

"I believe they couldn't pull it loose in time. She still had it around her neck, all twisted. That's what makes the Park Police think it was a mugging."

"You don't?"

"If they'd been muggers, they'd have left her on the towpath, not thrown her into the canal and turned a simple robbery into first-degree murder. And they'd have taken her watch. That was more valuable than the necklace. Somebody wanted the necklace with her name on it as a trophy. Proof for whoever hired them that they'd done the job."

"Why would anyone want to hurt Dr. Alsop?"

"You tell me."

"I don't know anything about what happened at the canal."

An elderly couple stops next to us, holding a paper guide listing the names of the dead engraved on the wall. The woman points to a name silently.

"Let's move on," I say. "We must talk."

"About what?"

"About the project you and Dr. Alsop were working on."

It seems wrong to be talking about a police investigation in this hallowed place, so we go up the inclined path to the National Mall level and walk toward the Capitol and the old Smithsonian Museum buildings until we find an empty bench.

"Is Zemlon what Dr. Alsop was investigating?"

"I can't talk about our projects. It's strictly forbidden."

"I'm a police officer investigating a murder. Two murders, actually. You must tell me what you know."

Malik seems to shrink a bit. "I could lose my job."

You could lose more than your job, I want to tell him. But not yet.

"Were you investigating Zemlon?"

"No. We were looking at a successor drug called Neuropromine."

"Is there a problem with Neuropromine?"

"Dr. Alsop was convinced that Neuropromine is not safe. She believed Altavista secretly changed the Zemlon formula so that it was more powerful than Zemlon and much more addictive."

Malik twists around to look directly at me. "I shouldn't be telling you any of this. I shouldn't even be talking to you. You're an outsider. Those are the rules."

"There are no rules, Dr. Malik."

"When I was hired, I had to sign documents about keeping our investigations secret to outsiders."

"I'm a cop. Dr. Young is dead. Dr. Alsop is dead. Tell me what Dr. Alsop found."

"She was convinced that something has been added to the Zemlon formula to create Neuropromine. But she could not identify it."

"What made her think that?"

"The figures Altavista submitted didn't add up. She thought she detected evidence that Altavista covered up data in their application. Dr. Alsop put a hold on the FDA approval process."

"Okay. She stopped it."

"Not quite. The Neuropromine application was then assigned to the 'accelerated approval' classification. The approval process was made less stringent. She couldn't hold out much longer."

"What changed things?" I ask.

"A whistleblower within Altavista contacted us." Malik clutches his arms around his body as if in pain. "If anybody found out I was telling you this, I could lose my job."

I twist around on the bench so I'm looking directly into Dr. Malik's face.

"Do you want Dr. Alsop's death to be pointless? She died trying to protect the American public from a plague. Do you want to help me nail the people who did this to Dr. Alsop?"

Dr. Malik nods silently.

"Who was the whistleblower?"

"Dr. Harvey Young."

"The man who invented Zemlon? And the man who had an appointment to meet with Dr. Alsop?"

"He was a senior company director at Altavista."

"What did he tell you?"

"He told us Neuropromine could lead even casual users to dependence and death. It was essential the FDA not approve it for sale. Margot was, by that time, the only person who could stand in the way of final FDA approval. She was under extreme pressure to approve the drug, you understand. From top management at Alta-vista. There was an army of lobbyists working the halls of Washington. Altavista also has its pet congressmen and senators who are demanding the FDA stop stalling and approve Neuropromine.

"Altavista got their phony doctors' and patients' lobbying groups up in arms. There were editorials in journals and letters to the editors in newspapers across the country denouncing FDA incompetence for creating bureaucratic red tape. These voices all demanded this new 'miracle' drug be approved." Dr. Malik makes air quotation marks with his fingers. "Dr. Alsop stalled as long as she could, but she couldn't hold out much longer."

Dr. Malik stops talking. He's clearly scared. I don't like to do it but I'm about to make him more scared.

"Listen to me carefully now. Your life is in danger. The people who killed Dr. Alsop will be after you. They may think you know the secret of the formula Altavista is using for Neuropromine."

"I don't know anything. Dr. Young never got to show us the evidence."

"They don't know that. They must assume the worst. Your best hope is to tell me what you know, and I will try to stop them."

Malik takes a deep breath.

"Dr. Young discovered that a variant of Neuropromine was already being sold illegally, off-label, and the effects were even more deadly than our worst nightmares. The new, illegal drug produces an almost instantaneous high and, in many cases, proves fatal. The user just stops breathing.

"He told Dr. Alsop he'd steal evidence from Altavista's confidential files and bring it to Washington. With that, she'd have evidence to stop the approval of Neuropromine. And maybe put Altavista out of business."

"What was in those files?"

"The records of how Altavista changed the Zemlon formula that made it so much more addictive and dangerous. Dr. Young was supposed to come to the lab and hand over actual samples of the new drug using the same additive as Neuropromine. Though many times stronger.

"What am I supposed to do?" Malik asks.

"Get out of Washington. Immediately. Go somewhere far from here. Altavista, or its agents, will be looking for you. Take the next plane out of Washington. Don't go home to pack. Go straight to the airport. And don't come back until you hear from me."

CHAPTER SIXTEEN

I WATCH AS Dr. Malik safely disappears into a taxi and is on his way to Reagan National Airport. I decide to walk the short distance back to police headquarters. My route takes me past the National Museum of Natural History and the Museum of Science and Industry. I'm facing the National Gallery of Art when a new thought occurs to me. There's somebody I must see, and this may be my best chance.

The rotunda in the National Gallery of Art looks spectacular this afternoon. The Mercury Fountain overflows with flowers. Tables, covered with white linen, are scattered throughout, laden with bottles and glasses and trays of food and chaffing dishes. Solicitous waiters weave in and out among the guests. This afternoon, the rotunda is filled with men and women, sipping wine, snacking on canapés, murmuring soft exchanges to one another. The men are dressed in business suits, the women, mostly younger than the men, wear fashionable cocktail dresses and spike heels. In the background, a five-piece string orchestra is playing Schubert.

I pause for a moment at the reception desk. Two stalwart ladies check in arriving guests. To one side is a neat stack of name badges, the kind you attach to your chest that says, "Hi! My name is . . ." Whatever.

I show the invitation Leland gave me. I palm one of the name tags with the name "Taylor" in bold print. I attach it to my jacket pocket and walk in.

The rotunda in the National Gallery of Art is one of my favorite places in the city. It is usually almost deserted, with just a few art students clutching notepads. It's normally so quiet I can hear the water flowing in the Mercury Fountain. It's a perfect place to soothe one's soul. Even now, Hermes flies above us, caduceus in hand, oblivious of the milling crowd below.

I recognize a few senators and men and women from Congress, and some senior members of the current administration. Nobody I'd want to talk to. There is one person here I must meet. There's no guarantee she's even here. Leland Taylor said she was one of the hosts of this affair, but that doesn't mean she's actually attending.

I scan the faces of the hundred or so people milling around me. I've never met her, but I have a vague recollection of her face from her pictures on TV. A roving waiter offers me a glass of white wine. I decline.

I spot her, standing behind a long table. She is stunning, even at a distance. Tall and willowy with shoulder-length dark blond hair. She is obviously working the room, watching the guests and the staff, ready to pounce instantly if a guest's glass is empty, their plate not heaping with canapés, or they have no one important to talk to. She disappears, and a moment later introduces two people who should know each other, and they are ushered to a quiet corner. A boring guest is gently pried away from a man and introduced to a woman who is presumably less important. Then I lose her and feel a momentary pang of disappointment. I was enjoying watching her move with grace, determination, and efficiency. She's doing her job and doing it well.

Placed around the rotunda are dozens of large photographs mounted on easels. They are beautifully shot, and tastefully printed and mounted. Many of them would easily belong in an upscale art gallery and would fetch high prices. The pictures are all of children, young children, mostly Black and brown, with large, soulful pleading eyes. The exploitation makes me angry.

"Looking for a good time, sailor?" The voice behind me is a warm, lilting soprano, with a built-in laugh. I turn, and the woman I've been watching is standing in front of me.

She holds out her hand. "I'm Rebecca Poole." We shake. Her grip is firm and assured. Her smile is attractive and amused. She has large brown eyes. She looks to be in her early thirties.

"I don't believe you are really Donna Taylor," she says, amiably. "Do you have an actual name?"

"I'm Marko Zorn. I'm a police officer."

"I don't remember inviting you."

"You didn't."

"My mistake."

I'm mesmerized by Ms. Poole. I can't take my eyes from her face, even though I know it's rude. What fascinates me is how expressive it is, as she shifts from quiet amusement to feigned shock to surprise. These emotions flash across her face in seconds.

A waiter rushes up to Ms. Poole and offers me a glass of wine from his tray. "We can only offer you white wine, Officer," she explains. "Red wine makes the curators here at the gallery very anxious."

"No wine for me, thank you. Seeing as how I'm crashing your party, it seems impolite to drink your wine. Besides, I'm here on official business, and I shouldn't be drinking."

"Are you here to arrest me, Officer Zorn?"

"Certainly not."

"Then why did you crash my party?"

"To meet you."

"Should I be flattered?"

"Probably not."

"Why do you want to meet me?"

"I'd like to ask you about the Poole brothers and their business empire. You are related to the Poole brothers, aren't you?"

"Distantly."

"I assume you are also employed by the Poole brothers in some capacity." I gesture around the crowded room. "Invitation lists. Ordering wine. Keeping unwanted intruders out. That sort of thing."

"Why are you interested in my uncles?"

"A routine criminal investigation."

"My uncles are not criminals, Mr. Zorn."

"If you say so."

She looks at me sharply. "Seeing as how you have already joined the party, even though without an invitation, feel free to circulate and meet people. There are many powerful men and women here this evening. You're a detective. You're bound to find a criminal among them."

"I'd prefer to talk to you. I have a feeling you're the most interesting person in the room."

"What would you like to talk about?"

"How about the Poole brothers' gift of their art collection? I believe you are involved in negotiating that gift."

"It's very generous, don't you think?"

"I believe they are demanding that, as a condition of the gift, a museum building be constructed on the National Mall."

"I'd love to talk, but I must circulate. I see the emir needs some companionship." She stops and then turns back to me. "I sense you do not approve of what's happening here this afternoon. This is a fundraiser for the International Fund for Disadvantaged Children. Surely, you're not opposed to helping children around the world?"

"Is that what the Poole brothers do?"

"Among many other things. They support schools, hospitals, and clinics everywhere."

"Good for them."

"Is something bothering you?"

"This. It must cost a fortune to rent the National Gallery of Art for an afternoon. And the catering bill must be astronomical."

"It's all for a good cause."

"It's all too much. Too much expensive food, most of which will go to waste. And a five-person string orchestra! Give me a break. Nobody's listening. You could hire one guy with an accordion. It'd have the same effect."

"You don't like Schubert?"

"The *Trout Quintet* is one of my favorite pieces of music. But this is obscene."

The muscles in Ms. Poole's jaw tighten. I know I've probably spoiled my one chance to get near the Poole brothers through her, but I can't help myself. These affairs make me sick.

"This is a charity function, Mr. Zorn." Her eyes narrow. "I'm sorry you can't get into the spirit of the occasion."

"I look around the room, and what do I see? Captains of industry, leaders in international commerce, surrounded by photographs of suffering children. Some of these men and women here tonight are responsible for the poverty these kids live under. Maybe your uncles are, too."

"Certainly not! Among other things, my uncles produce medications that cure terrible diseases."

"I hope you're right. But these people annoy me. They write a check to your foundations, and any flicker of guilt or remorse is washed away. And it's all tax deductible." I look around at the guests and, just beyond them, at the displayed photographs of desperately poor and diseased children. "If you must know, I find charity at this level philanthropic pornography."

Ms. Poole is not holding a glass of wine. Otherwise, she might throw it in my face. She would have every right to do so. I realize I'm being a pill.

"I apologize, Ms. Poole. I am being extremely rude."

She smiles at me, leans toward me, reaches out, and grasps both of my hands in hers. "You *are* being extremely rude. I attend dozens of these affairs every year. You cannot believe how deadly boring they are. Our little conversation is the most interesting exchange I've had in months. And you are by far the most interesting man I've spoken to. I'd love to continue our debate some other time. But, if you'll excuse me, I must attend to the emir. He needs feminine companionship—like most men. And if you want to know about my uncles' activities, why don't you ask them?"

"That's just what I'll do."

Ms. Poole disappears quickly into the crowd.

CHAPTER SEVENTEEN

MY PARTNER, TYRONE, slumps into the chair at his desk, which is next to mine. It's late and I'm tired. When I left the reception at the National Gallery of Art, I returned to police headquarters where I tried to see Chief Flynn only to be told she'd left for the day. I'm instructed to return first thing in the morning. Since then, I've been at my desk at my computer trying to get through to the Poole brothers. I'm blocked at every turn. All I get are clueless drones who shuffle me from one phone extension to another. After an hour of this I give up and decide instead to try to learn something about the players in my new drama using Internet search engines.

I start with Rebecca Poole. Parents deceased. Resident of Virginia. Graduate of Bryn Mawr. Employment listed with Magma Capital Investments as special administrative assistant. Whatever the hell that means.

I turn next to the Poole brothers themselves. Who are they really, and how can I reach them? Once again, the Internet fails me. I learn even less about them than I did about their niece. The information has been carefully scrubbed, so as to make it useless. I'll have to contact them the hard way. I do learn something about their financial empire from some articles in *The Economist*. It's complicated. Shell companies. Interlocking directorates. Intricate ownership arrangements. It's a high-stakes international three-card monte. And about as honest.

At first, I ignore Tyrone, other than to mumble some meaningless exchange of friendly greetings. I don't want to be interrupted by engaging in squad room gossip. Not that Tyrone is the gossip type. He's always dead serious. When he speaks it's only for good reason. And with as few words as possible. He's not here at the end of the day because we're buddies and wants me to join him at some local bar for a beer. He probably wants to go home as much as I do. Maybe curl up with the latest edition of "Federal Rules of Criminal Procedure." I know he's here to find out what I'm up to.

I turn away from my computer screen and smile in a friendly way. "How are things going?" I ask.

"The chief's pretty upset with you."

"I'll bet."

"What did you tell her?"

"She asked me where we were on the Dr. Young murder investigation. I've requested authorities in Indianapolis to follow up on Dr. Young. Find out what he was working on. What brought him to Washington. How were his relations with his wife."

Good luck with that. Tyrone is doing all the right things. Following standard police procedure. I don't want to tell him he's wasting his time. I don't tell him that normal police procedure is useless for a crime like this one. Obviously, a professional hit.

"Did the chief assign you another case?" Tyrone asks.

"Not exactly. I'm sort of working on an independent line of investigation." I might as well be honest with Tyrone. He's going to find out anyway. "You know there's a dangerous new drug circulating in town. Called Speedball."

"I've heard of it."

"I'm going to stop the production and distribution of Speedball."

"All by yourself? How are you going to do that?"

"Speedball is produced and distributed by a pharmaceutical company called Altavista. I'm going to persuade the owners of that parent company to stop producing the drug. The owners are businessmen. They negotiate. That's what businessmen do."

"Have you had any success?"

"I haven't been able to get to the owners personally. I've had to deal with subordinates. They don't have the authority to make a deal or even talk to me. So far, the owners won't let me in the door to hear my proposal. But that's all I need to do. Get in the door. What time is it in Chicago?"

"Five twenty."

Using my cell phone, I put in a call.

"Hello, Magma Capital. How may I direct your call?" the girl at the other end of the line in Chicago asks in a chirpy voice. She can't be over twenty.

"I must speak to Maximilian or Sabastian Poole," I say. "I don't care which one."

There's a slight gasp from Chicago. "Excuse me, sir. Who is calling?"

"My name is Peabody, Grover Peabody. I am the chairman of the Concerned Citizens Committee to Protect the National Mall. Please put me through to one of the Poole brothers."

"I will connect you with Mr. Ketchum. He's with our customer service division."

"I don't want customer service. I want Maximilian or Sabastian Poole."

"Nobody speaks to the Poole brothers. Not ever. Perhaps Mr. Marlow in Legislative Affairs can help . . ."

"Mr. Marlow in Legislative Affairs cannot help. If you won't put me through to one of the brothers, then get this message to them.

My committee has the final say on whether the Poole brothers will be allowed to build their confounded museum on the National Mall. If they want their gift to become a monument, I must speak with them. Personally. Tonight. My committee is scheduled to meet tomorrow to make a final decision on the location of the art museum. If the brothers want their heap built on the mall, they must deal with me. I have a proposition to make. Tell them to call me this evening or the deal is off. You have my number." I hang up.

"What was that about?" Tyrone asks.

"I just left my calling card."

I give the receptionist credit. She's a whiz at getting through what must be Magma Capital's byzantine organization chart. Within minutes I get a call from somebody in London described as assistant secretary in the management division. That takes less than ten seconds before I terminate the conversation. Then a lawyer type calls from San Francisco. He is very angry. We both hang up simultaneously.

I know I'm close when Rebeca Poole herself calls a few minutes later. I don't identify myself other than as Mr. Peabody. I explain to her, nicely, that I cannot speak with her. Only one of the Poole brothers. No one else will do.

"If this is about the location of the Poole Pavilion on the National Mall, Mr. Peabody," she tells me firmly, "you must speak with me. I'm in charge of these negotiations."

"This is not a negotiation, Ms. Poole. This is an ultimatum."

I can tell she's getting suspicious. "Do I know you?" she asks. "Have we met? Your voice sounds familiar."

I hang up.

At ten forty-five my phone rings. "Is this Mr. Peabody?" a very old, rheumy voice demands.

"I am Grover Peabody. To which Mr. Poole am I speaking?"

The speaker at the other end of the line ignores my question. The caller ID indicates he's calling from a Washington area code. "I understand you have a proposition to make in regard to the siting of the Poole Pavilion."

"I believe my committee may be able to help, provided you do something for us."

"We don't negotiate with strangers. We don't negotiate over the phone."

"I suggest we meet somewhere and talk in person. Then we won't be strangers."

"It's the middle of the night."

"I'm willing to meet with you right now."

"I've never heard of you, Peabody. Nor of your committee."

"We operate below the radar. Nobody knows us or what we do. That's why we have so much power."

There's a long silence at the other end of the phone. "Very well. You can come here now. Just you, Peabody. No lawyers." He gives me an address on Sixteenth Street.

CHAPTER EIGHTEEN

THE HOUSE IS located in an upscale Washington neighborhood.

A man waits for me in front of a set of massive iron gates. He wears a uniform with a Coldcreek Security patch on his shoulder.

"My name is Peabody," I announce brightly. "I'm here to help with the details of the Poole brothers' generous gift of their art collection to the nation. I'm expected."

The name "Gustavo" is embroidered on the guard's left breast pocket. A Beretta is at his waist.

"Stand real still," Gustavo commands. "No weapons, cameras, or recording equipment permitted." He pats me down. "I will escort you inside. Remember, I'll be right behind you at all times. Make no sudden moves. I don't care for sudden moves."

A twelve-foot-high stone wall blocks all sight of the big house and the grounds.

"They're waiting for you," he says, and opens the iron gates that squeak on their rusty hinges. He leads me into the grounds. "Don't speak unless spoken to. When you address the gentlemen, always say 'sir.'"

Inside the gates, there are more uniformed men carrying automatic weapons. Each man has a Coldcreek Security patch on his shoulder. I see others watching me from the darkness of a grove of trees, accompanied by fierce dogs, tugging at their leashes.

It's quiet here in this parklike area. The stone walls cut off much of the traffic sound from Sixteenth Street. A long, winding drive leads to an old mansion, once probably elegant and stately, now shabby and forlorn. Even in the dim light, I can see the window shutters need paint and some hang loose. There are missing tiles on the roof. The grass hasn't been mowed in years. The gardens have gone to seed.

I follow Gustavo along the drive until we reach a large stone bowl, which, I imagine, was once a part of an ornate fountain. Now, it's dry and filled with dead leaves. A dreary-looking bronze nymph stands in the middle of the empty fountain, holding a large urn from which water no longer flows.

We climb stone steps, enter the set of large front doors. I follow Gustavo down a dim corridor. There's a little illumination from a single sconce light. The bulb can't be more than forty watts. The walls are covered with purple, flocked-velvet wallpaper. Old furniture—dressers and wardrobes—are stacked on the floor and covered in dust. Mirrors in gilt frames, their backings dark and splotchy with age, hang on the walls. A rusting one-speed Schwinn bike, with upright handlebars, leans against the wall. It's old, probably from the 1950s, with a little bicycle bell attached to the handlebar. The balloon tires are flat.

Gustavo knocks softly at the door at the far end of the corridor. I hear a faint murmur from within. He opens the door and motions for me to go in ahead of him.

What I see takes my breath away.

The room must have once been a grand ballroom. There are floor-to-ceiling French doors leading to a terrace and garden beyond—now a jungle of weeds and barren fruit trees. Heavy, floor-length, faded damask curtains cover many of the windows. Two floor lamps with heavy velour shades cast a dim light.

The room is filled with cardboard boxes and crates that over-flow with papers, books, and a collection of junk. Some boxes are stacked shoulder high. In between are piles of old newspapers and magazines. There's a crate of Atari video games, on top of which rests a trombone. At the far end of the room is a stone fireplace stacked with logs. To one side of the fireplace stands a full set of armor complete with a closed visor. The armor figure grasps, in its iron gauntlet, a massive, double-edge, two-handed broadsword. The armor with its iron helmet and crest stands over seven feet high.

I step carefully through the maze of books and papers and accu-mulated junk. As I pass a grand piano, I catch a glimpse of a small painting lying on top. Even in the dim light, I recognize the image of three people gathered around a harpsichord. I'm stunned.

I've seen that picture before—probably hundreds of times—in reproduction. I'm looking at a long-lost painting that I seem to remember is called *The Concert*. This looks like an original oil on canvas. I want to stop and examine it, but Gustavo prods me on. Can this really be a genuine Vermeer? If it's the original, it would be worth well over a hundred million dollars. It's one of the most famous stolen paintings on record, second only to the *Mona Lisa*. Except the *Mona Lisa* was recovered. This picture has never been found. What is this treasure doing here in this junkyard?

"Keep moving," Gustavo whispers from behind me.

Two old men are waiting for me in the dim light. One, about twenty feet away, sits in a worn armchair, once covered in blue velour, now torn so the stuffing spills out. He's thin, and his hair is wispy gray, his face deeply creased and mottled with brown age spots. His legs are covered by a heavy lap robe even though the room is warm. He wears dark sunglasses.

The second man sits just a few feet away from where I stand. He is hunched over in a wheelchair, holding a plastic tube in his left hand attached to an oxygen canister. In his trembling right hand, he clutches a lit cigarette. He is frail. His clothes are too big for his body. His face is cadaverous, cheeks sunken. The skin like parchment. He is completely bald except for a few strands of hair at the back of his head. He stares at me through piercing, angry eyes.

"Are you the one I spoke with on the phone?" the man in the wheelchair demands. "The one who wants to make a deal about our new art museum?"

"That was me."

"Say 'sir,'" Gustavo whispers from just behind me.

"I'm here to offer you a deal," I say.

"What kind of deal?" the old man asks.

"Stop selling your poison drugs." I speak loudly to be sure the man across the room can hear me. "Stop selling Speedball. And stop your plans to market Neuropromine in its present form."

"What's that got to do with our museum?" the man in the armchair across the room demands. He does not look at me directly as a seeing person would. Leland Taylor of the *Washington Post* told me one of the brothers is nearly blind. I think he said that was Maximilian. The guy in the wheelchair must be Sabastian, then.

"I'm afraid I haven't been completely candid with you about the purpose of my visit," I say. "My name is not Peabody, and I'm not associated with any citizens committee. I'm here to come to an agreement with you about a drug one of your companies produces."

"Why do you care about what our companies do?" the man in the velour armchair across the room demands.

"Because," a voice from the dark announces. "This man is a fraud and a spy."

The speaker emerges from the dim light. He is tall and ramrod straight. His hair is bleached white-blond. The man who was watching me at the scene of the car fire where Dr. Young was murdered.

"Who the hell are you?" I demand. I'm not expecting company.

"My name is Hammer. And you look just like a nail to me."

Uh-oh. Bad news.

"His name is Marko Zorn." Hammer speaks to the two men. "He's a police detective. He's investigating the death of Dr. Young."

"You let this man in?" the man in the wheelchair, who must be Sabastian, screams at Gustavo. "Into our private sanctuary? Into our home?"

"He said his name was Peabody," Gustavo stammers. "He said you were expecting him."

"Did you inspect his identification? You broke the rules. You know what happens to people who break the rules."

"I'm sorry, Mr. Poole, I never—"

"There's no reason to act hastily." I sense something very bad is coming. I must not let this get out of hand. "I'm here to find a compromise. I'm offering a deal that will satisfy everyone."

"We don't do business with police spies." This is from across the room.

"Let's talk calmly."

"Damn your impertinence." Sabastian speaks directly at me. "I don't think I like you."

"If you don't agree to my offer," I say, "I'll put you out of business. That's a promise."

Sabastian reaches into a pocket on the side of this wheelchair. He pulls out an object. It's black and a foot long. I think it must be some kind of club.

Then I see it clearly.

"Holy shit!" I say aloud.

Sabastian is pointing a double-barreled, sawed-off shotgun at my head. His hand is shaking but at this close range he can't miss. With a shotgun, the effective spread of whatever shot he's loaded the gun with will be several feet wide and will destroy anything he points at.

Sabastian is too far away for me to reach him and get the gun in time. I think I stop breathing.

Sabastian turns the gun on Gustavo. "You first. You know the rules. You know what happens to those who break the rules."

"Please, Mr. Poole—"

The sound of two simultaneous blasts from the shotgun deafens me. For a moment, all I hear is ringing in my ears. But I seem to be alive and intact.

I breathe again.

So much for my theory that people, particularly businessmen, will negotiate before resorting to violence. I need a new theory.

Gustavo has vanished. I don't look around to see what's left of him. I don't want to know. I'm squeamish that way.

I should arrest Sabastian. He's just murdered a man in my presence. But the fact that he's holding a shotgun pointed at me gives me pause. Not to mention the fact that the man called Hammer is somewhere in the vicinity, almost certainly armed. And there is Maximilian across the room with God knows what weapon.

I need a plan B. Except I can't seem to think of one.

Sabastian is staring at the smoking shotgun clutched in his hand, looking a bit stunned. I suspect he meant to fire one barrel and save the second shot for me. His face and hands are covered with the residue of black powder. He coughs and snatches the plastic tube and sucks in oxygen.

Now's my chance, I think. If I move fast enough, I can disarm him.

Before I can make my move, Sabastian has emptied the barrels of the shotgun of the used buckshot rounds and has inserted two new rounds. Sabastian may be old and asthmatic, but he knows how to handle a shotgun. I'd guess he's had a lot of experience disposing of Poole family enemies.

"You're a fool, Sabastian," Maximilian calls from across the room. "How many times have I told you not to fire that damned shotgun in the living room? You could start a fire. And you've murdered a man in the presence of a police officer. Now we'll have to get rid of him, too. Mr. Hammer, you know what to do."

"Affirmative, sir."

I start to move silently toward the door.

"Stop him!" Sabastian almost pushes himself out of his wheelchair, his burning cigarette falling to the floor.

I step closer to the door.

"Mr. Hammer, I want the policeman dead," Maximilian shouts. "Do you understand?"

"Affirmative, sir," Hammer calls back. Hammer takes a gun from a shoulder holster and moves toward me.

I snatch up an oxygen canister. "Don't do anything stupid with that gun, Hammer," I say. "If you shoot in this poor light, you'll probably kill your boss here. Maybe you'll even puncture this oxygen tank and this place will go up in flames."

Hammer hesitates and looks from Sabastian to Maximilian for orders.

"Shoot the damn policeman," Maximilian calls from his armchair.

"What about Brother Sabastian?" Hammer demands.

"To hell with Brother Sabastian."

I twist the regulator on the tank. Sabastian snatches the plastic cannula tubing from his face as too much oxygen is flowing into his lungs.

"Stop!" Sabastian calls out furiously.

"Forget about him," Maximilian calls from his armchair. "Just shoot the policeman."

"No!" Sabastian leans down and gropes on the floor for his fallen cigarette. He anxiously stubs it out. "No, don't shoot. Not yet."

I take out my cigarette lighter and hold it high in the air. "One stupid move and I'll light this, and we'll all go up in flames."

Hammer freezes.

"Drop your gun," I tell Hammer as the sound of escaping oxygen fills the room. "Drop your gun and kick it toward me."

Hammer stands paralyzed, looking fearfully at Maximilian.

"Do what he says," Maximilian barks.

Hammer drops his gun. I suppose he's not eager to go up in flames, either.

"Okay. Now walk over and stand next to the guy in the iron suit." I point to the man in armor.

Hammer moves cautiously, weaving his way through the maze, keeping a careful eye on me.

I snatch up the gun Hammer dropped to the floor and toss the canister across the room to him. He catches it and holds it at arm's length as if it were a bomb.

"You know," I say. "You guys really ought to clean this place up. What with smoking cigarettes and the oxygen, this is a real firetrap."

CHAPTER NINETEEN

WHEN I ARRIVE in the morning at police headquarters, the pretty brunette who sits at the front reception desk, and who always has a bright smile for me, today seems obsessed with her crossword puzzle and doesn't look up when I say, "Good morning."

People turn away when I walk through the squad room. I'm getting a bad vibe.

Even Tyrone looks uncomfortable. He's obviously been waiting at his desk to talk to me.

"The chief's been asking about you all morning. She wanted to know where you were. I tried to cover for you."

"That's okay. I'll handle her."

I know I should report the death of Gustavo and organize a party to go to the mansion on Sixteenth Street to arrest the brothers. But I know an arrest would be futile. The Poole brothers' lawyers would argue self-defense. Gustavo was armed. Sabastian did what any real American would do. He defended his home. To hell with it.

"She's in her office," Tyrone tells me. "Waiting for you. She seemed very upset. You better go now."

Chief Kelly Flynn is at her desk when I enter her office. She looks up at me, and I know I'm in trouble.

"You needn't bother to sit down, Zorn. You won't be staying long." She leans back in her desk chair, arms folded. "Do you know how many complaints I've received from the Commissioner of the Food and Drug Administration? Two! Not one. Two! He told me he was visited yesterday by an employee of the police department. He said this employee was rude and disrespectful. Could that employee have been you?"

"It certainly sounds like me."

"And then I hear from Duncan Forest. One of the major financial leaders in the country. Did you break into a private meeting and accuse him of committing major crimes? Did you really threaten to call in a SWAT team?"

"I may have suggested something along those lines."

"Do you have any idea who Duncan Forest is? He's the CEO of one of the largest corporations in America. He's a major contributor to the president's reelection campaign. Do you have any idea what you've done?"

Someone has gotten to Chief Flynn. She's genuinely worried. Kelly's not the type to be scared off by some government bureaucrat. Not even by the head of the Food and Drug Administration. Certainly not some civilian. Duncan Forest would not be able to intimidate the chief like that. She and her department have a job to do, and she would never let an outsider interfere. Or let someone tell her how to do her job.

Something else is going on.

"I warned you," she goes on. "You're through."

This is probably not the best time to tell the chief about the incident last night at the Poole mansion.

I've been anticipating this moment, when my behavior has become too much for the system to bear. I could promise to change my ways. But who's going to believe that? I could plead for my job. That's out. Pleading is not in my character.

"Have you told Frank Townsend about your decision?" I ask.

"I spoke with the chief of Homicide. He was very unhappy with me. He told me you were the best detective in the department. He said he couldn't get along without you. He begged me to ignore what he characterized as your eccentricities and personality foibles. We had a long and very noisy row. In the end, I insisted there was no place for you in the DC Metropolitan Police Force. Leave your police credentials and your service weapon on my desk."

"I don't know where my service weapon is. I may have mislaid it."

Chief Flynn rolls her eyes. "You're fired, Mr. Zorn. You know the way out."

The chief's executive secretary, Gladys, glances up at me as I leave the office. She looks embarrassed and stricken. Neither of us says a word. What is there to say?

Well, that sucks, I think to myself as I wait for the elevator.

Okay, I'm a royal pain in the ass. So what else is new? Some people in the police probably find my style amusing. Although I can't think of any offhand. Nobody has a sense of humor.

I'll join the foreign legion. Does the foreign legion even exist anymore? They'd probably reject me because of my reputation as a troublemaker.

I should have seen this coming. But I figured I'd have time to sweet-talk the chief into giving me some slack. I know I've been out of line but not that much more than usual.

Something strange is going on here.

CHAPTER TWENTY

"Do I remember Sabastian and Maximilian Poole? It was a very long time ago—over fifty years now. But yes, I remember them well. They were unforgettable."

Erwin Schroeder and I are sitting on a bench on the edge of the broad expanse of lawn in front of Healy Hall, a neo-medieval building that dominates the Georgetown University campus in Washington. The Poole brothers may be done with me, but I'm not done with them. So here I am at my old school trying to find out who my enemies really are, speaking with the man who once taught me history a lifetime ago.

"I need to know anything that would help me understand them."

"Nobody could understand the Poole brothers. Except that they were evil." Professor Schroeder reflects a moment as he looks out at the young men and women strolling across campus on their way to classes. "Do young people even believe in evil anymore?"

"I do."

"What happened to the Poole brothers?"

"They're still active."

"I'm sorry to hear that. They should have been sent to prison or hanged long ago. Just proves there's no justice in this world. What's your interest in them?"

"A case I'm working on."

"You're still a policeman! I never understood that. You were one of my most brilliant students. I always thought you would become an academic and end up teaching and writing books. Like me."

"I chose a different path."

"You could have gone on to become a distinguished teacher and scholar but you dropped out of the university. And today you're a policeman. How could that happen?"

It's a question I'm often asked. I ask that myself. I don't have any good answers. It's a subject I don't like to talk about. It's much too personal. Being a teacher at a university was never in the cards for me. I'm too impatient, too outspoken, too much of a troublemaker to fit into the serene life of higher education. I would have been a pariah in the faculty lounge. By the end of my first semester teaching, the college president would have been in tears.

Why I chose to go into police work is a harder question. I realized, even then, I was not the straight arrow police departments want. My moral compass is on a different wavelength. If I ever worked with a law enforcement organization, there would be conflict and either I or the organization would have to adjust. And it wouldn't be me.

I feel I owe some explanation to my old professor who was bitterly disappointed with my decision to give up an academic career.

"There was an incident here at the university that changed my life," I say. "Do you remember the Watkins case? A student here at Georgetown."

"I remember."

"He was living off-campus. Somebody broke into his home and murdered him. Slashed him savagely with a knife."

"An awful business."

"I was profoundly affected by that crime. I didn't know Watkins, except by sight, but his death shook me deeply. It seemed as if the earth had been shifted off its axis and nothing would make that right again until his killer was called to account. This brought back a flood of memories of the murder of my sister Rose many years ago. Once again, I felt the need to see that things were made right. I could not rest until justice was done. It became an obsession."

"I remember how you were always deeply concerned with moral justice."

"That crime changed me. I knew then my life could never be fulfilled by teaching at some university. I understood that somehow my destiny had to be in finding justice for those who have been harmed. I knew realistically there was nothing I could do personally in the Watkins case. I had no idea who the murderer was or how to find him. I had to leave that to the police. That's when I understood that police work was my answer. That's why today I need to learn about the Poole brothers."

"I'll try to help. What do you need to know?"

"Were you friends with the Poole brothers?"

He shakes his head. "Sabastian and Maximilian had no friends. They had followers. They were very wealthy, you know. Some students gravitated into their orbit hoping to benefit from their fortune, maybe get jobs in one of their companies. Not that anyone ever got anything from the brothers. People who got close ended up being badly hurt.

"I arrived as a freshman here at Georgetown University the same year as the Poole twins. We shared some classes. Once in a while I might exchange a few words with one of the brothers, usually about coursework or something trivial. But I never got to know either of them as friends. I never wanted to.

"They were always together. I don't think I ever saw them apart. They went to classes together and ate in the dining hall together. They shared the same dormitory suite. They rarely mixed with other students."

"They sound strange."

"They were very strange. They were almost identical but had different personalities. Sabastian was affable and friendly. Until you got too close, and then he'd turn on you. Maximilian was unfriendly and withdrawn. He wore thick-lensed glasses. I think he had some eye problem."

"How did they do in their classes?"

"Maximilian was brilliant. He was always at the top of his class. The strange thing was, they both cheated. Even when they didn't need to. Just for the thrill of it. They also used to steal things, too. Even things they didn't really like."

"What kinds of things did they steal?"

"Anything that appealed to Maximilian. I then had a nice edition of Shakespeare's plays. It had no special value but I was extremely fond of it. One day, as we were leaving class, I mentioned the book to Maximilian. A few days later the book disappeared from my dorm room. I'm certain Maximilian stole it. Not because he wanted it, but because it was important to me. It gave him a kind of power. Later on, when they were expelled, the university authorities found my Shakespeare in the trash in Maximilian's room."

"Maximilian was expelled?"

"They were both expelled in their sophomore year. I never learned the true reason. According to one rumor, it involved missing funds from the soccer team account. According to another story whispered behind closed doors, it was something far worse. Who knows? I'm not a religious person and I'm not sure I know what evil means, but whatever it means, Sabastian and Maximilian were it."

I now know the Pooles are part of the malign brotherhood that lives for cruelty and oppression and death. These guys are psychopaths.

CHAPTER TWENTY-ONE

A STRETCH LIMOUSINE is waiting for me in front of the gates to Georgetown University. A large man, built like a dumpster, stands next to the limousine with his arms crossed, eyeing me. He looks like a professional prizefighter. Middleweight. He has a broken nose and battered ears. Perhaps a prizefighter who went one round too many.

"The man wants to speak with you," the prizefighter says to me.

"What man is that?"

"The man who wants to speak with you. Don't make me tell you again."

"And if I don't want to speak with this man?"

"I'll have to insist. And that may result in you visiting a hospital."

I shrug and brush past the knuckle-walker. A second bruiser opens the rear passenger door, and I climb in.

"Let's make this quick, Zorn. I'm in a hurry."

"And a good morning to you, Mr. Forest."

"Skip the pleasantries," Duncan Forest snaps. "I'm not a pleasant person."

"Okay. No more pleasantries."

"Who sent you after me?"

"Nobody sent me."

"I don't believe you."

"Do you want to elaborate on that?" I give him my best smile.

"You're talking to the wrong people. About the wrong things."

"What things?"

"You're telling people that one of my companies is manufacturing dangerous drugs. You've claimed one of our products can result in narcotic addiction and death. That is a calumny and a libel. I'm warning you one time, and one time only—cease spreading these lies or face severe consequences. And stop harassing me."

"I have reason to believe that your new product, Neuropromine, is addictive and deadly."

"There is no truth to those claims. Taken as directed, Neuropromine is no more dangerous than plain aspirin. Stop bothering people. You have seriously upset the Poole brothers. And you are annoying their niece, Rebecca. Rebecca knows nothing about any of our companies. She's just an ornament, there to handle the brothers' charitable work. As I'm sure you were told when you were a child, don't play with the ornaments. They break easily. I'm warning you, stop spreading false rumors. Or else."

"Or else what?"

"Get out!"

"I want you to understand that I know what you are doing."

"You don't scare me at all, Detective."

"I want to give you a final chance. Drop the production and marketing of Neuropromine and the illegal sales of its clone that's known as Speedball and I'll see to it the investigation into the deaths of Harvey Young and Margot Alsop go no further."

"Out!"

The limousine's passenger door is yanked open, and one of the prizefighters reaches in for me.

"I take that as a no." I slip away from the meathead's grasp. "Are you the one responsible for their deaths, Mr. Forest?"

"If I ever hear your name again, you're finished."

One of the goons is now holding a snub-nose revolver, aimed vaguely at me. I'd hate to see the interior of this nice car ruined, so I get out and stand on the street while the limousine pulls silently away.

CHAPTER TWENTY-TWO

I'M BACK HOME, secure in my basement office. I promised myself I'd pursue the Poole brothers, so I better get started. I dismiss my encounter with Duncan Forest. He's a lackey. Albeit a very well-paid one. I need a better point of attack. I write out the names of seven men and two women on a sheet of paper.

Men and women I've investigated in the past, or had business dealings with. I don't make use of the dark web for these calls. I want there to be a record of my search. It's time to stir the pot.

Two of the people I call are dead. One is serving time in a Turkish prison for receiving stolen property. One refuses to speak to me on advice of counsel. My first hit is Antonelli in Milan.

"*The Concert*? On the market?" Antonelli is breathless. "That's impossible. Where did you hear that? What price are they demanding? It must be astronomical."

It takes fifteen minutes to convince him I don't have answers to his questions. But I've done what I need to do. I've planted the seed. I'm certain he'll be on the phone in minutes to his buddies in the business, demanding to know anything about *The Concert* being on the market.

Corman in Hong Kong swears that he's completely out of the business. He has clean hands. Then he tries to interest me in a rare

Ming case stolen from a private collector in Jakarta. After which, he cross-examines me about the Vermeer. He asks who is handling the sale and what price is being asked.

Louise Benton is extremely cautious. She doesn't want to talk about the Vermeer on the phone. She urges me to take the next plane to London so we can talk face-to-face. It's obvious she's heard something recently about *The Concert*.

With some trouble, I reach Mikimoto. I think he's in Dakar. He insists I tell him where I heard about a possible Vermeer sale. I plead ignorance.

"Something like that would be in the range of many millions of dollars," he says. "There are few dealers who could handle anything on that scale."

"Would you be interested?" I ask.

"That would be too hot to handle, even after all these years. But I might be interested in getting a piece of the action."

"Have you heard anything about *The Concert* being on the market before?"

Long silence. "Maybe. About ten days ago, O'Brian called from San Francisco and asked me whether I'd heard anything about the picture being in action. After thirty years! It sounded like someone's been making inquiries, but he wouldn't say who."

Enough games, I decide. I've made my play. I've left my bread crumbs. I just have to be patient and wait for the vultures to arrive. By this afternoon, the network among dealers in high-end stolen art will be burning up. Maybe one of them will be desperate enough, greedy enough, or foolish enough to contact me.

CHAPTER TWENTY-THREE

My cell phone rings. It's an Illinois area code. Chicago is where the headquarters of Magma Capital Management is located. Maybe it's one of Duncan Forest's stooges, wanting to apologize and telling me our recent contact was all just a terrible misunderstanding.

"Detective Zorn?" a soft woman's voice asks. It's familiar, but I can't yet place it.

"That's me."

"This is Rebecca Poole calling. Do you remember me?"

"How could I forget? Of course, I remember you."

"Among all my phony friends?"

"I never met any of your friends, Ms. Poole. What can I do for you?"

"I'd like to invite you to have lunch with me."

"Lunch? I thought I was acting like a jerk when we last spoke. You probably wanted to see the last of me."

"Not at all. I thought you were really fascinating. For a jerk. Can you join me for lunch? In an hour."

"Today?" I ask.

"At my home in Virginia. I find I must go to Chicago this afternoon. I need to talk with you before I go. Can you come here to my home? I'm having an especially nice wine."

She gives me an address on the Virginia side of the Potomac River. The call ends.

I find Ms. Poole's house tucked away in a dense forest just off the George Washington Parkway. I drive along a narrow, winding road and emerge from the trees into a clearing on which sits a large stone house, surrounded by carefully maintained lawns, some stables, and an Olympic-size swimming pool. As I pull up to the front door, a man emerges from the house and opens the door to my MG. He stands silently to one side, as if at attention, as I get out. A butler, I suppose, or whatever they call these attendants these days.

"Ms. Poole is awaiting you in the rose garden," he murmurs. I see no other cars, so I assume there won't be a crowd this afternoon, which suits me just fine.

The butler, or whatever he is, leads me into the mansion, through sitting rooms and cozy drawing rooms, and under many arched entryways. I'm a sucker for arched entryways. The attendant takes me out into what I assume is the rose garden. It turns out to be a broad terrace with a spectacular view of the Potomac River and Maryland on the far side.

In the middle of the terrace is a round table set with two chairs. Dishes and glasses have been arranged along with a large bowl of fruit, several bottles of wine in coolers, and silverware. Platters heaped with cold cuts and salads rest in the center.

Rebecca Poole rises from her chair. She is dressed in a casual summer frock and wears sandals and a silk scarf around her head. She strides across the terrace to me, smiling warmly.

"I'm so glad you were able to come, Detective. I apologize for the short notice." She invites me to take a seat at the table.

"I was intrigued by your bolshie attitude the other afternoon at the National Gallery," she says in her soft, musical voice. "I looked forward to meeting you again for a lively debate. But I'm afraid that will have to wait until another day. There's an emergency meeting of the Magma Capital Management board of directors. Something serious has come up, it seems."

I wonder whether I am the "something serious" that has come up.

She starts to pour me a glass of wine then hesitates. "Forgive me, Detective. Are you allowed to drink while you are on duty? You are on duty this afternoon, are you not?"

"I'm definitely on duty while I'm here."

"I wouldn't want to violate police regulations . . ."

"Perish the thought. I never let police regulations stand between me and a glass of wine and good company."

"Excellent! I admire a man who knows his own priorities." She pours me a glass of white wine and I take a sip. It's a marvelous Moselle and it's properly chilled. She serves me thin slices of ham and some kind of mushroom salad.

"What kind of issue sends you to Chicago on such short notice?" I ask.

She studies me carefully, a smile on her lips. "Who knows?" She shrugs. "All I can say is Duncan Forest has directed all board members to attend an emergency session at Magma headquarters in Chicago this afternoon. And you never say no to Duncan."

"You're a member of the board?"

"Of course."

"Are you going to take a vote on something?"

"Are you asking as a police detective or as a guest?"

"Is there a difference?"

"There are no votes on our board. Everything is unanimous. Just as Duncan dictates."

"How is it you're a member of the board of directors, Ms. Poole?"

"Please call me Rebecca. Everybody does. And may I call you Marko?"

"Of course."

"I think I may have left you with a false impression when we spoke at the gallery reception. You said I was an employee of Magma Capital Management."

"You're not?"

"I am an employee—in a manner of speaking. I handle all the charitable trusts for my uncles, and I serve as the company's public spokesperson. I'm Magma Capital Management's official shill."

"You're a very attractive shill."

"Why thank you. It's not quite that simple, though. The fact is, I own Magma Capital Management. Well, I own almost half of it. I inherited a large share from my grandmother."

"How did that happen?"

"Many years ago, my uncles, Maximilian and Sabastian, wanted to buy a company called Altavista, but they were short on cash at the time. Altavista made one product then. A painkiller called Zemlon. My uncles thought Zemlon had a huge potential—a blockbuster drug. But they couldn't afford the price the original owners asked. So, they made a deal with my grandmother. She, like my uncles, inherited a fortune from her father who founded the Poole empire. She bought Altavista herself and transferred control to my uncles."

"What happened to your parents?"

"They died in a car accident in Bermuda when I was seven. I was brought up by my grandmother and then stayed in a series of boarding schools after she passed away."

"Did you live with your uncles?"

She shakes her head vigorously. "I had nothing to do with either of them. They hate children, particularly me. They hate everybody."

That sounds right, I think.

"Plus, they're major creeps."

"You're a partner in Magma Capital Management?"

"A silent partner. Very silent."

"What's your function on the board?"

"I'm supposed to give late-stage capitalism a human face. All I do for Magma Capital is schmooze corporate leaders and government officials. And give away scads of money. I get a very generous budget for a fashionable wardrobe and for entertainment."

"I'm sure you're an outstanding schmoozer. Do your uncles still operate the businesses?"

"When they were younger, they did. My uncles don't actually run their companies much anymore. They buy companies and hire super competent Nazis to run them."

"Men like Duncan Forest?"

"Exactly. Maximillian and Sabastian are pretty much retired. They're both quite ancient and they never leave their home, which is a horror. It's not a home—it's a mausoleum. I used to go there with my grandmother when I was a little girl. I was scared to death of the place. It's filled with the oddest assortment of things. They collect stuff." She pours me more wine.

"Now Duncan Forest runs everything?"

"If you want to know anything about Magma Capital, you're going to have to ask him."

"Does Duncan Forest run Altavista?"

"My uncles still make the executive decisions regarding Altavista. The day-to-day stuff is left to Colin Stone. But he's their stooge."

"What do your uncles do now?"

"They buy things. Whatever strikes Uncle Maximilian's fancy. He once bought an entire theater set from a Broadway show. He never even saw the production. They're weird that way. According to Forest, they're bankrupting the companies with their obsessive collecting."

"I thought your uncle Maximilian was blind."

"He's legally blind. He used to be able to see some, but I believe in recent years his sight has deteriorated. His vision is good enough to see his pictures, they say, but he must use a powerful magnifying glass to do so."

"What are your uncles giving to the Smithsonian Institution?"

"Their life collection."

"Does that include a painting by Vermeer?"

Rebecca's face freezes for a split second.

Does she know about the Vermeer?

"I know nothing about individual pieces in the collection." She sips her wine. "I understand that they are excluding a few items that have special significance for them."

She pauses and watches me over the mushroom salad.

"Why did you want to see me before rushing off to Chicago?" I ask.

"I wanted to warn you about Duncan Forest. Duncan is a dangerous man. If he senses somebody is interfering in one of his ventures, even showing too much interest, he will destroy them. I've seen that happen. I wouldn't want to see you get hurt." She sips her wine. "There was another reason, to be candid. When we met at the National Gallery, we parted on such a sour note. I didn't want to leave our relationship like that."

"What relationship?"

"I'm a friendly girl. I like to get along with other people. That's my job. I felt bad about our little contretemps. I didn't want to leave it that way."

"But we may never see each other again." I wave at the mansion behind us, the fabulous view of the river below. "We lead different lives. We move in different circles."

"That's a pity, isn't it? Have some more wine." Without waiting for a reply, she pours wine into my glass.

"I think you should know," I say. "I'm investigating a dangerous drug that has recently appeared on the market. At least on the illegal market. It's called Speedball. It's a version of a drug made by Altavista that will soon be sold on the legitimate market as Neuropromine."

"I'm afraid I can't help you. I don't take drugs myself. I never put synthetic chemicals into my body. You'll have to talk to Duncan Forest. He handles everything."

At this point the butler arrives at the table. "Your car is ready, Ms. Poole. I've packed your luggage. You must leave as soon as possible to catch your plane."

"It's my plane. It will leave when I say so. But you're right. Duncan will be very annoyed with me if I'm late to a board meeting and will skin me alive."

Rebecca Poole reaches across the table and grasps both my hands, just the way she did at the National Gallery. Her grasp is strong. It's a nice feeling. Our hands seem to fit together. Her bright smile shifts in an instant to one of regret and sadness. I can't keep up with her emotional journeys.

"I'm so sorry I have to run off like this and leave you," she says. "I so wanted more time with you. I want to know all about you. I'll be back in Washington in two days. Let's have a proper lunch then. I'll call you."

Members of Ms. Poole's staff are loading suitcases and garment bags into a limousine. She leans down and kisses me on the mouth. "Please watch out for Duncan."

Then she's gone.

CHAPTER TWENTY-FOUR

I HURRY UP the front steps of my house.

And freeze. An electric shock runs through my body.

My front door stands wide open. I'm sure I double-locked it when I left the house.

The lights in my living room are out. But I can just make out the form of a woman sitting in semidarkness.

"You broke into my home. That's criminal trespass, Carla. Or something. Should I call the police?"

"Shut up, Marko." Carla, the head of the FBI's Criminal Investigation Division, does not seem impressed by my threat about the police. "Criminal trespass is the least of your problems."

"How in hell did you get in?"

"That's a trade secret."

"The locks on my doors are supposed to be impenetrable."

"Guess again. Sit down! You're making me nervous pacing around like that."

"May I ask why you broke into my house and are sitting in my living room?"

"We need to discuss the Stewart Gardner Museum robbery."

"That was thirty years ago."

"That theft is a black eye for the FBI. And for me personally. I want to clear the record."

"Why is it a black eye for you?"

"A few years after the robbery, I was assigned to the FBI's Boston field office. I was a brand-new recruit in those days and a very junior officer. I was assigned the Gardner case, among others. We never solved the robbery."

"What's your real interest? There have been hundreds of robberies since then."

"Nothing on the scale of the Gardner Museum robbery. The largest art theft in American history. On my watch. I can't let it go."

"What's that got to do with me?"

"One of the pieces of priceless art stolen was a painting by Johannes Vermeer called *The Concert*. You've recently been talking with some very unsavory characters involved in buying and selling stolen art. *The Concert* keeps coming up."

I was expecting the vultures to show up. Not this particular bird. "Have you been listening in on my phone calls?"

"Don't flatter yourself, Marko. We may have been monitoring some of your scuzzy friends, though. *The Concert* keeps being mentioned in your conversations. What do you know about the Gardner robbery?"

"Just that some guys broke into the museum and stole some paintings."

"The details are important. On March 18, 1990, at one twenty-four in the morning, two men entered the Isabella Stewart Gardner Museum in Boston dressed in Boston police uniforms. There were two guards on duty at the museum that night. They were essentially rent-a-cops. The thieves specifically targeted one painting. *The Concert* by Johannes Vermeer. We think the other paintings were just picked up as random targets of opportunity.

"Whoever planned the robbery was highly professional. The thieves knew the museum's security system, the routines of the museum guards, when they were on their rounds, and how they communicated. The FBI suspected that a man named Digger Granger was somehow involved."

"I've never heard of him."

"He was a low-level, Boston crime figure at the time. We were never able to nail him. Digger Granger is now in prison serving two life sentences for a double murder."

"Nice guy."

"What we want now are the paintings themselves. And for that, we need to know who organized and financed the theft. There was big money behind this. People to plan the robbery, people to hire, people to bribe, people to hide the stolen property."

"I suppose you've asked this Digger Granger about all that."

"Many times. During the years when I was assigned to the Boston field office, the Gardner case was one of my many assignments. But we never solved it. That bothers the hell out of me, still. I met with Digger often. We actually got along pretty well. He can be quite charming when he wants to be. Charming for a multiple killer. We saw each other so often we established a kind of working understanding."

"But I take it he never revealed anything about the robbery to you."

"Not a word. He's afraid."

"Afraid of what?"

"He would never tell me. From time to time, when I'm in the Boston area, I still see Digger. Mainly because I keep hoping he'll break and reveal what happened to the paintings. He once said to me 'If I told you, it would mean my death warrant'. Marko, if you know anything about the robbery, tell me now."

"I can't tell you anything about the robbery."

"I don't believe you."

"Carla, you must learn to trust people more."

Carla studies me carefully but remains silent.

"Do you believe Digger knows who the principals are?" I ask.

"I'm convinced he does."

"Maybe it's time he confessed before he meets his maker."

"I've tried that. He won't bite."

"There must be something he wants badly. Is he interested in the reward money?"

"Not at all. What's he going to do with it in the remaining time he has left?"

"There must be something. There always is. For every man and every woman there is something they want, something they've longed for all their lives, just beyond their reach."

Carla looks at me intensely. "What is it you long for beyond your reach?" She waits a beat. "Never mind. I don't think I really want to know." She leans forward in her chair. "If Digger Granger has some secret passion in life that he wants to achieve so he can die happy, I don't know what it is."

"Maybe you didn't ask him the right question. Let me talk to him."

Carla stares at me. Astounded. "You? You want to talk to Digger Granger? Not a chance."

"Why not?"

"Because he doesn't talk to anybody except his lawyer, and he doesn't talk to him much. He sometimes sees a few old friends who aren't in jail and haven't been murdered yet. That's all."

"You see him, Carla."

"I'm special. That's a relationship developed over a period of many years."

"He'll talk to me if you ask him to."

"I won't ask him. Don't bug me."

"Call him. Tell him your good friend wants to meet with him."

"You're not a 'good friend.'"

"Tell him I can help him get the one thing he really longs for. Something so he can die happy."

"What are you talking about? You don't even know the guy. You know nothing about him."

"I know what kind of man he is. He's a killer. That's all I need to know."

"Even if I agreed, at least somebody from the FBI would have to be there."

"We can't have strangers involved. Carla, this is your last chance to solve the Gardner Museum robbery. Digger must be an old man. He won't last much longer. This is your chance to retrieve the Vermeer. Your chance to clear your personal record."

She sinks back in her seat and stares out the window. "I'll talk to some people. I'll try to arrange for you to talk to Digger. On two conditions. You behave yourself."

"I always behave myself. And the second condition?"

"I go with you."

"Deal."

CHAPTER TWENTY-FIVE

ONCE CARLA AND her entourage have left, I decide it's high time to find out something about Mr. Hammer. I go to my subterranean office and fire up the computer. One of the Poole brothers is desperate, and the other homicidal, so I know I have to take precautions, and must also pay close attention to their enforcer. The Internet provides me with a wealth of information.

Hammer was once a much-decorated senior enlisted SEAL. He was also dishonorably discharged from the service and was charged with the murders of seven Iraqi civilians, including three small children. The charges against him were dropped before the end of the trial when two key witnesses, members of his own unit who were to testify against him, mysteriously died. With this background, one might ask, how could the Poole brothers employ him? It's simple—all organizations like Magma Capital Management need a resident psychopath. It's an essential part of their business plan.

It's late, and I think about an old man alone in a prison cell. A man named Digger Granger. I've never met him, but I know him well. I've met too many men like him. I need music and a drink to help me concentrate. I decide on Chet Baker performing "But Not for Me."

I pour myself a glass of Laphroaig, sit back in my living room armchair. I shut my eyes and listen.

Chet's just completed the horn solo bit and is beginning the chorus when my front doorbell rings. I check the central monitoring system in my office that shows me what the CCTV cameras are recording around the perimeter of my house. A single figure stands on my front doorstep. A woman. The figure wears a poncho and a ball cap. Her face is obscured by the hat's brim. When she turns, the street light strikes her directly. I read the logo on the cap—Washington Wizards. My heart sinks. There's one person I know who is a fan of Washington's professional basketball team. If it's who I fear it is, she's the last person I want to see.

But I can't just leave my visitor standing outside in the night. That's not very gallant and, besides, I know she'll just lean on my doorbell until I answer it.

I open my front door.

Kelly Flynn, the chief of the Metropolitan Police Department, is waiting on my doorstep.

"Can I come in?" she asks, her voice shaking. She pulls the cap from her head.

There's no sign she has company. There's no police protection with her tonight, and no sign of Hammer and his friends.

My first instinct is to shut the door. I figure the chief and I have nothing left to say to each another. Not after what happened in her office. My instincts tell me I should have nothing to do with Kelly Flynn. Stop this now, before it's too late. I know she means trouble. No good can come of this. But every time a beautiful woman comes to me in distress, I go all wobbly. And I know she's in distress. I can't seem to help myself. I gesture for Chief Flynn to step inside. She stands just within the small vestibule while I close and secure my front door with heavy dead bolts.

"I need your help," she says.

"Let's go where we can talk."

She nods, and I lead her down the hallway into my living room. She's not in her police uniform tonight. She's wearing stonewashed jeans and a gray wool sweater. She sits on a straight-back chair with her hands twisted, her knuckles white, her hair uncombed. I take my seat in the armchair opposite her.

She doesn't examine the room the way people who come for the first time normally do. Particularly women. Instead, her eyes are focused on me.

"Can I get you a drink, Chief Flynn?"

She shakes her head impatiently. "I'm not here on a social call. I'm here because I'm in trouble."

I thought *I* was the one in trouble. "You fired me. Remember?" I sip the Laphroaig.

Flynn leans forward toward me. "May we speak in confidence, Mr. Zorn? No one knows I'm here. And no one must ever know I've talked to you. This meeting never happened. What I say tonight is completely off the record. Do you understand? Are we clear on the ground rules?"

"Okay, we never met this evening. What's this all about?"

"It's Angela. My daughter." Flynn takes a deep breath. "Angela's been kidnapped." Flynn wipes away something from her cheek. "I want you to find her and bring her back to me."

"You have four thousand people in the DC police department under your command. They are professionals and are trained to deal with matters like this. Or you could go to the FBI. They have expertise with kidnappings. Carla Lowry, the chief of the Criminal Investigative Division, will give you the bureau's full support."

"I can't go to anyone in the police department or the FBI for help. I can't tell anyone about the kidnapping. If I do, she will die."

"What happened to your daughter?"

"Angela went to school this morning, as usual. She's a junior at Saint Anthony's School. She attended her morning classes, but this afternoon she didn't show up for a rehearsal of a play she's in. At three forty-five, I received a phone call. A man told me his men were holding her captive. He said she was safe and unharmed—for the moment—and they would return Angela to me, but only if I did exactly what he demanded."

"What were his demands?"

"Call off all investigation into the deaths of Dr. Young and Dr. Alsop. There was to be no further investigation into these murders. Both are your cases."

"That's correct. I'm pretty certain the brothers Sabastian and Maximilian Poole are involved in your daughter's kidnapping."

"Who are the Poole brothers?"

"They're owners of several corporations, including a large pharmaceutical company."

"What's this got to do with Angie?"

"I'll find out. Tell me exactly what the caller said."

"He said if I told anyone about the call, Angela would be killed. 'Just like Young.' I take that to mean they would burn Angela alive." She clenches her jaw. I can see she's forcing herself not to go to pieces on me. "That's the reason I fired you. I had to demonstrate publicly that you no longer worked for me, or for the police. And that there would be no further investigation into those murders."

She stops abruptly. She looks desperate. Takes a deep breath and goes on. "I received a second call at home from the same man this evening. He repeated the threat against Angela. He said you—and he mentioned you by name, Mr. Zorn—had been talking to certain people you should not have been talking to."

This must refer to my meeting with the Poole brothers.

"Why are you telling me this?" I ask.

"I want you to find my daughter. And bring her back. I don't care how you do it. I want my daughter back."

"It may not be that simple. It would involve extracting your daughter from some very dangerous and nasty people."

"Do whatever you need to do."

"Even if that requires violence? Which it probably will."

"This time, there are no rules."

"I thought you said—"

"I know what I said. And I meant every word of it. But the situation is different now. My daughter's life is at stake."

"Do you believe the kidnappers will return your daughter to you if the investigation is terminated?"

She shakes her head. "There's no way they'll let Angela go. I know that. She'd be able to identify her captors. They'll keep her alive only as long as she is useful to them. That means long enough to see that the murder investigations are terminated. After that, Angie's just in the way."

"Why come to me?"

"Because this job requires special skills. Skills only you have." She takes a deep breath. "I think you're a man of honor, Mr. Zorn. You lie, you cheat, you steal, you do not obey rules, and you don't accept authority. But, in the last analysis, you're a man of honor. I've read your files. I've talked to Carla Lowry at the FBI. I know what you can do and who you are."

"Do you know what you're asking?"

"Of course. I'm asking you to do something that will be illegal and very dangerous. You no longer work for me, and I can't order you to do this job. There will be no reward. If you succeed, there'll be no recognition. And if you fail, I won't be able to help you. This operation must be completely off book. You'll be on your own." She smiles a regretful smile. "Will you do this? Will you save Angela for me?"

I don't hesitate. "Of course. I will try."

What else can I say? I know what the Poole brothers do to people who cross them. Alsop drowned in the canal. Young burned alive. I know what the Pooles' people are capable of. The kidnappers will keep her daughter alive only as long as she can be used to ensure that the FDA approves Neuropromine. Once the FDA makes a final decision, which should happen in days if not hours, the girl is useless baggage and will be disposed of.

"I'll do what I can to get your daughter back," I say.

Kelly leans back in her chair, relaxing just a bit. She unclasps her hands. For the first time she glances tentatively around the room. "Maybe I'll take you up on that offer of a drink. I could use one."

"I'm drinking Laphroaig. I can get you something less peaty if you like."

"Laphroaig is fine. Neat. Just a little though. I'm driving."

I pour her half a glass. Holding it in two hands, she takes a swallow. She doesn't wince.

"Have you talked with anyone at your daughter's school?"

"I spoke to one teacher early this afternoon. She's an English teacher who's directing the play Angie's in. I've spoken to no one else."

"Did this teacher observe anything unusual this morning?"

"She told me she'd seen nothing out of the ordinary. The first time anything wrong was observed was when Angie didn't show up for the play rehearsal. Some of Angie's friends saw her at the theater just before the rehearsal was to start, then she disappeared. Her teacher called me, wanting to know if I knew where Angela was."

"Did anybody see any strangers around the school today? Any cars parked nearby that aren't normally there?"

"None the teacher told me about. I didn't cross-examine her. I've been involved in kidnapping investigations many times. I know the drill. I know the questions. I didn't dare."

"What play is she in?"

"*Romeo and Juliet.*"

"What part does your daughter have?"

"Is it important?"

"Probably not, but I'd like to know."

"She's Juliet."

"Is Angela a budding actress?"

"Not at all. The kid playing Romeo insisted Angela be cast opposite him."

"What's this kid's name?"

Flynn thinks a minute. "Hamilton. Hamilton Towne. I've never met him."

"Is this Hamilton your daughter's boyfriend?"

"Of course not."

"Does she have any boyfriends?"

"No. She's just a child."

"Would you know if there were any boys in her life?"

"I'd know. Angela and I have no secrets from each other."

"You believe she's not having a sexual relationship with anyone?"

Her face flashes with momentary anger. "She's never had sex with anyone. I would know if she did. The mother is always the first to know."

I decide not to tell Chief Flynn that, in my experience, mothers are often the last to know.

"How about girlfriends?"

"Angela has lots of girlfriends. You know how girls are at her age with their slumber parties and that sort of thing."

"Any special girlfriends?"

"This semester that's probably Yardley. Angela's in the play with Yardley, and they've been running lines together."

"Is there somebody in your own life?" I hesitate. "Are you dating anyone?"

"For heaven's sake, women my age don't date—they socialize. What you really want to know is if I'm currently having sex with anyone. If you exclude my plumber, electrician, and computer guru, there are no men currently in my life."

"What about Angela's father?"

"Forget about Bob. He's an orthodontist and lives in Austin, Texas. He's a pussycat."

"Are you divorced?"

"The divorce was amicable. Neither of us had any money, so that was never an issue. All we had was Angela. We both agreed it made more sense for a girl to be brought up by her mother."

"Does Bob know about the disappearance of his daughter?"

"Nobody knows."

"Are Bob and Angela close?"

"When she was little, he doted on her. He has his own life now. He's screwing his dental hygienist these days, and that keeps him occupied. If you're thinking he wants custody of Angela, you're on the wrong track. She's a handful and he's happy to be an absentee father. Angela is a teenage girl and can be quite difficult. She takes after her mother."

"Tell me about the phone call."

"There were two calls. One this afternoon. The second an hour ago."

"Who was on the phone?"

"A man. Not young—maybe thirty or forty. No identifiable regional or ethnic accent."

"Did he sound angry or belligerent? Nervous?"

"Not at all. Both times he spoke slowly and calmly. I think he was speaking from a written script. You can listen to the second call for yourself. I was able to record it." She hands me her phone.

"Tell me what the man said on that first call."

"He said they were holding Angela and she was okay. He told me not to try to find her. I was to make absolutely no contact with anyone in law enforcement. Secondly, I was to see that all investigations into the deaths of Young and Alsop were suspended immediately. All records of the investigation you and your partner have made were to be destroyed. He said I was to immediately call off my 'pit bull'—I think that means you, Mr. Zorn. If I failed to do any of these things, he would kill Angela immediately."

Flynn swallows hard. "It was then I decided to fire you. It was the only way I could think to demonstrate to Angie's kidnappers that you were off the investigation and that I didn't trust you."

"Let me hear the call." I open her recorded calls and press PLAY.

"Chief Flynn?"

"Who is calling?"

"I have Angela here with me."

"Is she okay? Have you hurt her?"

"She's okay. She'll stay okay as long as you do exactly what I say."

"I want to talk to Angie."

There's a pause and then another voice comes on the line. It's the voice of a young woman.

"Mom?"

"Angie, are you hurt?"

"No. Can you bring me home? I'm scared."

"Of course, darling. I'll bring you home. Don't be scared. I'll take care of you."

"They said if you don't do what they want, they'll hurt me."

"Where are you, darling?"

There's a muffled sound at the other end. Then the man's voice is on the line again.

"*That's enough. Shut your pit bull down. Understand? Zorn must stop all further investigations. If you don't stop him, we will. And if you don't do as instructed, you'll never see your daughter again.*"

"*Don't hurt my daughter. Please . . .*"

"*Mom?*"

The line goes dead.

We listen to the recording a second time.

"I must keep this recording."

"Of course."

I try to identify the male voice on the call. Is it Hammer? Hammer didn't say enough when I was with the Poole brothers, so I can't be sure. But of one thing I think I *am* sure. There was something off about the sound of the recording.

I retrieve a notebook from the sideboard and give it to Chief Flynn. "Write down every word the man said during that first call this afternoon. Were there any other sounds at his end of the line? Any other voices? Were there traffic sounds? Passing aircraft? Anything that could help me pinpoint where the phone call was made."

She nods, takes a sip of her drink, shuts her eyes, then writes. After ten minutes, she passes the notebook back to me. "That's it. I can't think of anything else."

Her handwriting is strong and clear. The words feel like a verbatim transcript of her conversation, as if taken by a professional stenographer. Kelly Flynn seems to have total recall. She obviously has many talents.

She looks at her watch. "I must leave soon. I don't want to draw attention to the fact that I'm away from home."

"You've given me what I need. Go home. Try to get some rest."

"Before I go," she says, "I have one question for you. A very personal question."

"Go ahead."

"When we met in my office and I asked you whether you were ever afraid, you told me you were afraid of only one person: yourself. What did you mean by that?"

"It's not important."

"It is important. Otherwise, you would not have said it. I'm trying to understand you. To know who you really are."

"Good luck with that."

"What did you mean when you said you feared only yourself?"

I take a gulp of my Scotch. I never talk about this part of my life. Not with anyone. But this situation is different.

"I killed a man once."

"You're a police officer, licensed and trained to use weapons. That doesn't explain what you meant when you said you were afraid of no one but yourself."

"Something happened long before I became a police officer, and long before I wore a badge. It happened when I was little more than a kid."

"Go on."

"I shot a man in cold blood. There was no trial, no jury, no judge. Just me. Executioner. Me and my gun. And my victim. My sister Rose had been raped and murdered by a man who lived in our small town in Maine. The police thought they knew who killed my sister, but they had no evidence. The man escaped, hid in the forest, and disappeared. Growing up, I'd spent years in the forest, hunting and fishing. I knew the territory well. I hunted the killer on my own. When I found him, I shot him dead on the spot. I was the executioner, judge, and jury."

"Thank you for telling me this."

"There's something more. When I killed that man, I felt no remorse. I've never felt guilt about what I did that day. When I pulled the trigger, I felt only deep satisfaction. Even an inner peace. I understood then that I'm capable of extreme violence. I know if I'm confronted with a hostile situation and am armed, I'm capable of anything."

"I think I understand you now." She stands up. "Thank you."

I accompany her to my front door, where I check outside to be sure no one is watching the house.

"Please find my daughter. She's the most important thing in my life. She's the only important thing. I realized that today. I hope I didn't realize that too late. I know I'm asking a lot of you." She puts on her cap with the Washington Wizards logo, adjusting it so her face is hidden. "I'm putting you in great danger. I hope someday to be able to repay you."

CHAPTER TWENTY-SIX

THE SIGN ON the door reads "Slipped Disks."

The office is not much more than a crowded walk-in closet and is filled, floor to ceiling, with electronic equipment. Computer monitors, a dozen speakers hanging on the walls or sitting on the floor, tape decks, earphones hanging from hooks, and old radio transformers. The sole piece of office furniture, in addition to a wooden chair, is a desk holding two turntables, almost lost in a snake pit of wires and cables, several circuit boards, a stereo amplifier, and three power strips. There are two antique radio vacuum tubes perched on the desk.

I've often observed that engineers have eccentric tastes in interior decorating.

Ernie Levado is a sound engineer. He creates sound effects for television. He does this mostly through computer manipulation and sounds he downloads from the Internet, but scattered around his cramped space are remnants of ancient devices he once used to make these same sounds. They're relics, I suppose, from the golden age of radio. On the floor next to the desk is a sandbox for recording footsteps, and next to that is a miniature door used to capture the sound of a door closing. There's a doorbell and a siren on a shelf above my head.

Ernie is also a genius at analyzing recorded sounds.

"What brings you here to my humble abode?" Ernie asks, pulling a set of headphones from his head.

"I have a job for you, Ernie."

"I hear you've been fired from the police department. Way past time, I'd say."

"It's just a temporary speed bump in my career path. Will you listen to a recording for me and tell me what I'm hearing?" I put my phone, where I copied the call Flynn received from the kidnapper, on Ernie's desk. "Tell me what kind of room this call was made in. Or if there's anything you can tell me about the location of the call."

Ernie pops his speaker cord into my phone jack and presses PLAY. His office is instantly filled with the voice of the man I'm searching for. Ernie has a dozen speakers, so I'm hearing the voice from all sides. Now that I'm hearing it with better sound equipment, I'm pretty sure it's Hammer. Ernie shuts his eyes in concentration and listens. Then plays the recording through a second time.

"That's heavy," he says. "This girl whose voice I just heard, is she in trouble?"

"I'm afraid she is."

"My God, Zorn, what have you gotten into?"

"Don't listen to what the man or the girl are saying. Just tell me where this call came from. When I listened to it, I thought there was something off about the way it sounded. Something didn't seem quite right, but I can't tell why."

"That sound you're hearing is off because the room this call was made from has walls that do not absorb sound. Or they hardly absorb it. It wasn't recorded from a normal room, one with furniture and books and curtains. The walls here must be made from some very hard, rigid material."

"Like maybe from inside an airplane."

Ernie shakes his head vigorously. "Not a plane. Aircrafts normally are equipped with padding or absorptive material. Even commercial freight jets have some for insulation purposes. I'll check the sabin sound absorption rate." Ernie switches dials, flips switches, and turns on several devices. One has a small, round black screen on which appear wiggly white lines I seem to remember representing sound waves. Ernie places the headphones onto his head, squints his eyes, and stares at the round screen. After almost five minutes, he turns off the device, closes the switches, removes his earphones, and swivels around in his chair to face me.

"The absorption reverberation time is minimal. There's a flutter echo, which is causing a repetitive pulsing sound."

"What does any of that mean?"

"It means the call was made from inside a 'dead room.'"

"I assume when you say 'dead room,' you mean something other than what I might mean."

"These walls were made of iron or steel."

"The man speaking was in an iron room? Maybe the call was from a prison cell?"

"Maybe." Ernie puts his earphones back on his head and closes his eyes. "Maybe if it was an isolation cell, but that's not likely. Those cells normally have some kind of ventilation system you can pick up in the background."

"From a ship's cabin?" I suggest hopefully.

"That's close." Ernie holds up his hand to stop me from speaking. He closes his eyes in concentration. "It's not a ship's cabin. There's no sound of a ship's engine. And there are always other boat sounds in the background."

I start to say something.

"Shut up! I can't hear." He hunches over, eyes closed, and I stay silent.

"I can just make out wave sounds. Not sound waves. I mean real water waves. Big ones. This call was definitely made somewhere on or near the ocean."

"I told you it was a boat. I was right."

"As usual, you're wrong."

"I give up. Where did the call come from?"

"I thought at first it might be a lighthouse. But no. Why would a lighthouse have an iron room?"

"An island prison, then."

"I don't think the Count of Monte Cristo is making calls these days. And how many island prisons are there, really?"

"I don't know."

"The answer is simple. Your call was made from a stationary structure in or near the ocean. One surrounded by heavy seas. An oil-drilling or pumping installation somewhere. Find that rig and you'll find your girl."

"There must be hundreds of rigs out there."

"You're the brilliant detective, Zorn. You figure it out."

"Not a problem."

I know I don't really have to check out hundreds of different oil and gas rigs all around the globe to locate Angela. I just need to find one that's within easy transportation distance of Washington. The kidnapper snatched Angie yesterday afternoon in Washington, and by last night she was in an iron room in the middle of some ocean. I don't know which ocean, but I know it can't be that far away. I know someplace to look.

As I'm about to leave, Ernie asks, "That girl—the girl whose voice I heard on the recording—is she going to be all right?"

"I'll see to it she's all right."

"I thought the police fired you. Why are you even involved?"

"I made a promise to someone. And I always keep my promises."

"I don't understand you, Zorn. Not at all."

"Sometimes I don't understand me, either."

CHAPTER TWENTY-SEVEN

THE CAMPUS OF Saint Anthony's school is pleasant, adorned by trees, hedges, and winding, broad walkways. There are a dozen cream-colored brick buildings with porticoes and fake Greek columns. It's a warm afternoon, and the campus is thronged with young women—most wearing what I take to be the school uniform: skirts in blue and green plaid, and black and green blazers. Many of the girls carry lacrosse sticks or tennis rackets, presumably on their way to or from the courts or playing fields. Some have inline skates slung over their shoulders. Two girls stand in the shadow of one building, furtively smoking a cigarette.

Baxter Theatre is approached by shallow stone steps. Sitting on the top step is a young woman, the school tartan skirt tucked around her legs. Her knees show grass stains. She's probably sixteen or seventeen with a round face.

"Is this where the rehearsal is taking place?" I ask, smiling in a friendly way.

The girl shrugs uninterestedly. "You'll have to ask Ms. Drew. She's in charge of the play."

"Where is this Ms. Drew now?"

"The last I saw, she was in the ladies' room crying."

"What's your name?"

"Yardley Hopkins. Who are you?"

Great. The girl Chief Flynn said was her daughter's friend.

"I'm interested in this here play production. Are you in the cast?"

She shrugs and eyes me suspiciously. "Whatever."

"I work for a publication called *Ars Dramatica*." I have no idea whether such a publication exists. But it's doubtful whether Yardley knows either. Or cares.

"You a reporter?" she asks sullenly.

"I'm here to do a story on the production of *Romeo and Juliet*."

"You are?" She sits up a bit straighter.

"Can I get an interview with you? It might be published in our May issue. Maybe with pictures."

"Pictures?" She smooths out her skirt. "Cool."

"Who's playing Juliet?"

She gives me a sour scowl. "Angie Flynn got that part."

"You mean the police chief's daughter?"

"Yeah, right."

"Is that how she got the part?"

"She got the part because she's fucking Hamilton. Hamilton is Romeo. He insisted Angie be cast as Juliet. Ms. Drew does everything Hamilton says."

"Why does Ms. Drew do that?"

"This is a girls' school and it's hard to cast men's roles. Most of the boys who show up for casting calls drool and look like the Swamp Thing."

"Why aren't you rehearsing the play today?"

"Because Angie hasn't shown up. We can't have *Romeo and Juliet* without Juliet."

"When did you last see Angie?"

"Yesterday afternoon. It was just before rehearsal was supposed to start."

"What happened to her?"

"Why are you so interested in Angie?"

"I'm a reporter. We have inquiring minds."

"Angie and me and some of the girls were sitting right here on the steps. Hamilton waltzes up. He took Angie away even though he knew rehearsals were about to start."

"What do you mean? 'He took her away'?"

"He just came up and pulled Angie away from us, like he was angry or something. He said there was somebody she had to meet. They argued for a while, and then Angie went off with Hamilton. She never came back. Neither of 'em did."

"Who is Hamilton?"

"He's a sophomore at George Washington University. He's a dork."

"Where can I find this dork?"

"He must have decided, what with Angie away, there'd be no rehearsal this afternoon and no need for Romeo, and he might as well go somewhere and drink with his buddies."

"Where would he do that?"

"Why do you want to know? You gonna interview him? I told you, he's a dork."

"I might have to talk to him."

"At this hour, he's probably at Bojangle's. That's where he usually hangs out."

*   *   *

Bojangle's is in the basement of an office building on Wisconsin Avenue. On the street level, there's an electric supply store and a dry cleaner's and a small gift shop that sells greeting cards. To get to Bojangle's, you walk down a short flight of concrete steps, littered this afternoon with empty cigarette packs and condom wrappers, and enter a dingy and dark bar. I remember Bojangle's from my tour in vice a few years back. It's patronized by college kids and sometimes by their high school dates. There's nothing appealing here, except for lots of dark nooks and corners. The place smells of spilled beer and weed. It's the kind of place where management is carefree about checking IDs and who's smoking what.

There are two kids at the bar nursing Buds, a cluster of what looks like jocks at a table, and a couple sitting in a corner booth talking quietly and surreptitiously feeling each other up.

"You know someone by the name of Hamilton?" I ask the bored bartender.

"Who's asking?" the bartender replies in a tone of voice that says he's in no mood to tell me about his customers.

Under normal circumstances I'd flash my police ID and bully the man into telling me what I want to know. That won't work today as I have no police ID to flash.

"*I'm* asking. It seems that Mr. Hamilton's been seen on these premises with a young woman."

"So?" the bartender asks, without interest. "We have lots of customers here."

"My name is Jones," I announce officiously, "and I am a concerned citizen and a member of the neighborhood watch. Twice the young woman in question was brought home by this Hamilton boy very late at night and in an inebriated state—as recently as last night."

Of course, what I'm saying is probably not true, and it's possible the bartender might have been on duty yesterday and might remember his customers. I'll take that chance.

"She and Hamilton spent the afternoon here. They consumed many drinks. The legal drinking age in the District of Columbia is twenty-one. Are you aware of that fact? The young lady who spent the evening drinking here was seventeen. Seventeen! Does that ring a bell with you? Does that get your attention? As in, we could have your alcohol beverage license lifted. As in, we could close you down."

"All of our customers have IDs."

"Most of those IDs are phony, you know. There's a cottage industry around here providing underage kids with fake IDs to use in dumps like this."

"I can't help it if these kids break the law and use fake IDs."

"That's the most pathetic excuse I've ever heard. Try for a better one when you're in court, standing before a judge. You might be interested to know that the young lady in question is the daughter of the chief of police of Washington, DC. That would be Chief Kelly Flynn."

"You say the daughter of the chief of police was here?" All bluster deflated.

I now have the bartender's full attention. He carefully puts the glass he's drying onto the bar.

"Is Hamilton here?"

He nods at the group of jocks sitting at the table. "Hamilton's the one in the tweed jacket."

Hamilton is a skinny kid who can't be much over twenty. He clutches a cigarette in one hand and is speaking loudly to his buddies. He has tattoos on his arms in a desperate effort to look cool and dangerous. He fails on both counts.

"Hamilton." I approach the table. "You and I need to talk."

The kids swivel their heads to stare up at me.

"We're busy," Hamilton says. "Butt out."

"Sorry. It's important that you listen to what I have to say."

"You deaf, old man?" another kid says. "My friend here just told you—we're busy." This one has a scraggly, unpromising beard.

I study the other kids intensely. "I don't know who you are. For all I know, none of you are wanted criminals—unlike your buddy Hamilton here. Unless you want to become involved in a serious criminal case, you will all leave quietly now and go home. Except for Hamilton. He belongs to me. If you don't, I hope your fathers have lots of money for lawyers."

The others around the table straighten up sharply. I don't know whether it was the word "lawyers" or "fathers" that gets their attention.

"Look, Hamilton . . . ," the one with the beard protests.

"Beat it!" I lean in close to the beard.

They slip quickly and silently away, looking sheepish as they go.

"I don't want to talk to you." Hamilton tries to assume a brave, hostile front. It doesn't work for him.

"Too bad."

"Who the fuck are you?"

"A concerned citizen. I'm here to talk about Angela Flynn. You know Angie Flynn, don't you?"

He studies a half-drunk bottle of Coors on the table in front of him.

"The minor you're bonking. The daughter of the chief of police here in Washington?"

"You can't intimidate me."

"Want to bet?" I sit down at the table, so I'm facing Hamilton directly. "Yesterday afternoon, you met Angela at the theater at her school. You took her someplace. Maybe by force. Where did you take her?"

"I don't know what you're talking about."

"Hamilton, when people lie to me, I tend to get grumpy. You don't want to make me grumpy. Trust me. We're dealing with kidnapping and maybe murder charges. You hear me, Hamilton?

You're in deep shit. We're talking about the daughter of the chief of police. You listening to what I'm saying? If you want to stay out of trouble, tell me what you know."

"What if I do tell you?"

"Then you may not spend the rest of your miserable life in prison. You're too stupid to organize this snatch yourself. Somebody was paying you. Who was it?"

"Nobody." I can see in his eyes he's seriously scared now.

"You're trying my patience. Who paid you to get to Angie?"

Hamilton looks around the dark room now, trying to see if anyone is watching us. No one is.

"Who paid you?" I repeat, louder.

"Who are you?"

"Right now, I'm your worst enemy. Or your best friend. You decide."

"I don't know what you're talking about."

"Have it your way. I'm sure you'll have no trouble getting dates in prison. A pretty boy like you. You're going to be real popular inside."

Hamilton stares at me, open-mouthed.

"Who paid you?"

Hamilton clutches his Coors but doesn't drink it.

"A guy ... he met me here yesterday and we just started talking."

"Guy? What guy? Did this guy have a name?"

"I never caught his name."

"What did he talk about?"

"He asked me if I knew a girl named Angela Flynn."

"And you said?"

"Sure, I know Angie. Everybody knows Angie. He said he wanted to meet Angie. That's all."

"So, this guy with no name tells you he wants to meet Angie. Did he say why?"

"He just said he'd seen her around and thought she was cute and said he'd like to hook up."

"How much did this man pay you to get to Angie?"

Hamilton looks away, now thoroughly frightened.

"How much, Hamilton? How much did you sell your girlfriend for?"

"I never sold Angie. It was just for an introduction." His voice squeaks.

"Okay, you're just a procurer then. How much?"

"He paid me a thousand bucks."

"In cash?"

"Sure. I'm no fool."

"I'd take issue with that, Hamilton. And when you delivered the product, by which I mean Angela, you just disappeared."

"I didn't want to be in the way."

"You're a proper gentleman. Old-school, right? So, you quietly slipped away with your money, leaving Angie with this man with no name?"

"He just said he wanted a date with Angie."

"What did he mean by 'date'?"

Hamilton stares at me wild-eyed.

"Where is she now?"

He shakes his head helplessly. "I don't know."

"Take a guess, Hamilton."

"She probably went off with him. She does that kind of thing. She's pretty wild, you know."

"I don't know. You realize you're involved in a kidnapping. That's a capital offense. I hope you don't have any plans for the rest of your life."

"He just said he wanted to have sex with Angie. That's all."

"What did he look like?"

"You some kind of cop or something?"

"You should hope I was a cop. Cops have rules. If I were a cop, I wouldn't be allowed to haul you out into the alley behind this place where they keep the rest of the garbage and beat you to a pulp and shove you into the dumpster headfirst with the other rats. That would be against police regulations, but I don't have to follow those. So I repeat my question: What did the man who took Angela look like?"

"I don't know."

"Tall? Short? Fat? Thin?"

"I can't remember."

"Try harder."

"He was a big guy. Thin." He swallows hard. "He had white-blond hair." Hamilton looks at me desperately. "Can I go now?"

"Go. And stay away from St. Anthony's school. Far away."

He disappears into the gloom.

CHAPTER TWENTY-EIGHT

THE BISMARCK MOVING and Storage Company is located in a commercial strip mall in Herndon, Virginia, just outside of Washington. The company's neighbors include a Vietnamese restaurant called Saigon Palace. On either side are a nail salon and a check-cashing office—both out of business—and at the end of the block, a tattoo parlor. It's three in the morning, and the area is deserted. The mall is dark and desolate. I see no lights in any of the buildings in the neighborhood.

"There'll be a night watchman," Stryker tells me as he guides a beat-up SUV to the rear of the strip mall.

There are dumpsters in the parking lot behind Bismarck Moving and Storage, some overflowing with cardboard boxes. At the rear of the Bismarck property are five loading docks edged with thick, black rubber bumpers. Some docks are large enough to accommodate a sixteen-wheel rig. Waste paper litters the ground, blown by a light breeze.

I stand in the shadow of a dumpster and watch for the night watchman or for anybody else who might be taking an interest in me or in Bismarck Moving and Storage. I see nothing suspicious. I know I'm about to break into a private property, and that's a felony.

This shouldn't make me anxious. It doesn't normally. I guess I'm on edge. "Let's get to work," I say.

We cross the parking area and climb a set of iron stairs. A sign tells us this is Bismarck Moving and Storage and the hours are seven in the morning to six in the evening. The door is covered with sheet metal, but the lock is old and cheap. It's a simple key-in-the-knob lock, and there's no dead bolt. I'm pretty certain Bismarck is a distribution point for Speedball, but considering the building's weak security, the drug is probably not stored overnight here. It must be delivered from some other facility first thing in the morning. That's not a problem. I'm not here for the drugs. I'm after something far more valuable.

I push the door so there's a slight gap between the door and the jamb. I insert a credit card into the gap and shift it around so it's properly placed and shimmy the card for a couple of seconds until I feel the bolt slide open. Stryker and I step into a small office furnished with a metal reception desk, a desk lamp, and two metal office chairs.

"What we lookin' for?" Stryker whispers.

"Business records. This place is the distribution point for Speedball. They must schedule deliveries and pickups from here."

I work my way through a series of back offices and mostly empty storage areas. In what is probably the front office is another desk and a couple of chairs. A calendar on the wall features a naked blond woman holding a dictation pad. Next to the desk is a large industrial shredder, its bin half-filled with torn paper. Tucked in the back of the office is a vertical, three-drawer steel filing cabinet secured by a three-way Lee & Cross combination lock. No problem. I've dealt with a lot more challenging locks.

The only illumination comes from a street light in the rear parking area streaming through the dirty windows. I turn on the light from my cell phone, shielding the glare with my left hand so it can't be seen from outside. I examine the padlock dial and make out faint smudges—fingerprints users have left when they spun the combination dial and needed to stop the rotation when they reached the number they were looking for. I count four of these faint prints on the dial. These prints should have been wiped clean after each use. They should have emptied the shredder bin and had dead-bolt locks installed on the front door, too. Coldcreek, or whoever is responsible for the security for this building, is doing a sloppy job.

One number the fingerprint reveals is obviously for zero. The other numbers are eleven, twenty-three, fifty-four. I just don't know the correct sequence, so I have to try each of them. The sequence turns out to be twenty-three, fifty-four, and eleven. I snap open the lock. The file drawers and their contents are ours.

The bottom drawer is empty. The middle drawer is filled with what look like business documents. Why are they secured in a heavy-duty locked file drawer? There must be something here somebody doesn't want others to see.

Stryker and I lay the documents out on a desktop and we go through them, using my cell phone for light. It takes an hour before we find what we're looking for. A single page that looks like it had once been a PDF attachment to an email message.

It's labeled TRANSPORTATION MOVEMENT AUTHORIZATION SCHEDULE and has yesterday's date. This is what we are after. At least I hope so.

The page contains columns of meaningless letters in groups of three and what seem like random numbers. Stryker and I quickly figure out that they must be abbreviations of the names of cities and, in some cases, airports. The numbers turn out to be times and dates.

"This a dispatch order," Stryker says. "A record of scheduled shipments of goods and people. It doesn't identify what is being shipped."

I figure out the letters are abbreviations of departure and destination locations. And vehicle types: long-haul trucks, local, last-mile delivery trucks, and pickups. There are records of dates and costs for rented and leased passenger cars. There are also airline reservations and plane departures and arrival times.

"It looks like the aircraft departure and destination locations are all over the country and include Mexico and Canada," Stryker observes.

We examine the list in silence. "Look for departures from Reagan National Airport in the last twenty-four hours, not using a commercial airline."

"Maybe the people you want left from Dulles or Baltimore/Washington Airport."

"We're looking for people who needed to get out of Washington fast. They would've picked the nearest airport." I run my finger down the column of abbreviations. There's a notation of a leased Lear business jet leaving from Reagan National, destination Gulfport-Biloxi International Airport in Mississippi at 4:42 p.m.

"This's got to be our guys," I whisper. "The timing is right. There's also a local, short-haul flight to something referred to as BAT. What's BAT?" I ask, not really expecting an answer.

"That's Beeson Air Terminal," Stryker tells me.

"And that is?"

"The oil rigs in the gulf use BAT as a staging area for supplies and crew rotations. When I worked the oil-drilling platforms, I used to fly back and forth between the rig and BAT on the mainland for shore leave."

"These helicopters—where do they go?"

"They service the rigs in the eastern gulf area."

"Were any of those gas and oil rigs owned by a company called Gulf Deepwater?"

"Deepwater used to operate a lot of rigs in the gulf. I never worked on Deepwater rigs myself, but they were all over the place. What's a moving and storage company in Virginia got to do with offshore oil rigs in the gulf?" Stryker asks.

"What do you say we go to Mississippi and find out?"

CHAPTER TWENTY-NINE

STRYKER AND I meet at Reagan National Airport at six in the morning. We have one layover on the way and Stryker and I sit in a dreary terminal and drink weak coffee and watch CNN news on the TV monitors. There is nothing about the Bismarck break-in. No surprise there. A burglary in the Washington suburbs is not a newsworthy story even if it were reported to the police, which I seriously doubt it was.

During the flight to Gulfport, I study the paper I took from Bismarck Moving and Storage and try to decipher its further meaning.

"This tells us that three people flew from Washington yesterday to Gulfport. From there, they took a short connecting flight to Beeson Air Terminal, where it looks like they were scheduled to board a helicopter. It doesn't say who they were, why they needed a helicopter, or where they were going. We need to find out about that chopper flight."

"They had to be going to one of the rigs in the Gulf. But there are hundreds of them in the Gulf," Stryker protests.

"We can narrow it down to one of the rigs owned by the Gulf Deepwater Company. How many rigs does Deepwater own and operate in the gulf?"

"A lot."

"They must have filed a flight plan. Can we get our hands on that?"

"We'd have to break into the flight control center."

"They probably have better security than Bismarck Moving and Storage. We don't have time for that."

"There's a bar just outside BAT called Ella's where roustabouts get together when they come back to the mainland for shore leave," Stryker tells me. "A lot of the guys work on the flight deck, and they gossip about what happens on the rigs and about job openings. I'll see if there's any talk about that helicopter flight."

When we arrive at the airport in Gulfport, I rent a car and we drive to a small, out-of-the-way motel near the waterfront. A battered sign reads "Sea Foam, Just Like Home." It's used, Stryker tells me, by rig workers and local fishermen. While Stryker heads off to Ella's, I check into the Sea Foam. I collect my door key from the surly manager and find my room.

It's a single room with a minuscule bathroom attached. The place doesn't look like it's been cleaned any time recently. I don't care. All I really want to do is lie down and sleep. I examine the sheets and decide to lie on top of the outer blanket. The TV seems to receive only one channel, currently showing a program on bass fishing.

Stryker shows up a little after five. "A chopper did go to one of the rigs and it hasn't come back. They must be stayin' at the rig for the return flight. They not gon' fly anywhere tonight, that for sure. They say a big storm comin' in. Might even be a hurricane."

"Who owns the chopper?"

"Owned and operated by Coldcreek Security. The chopper carried six people plus a flight crew of two. One of the guys who works the flight deck saw the passenger manifest. Five listed as a security detail plus one passenger."

"Who was the passenger?"

"He didn't see no names. He thinks it might be a woman."

"Where did the chopper go?"

"That's the strange part. It was goin' to Deepwater Two."

"Why's that strange?"

"'Cause Deepwater Two was decommissioned three years ago. There's nobody on Deepwater Two no more. Why they sendin' a security detail to an abandoned rig?"

"Let's find out. We have to get onto that rig."

"We can't hire a chopper. They all grounded because of the weather. The only way to get out there is by boat."

"Can we hire a boat in the middle of the night in this weather?"

"I think I can find one. I'll make a couple of calls."

Stryker calls several different numbers. The conversations lead to prolonged talk about old friends, some seemingly deceased, fish prices (deplorable), and the riffraff found at Ella's bar these days. That takes almost forty minutes. At the end of the last call, Stryker looks very pleased with himself as he puts down the phone.

"We've got us a ride, partner. I got in touch with an old friend with a boat. He my buddy from way back when I worked the rigs. A bunch of us used to go fishing when we were on shore leave, and we used to rent this fella's boat, and he'd take us out into the gulf. Duke can take us to the rig. There's nowhere Duke can't go."

"What about the storm?"

"Weather don't bother Duke none."

CHAPTER THIRTY

STRYKER DRIVES ME to the marina, and we walk along a wooden pier. It's getting dark and a wind suddenly picks up. Dozens of boats are lashed to the pier, bobbing in a troubled sea. Stryker takes me to a beat-up, forty-foot motor launch that's rising and falling in the sea swells. A small, elderly man emerges from the wheelhouse.

"Welcome, old friend," the man calls to Stryker, climbing onto the pier. "I hope you been staying out of trouble." He smiles brightly.

"Duke, this my partner." Stryker pushes me forward so I stand in front of Duke. "The man I tole' you about."

The old man makes a slight bow and smiles welcomingly. We shake hands. He appears to be Asian, but it's hard to tell anything about him in the dim light. His face is brown and deeply weathered.

"Stryker tells me you can take us out into the gulf."

"I sure can. Anything for my old friend Stryker and his partner." Duke speaks with a distinct accent that I can't yet place. "When do you want to leave?"

"Right now. We need to get out to the rig tonight and get back to land before daylight."

"We can leave now. The sooner the better. We're in for bad weather."

I look up at the clear sky. "It doesn't look bad to me. What makes you think there'll be a storm?"

"Pressure's dropping. We better get started."

I follow Duke onto the boat, which rocks under our feet, and I grab on to a stanchion supporting the roof of the wheelhouse to keep from falling. Duke has no trouble keeping his balance. The craft smells of motor oil and shrimp.

"You want to go to Deepwater Two?" the old man asks me.

"That's right."

"You know there's nobody on that rig. It was abandoned years ago."

"Let's go find out," I say.

Duke looks at me with commiseration as Stryker releases a rope from a bollard on the pier. He tosses the rope to Duke and jumps into the boat after us. Duke disappears into the wheelhouse and a moment later the big outboard motors sputter to life. Duke steers the craft out of the marina and into the gulf.

The only light I see on the boat, in addition to the running lights, is a faint glow on the navigation panel. There's a certificate of some kind, beat-up and water-stained, taped to one side of a compass. It lists the boat operator as Lee Dinh Duke.

"How do you know the pressure is dropping?" I ask Duke. "I don't see a barometer."

"I don't need no barometer. I can feel the pressure right here." He taps his chest.

A few minutes later, we run into heavy chop and the boat rolls and pitches. I sit down and hold tight to keep from being thrown around. The wind is stiffer now that we're out in the open sea. Stiffer and colder.

I don't normally suffer from seasickness, but this sea looks bad. And there's always a first time. It would be embarrassing if I had to throw up in the middle of our operation. Duke and Stryker look unfazed. I breathe deeply and hope for the best.

Duke turns to me. "Stryker says you a cop."

"You could say that."

"You not here because of that casino business, are you?"

"I don't know anything about a casino."

"I wasn't really involved. That was Torres."

"Don't worry about it, Duke. I'm not here about the casino."

Duke, satisfied, turns back into his wheelhouse and concentrates on navigating.

A wave splashes over the prow, drenching us with cold spray. I move to the back of the boat and sit next to Stryker. The move doesn't give me any real protection from the weather.

"What are we looking for when we get to the rig?" Stryker asks me.

"A young girl, aged about seventeen, was kidnapped in Washington. I think she's on the Deepwater Two rig. I'm going to find her and take her back home."

"What makes you think she's there?"

"Her kidnapper made a call to her mother. The call came from an oil rig, I'm pretty sure. We know some people went to Deepwater Two yesterday. Why would anyone go to a decommissioned and abandoned oil rig? They must be hiding. The girl's there, I'm certain. And so are her captors. All we have to do is find her and get her off."

Stryker nods thoughtfully. "The men who snatched this girl—they gonna be armed?"

"Heavily armed. The people who took the girl are dangerous killers. And they're desperate."

"Do you have a plan?" Stryker asks.

"Sure. We go to the rig, find the girl, and escape."

"That don' sound much like a plan to me."

I realize Stryker's too smart to buy my bullshit anymore. I'm going to have to be square with him from now on—or at least a bit more honest than I'm accustomed to.

"The people who kidnapped the girl have no idea we know where they are. They don't know we know where the girl is being held. And even if they did know, they're certainly not expecting visitors to show up in the middle of the night—in a hurricane. They're thinking the only way to get to the rig is by chopper, and nobody's flying a chopper in these conditions. So they figure they're safe. We have the advantage of surprise."

Stryker studies me skeptically. "Don't seem like much of a plan to me."

"Do you believe in magical thinking?"

"No, sir. I put my faith in God."

"You don't have to go with me onto the rig to find the girl. You never signed up for that."

"I've gone this far. I'm with you all the way. You my partner an' I don' let my partner down. I promised Sister Grace I'd look after you."

As if in a comment on this observation, our boat rises and pitches violently with heavy sea swells. Another large wave splashes over us, soaking us with freezing seawater. I'm soaked through to the skin and having a hard time catching my breath. Both Stryker and I hang on to whatever is secure. Duke, in his cabin, is untroubled.

After an hour of wind and rain and rough seas, the skies momentarily clear, and the moon and a sprinkling of stars appear. I didn't embarrass myself by throwing up. Before us, a massive structure rises from the sea. Forty stories tall. It's the derrick of an offshore oil rig. There's no sign of a light anywhere.

"Slow down," I say to Duke. "And keep the engines as quiet as you can. I don't want anybody on that rig to know we're coming."

Slowly, we approach the giant rig. Duke maneuvers the boat up close to a landing platform at the base of the rig. Stryker leaps onto the landing. Duke tosses him a rope. Stryker grabs it and secures the boat, lashing the rope around a massive steel beam supporting the structure. I jump out after Stryker and onto the platform.

"Stay here and wait for us," I yell to Duke. "If you see anyone who doesn't look like us, cast off and get the hell out of here. Don't hang around to find out what happened."

Stryker and I head for the base of a circular iron staircase. It's raining hard again, stinging my face. I'm almost blinded. The steps are wet and slippery, and we have to grip the railing hard to keep from being blown off. I'm numb with cold when we reach the top of the structure, and I'm deafened by the wind, which howls around us with a noise like a freight train.

At the top is a wide, circular deck. In the middle stands a Bell 407 turbine helicopter lashed by heavy cables to the landing deck. The emblem of Coldcreek Security is on the side of the chopper. There's no barrier on the edge of the platform. The wind is so strong we could be easily blown over the edge into the ocean below.

I grab the iron rail and my head spins. I turn away, not looking over the edge, until I regain my balance. As if the wind and the rain weren't bad enough, I have a deathly fear of heights. Even Stryker looks nervous and clutches the railing.

There's no sign of the security detail or the helicopter crew. They've presumably sensibly retreated to someplace dry and protected from the storm. The wind suddenly picks up again, and I feel cold to my bones.

"Where is the security detail?" I yell.

Stryker points at his wristwatch. "Probably asleep on one of the upper decks." Stryker shouts over the shrieking wind and signals for me to follow. He leads me around the chopper, keeping far away from the edge and the dizzying drop beyond. We duck down, careful to stay out of sight in case some unknown person is watching. I follow Stryker through a steel door, and we're standing in a spacious room. A large window looks over the helipad and, beyond that, to what I think was the rig's drilling floor.

"We're on the bridge," Stryker whispers.

For the moment, we're protected from the wind and the rain, but we're both soaking wet. Puddles of rainwater pool around us as we move, shivering, through the bridge.

We go quickly into an adjacent room filled with work outfits. Heavy-duty overalls, hard hats, thick gloves, boots with steel toes. Then we reach the intersection of two dark corridors.

"She's probably being kept in one of the bunk rooms they use for VIP visitors," Stryker whispers. "Security is probably in the dormitory used by the drill teams."

"Where are these VIP rooms?"

"They'll be down one of these two hallways."

I indicate silently to Stryker he should go to the right. I go to the left.

I move down the corridor, feeling my way from door to door. The first five doors are unlocked, and I don't bother to look inside. If they're keeping Angie Flynn prisoner, her captors wouldn't leave the door unsecured.

The door to the sixth room is locked. The door and frame are flimsy, more for privacy than security. I give a fierce kick to the door, and the bolt tears through the thin metal frame. I step quickly into a small room.

Somewhere in the dark, I sense rather than see someone moving. I hope it's the girl rather than an armed guard.

"Angie?" I whisper. "Are you here?"

"Who the fuck are you?" a girl's voice demands.

"My name's Marko. I'm here to get you out of here. Come quick."

A small bedside light flashes on across a small two-bunk bedroom revealing a young woman. She's still wearing the tartan plaid outfit I saw the other girls wearing at her school. Even in the shadows, I recognize her as Chief Flynn's daughter.

"What do you want?" she demands loudly.

"I'm going to get you off this oil rig."

She doesn't move from her perch on the bunk. "Did my mother send you?"

"I promised her I'd get you home safely."

She eyes me suspiciously. I know instinctively what's coming. I jump forward to stop her.

I'm too late.

"Help me!" she screams. "Somebody help me! There's a man in my cabin and he's going to rape me."

By now, I have my hand over her mouth. She struggles to free herself and bites my hand savagely, but I don't release her. I stop her scream. From a distance comes the sound of voices yelling and emergency Klaxons blaring.

Harsh, bright light fills the room, and two armed men are standing at the door, both holding Heckler & Koch machine pistols pointed at me. Behind them the corridor is filled with pulsing, white strobe emergency lights.

Angela crouches on her bunk bed and points at me with a trembling hand. "He attacked me! He tried to strangle me."

"It's all right, miss," one of the armed guards says. "We'll take care of him."

I pull away from the angry girl. He's the man I encountered in the department store men's room. He obviously remembers me and his face flushes with fury.

"Who is this man?" Angie asks, pointing at me. "Why is he in my room?"

The second man speaks into a radio transmitter hanging from his shoulder. "We've got company, Mr. Hammer. Zorn is here with the girl. Situation under control." He listens for a moment, then waves his submachine pistol at us, indicating we should leave the room with him. Spencer points the Heckler & Koch at my head.

I stumble toward the door, clutching my throbbing right hand that's beginning to bleed from the girl's bite.

"You, too, lady," Spencer barks at Angela.

"I want to stay here."

"Now! Mr. Hammer wants both of you on the helipad," the second man says.

"It's raining and it's cold—"

"On the helipad! Both of you."

Angela slides off her bunk, and we leave the room. We hurry down the corridor, now brightly lit, with one of the gunmen ahead of us and Spencer behind, poking his machine pistol into the small of my back. We go past the entrance to the bridge, out through another door. We're out on the helipad, slammed against the bulkhead by a violent burst of wind and rain.

A man is waiting for us on the far side of the pad. He stands with his feet far apart, bracing himself in the gale, gripping a railing. His spiky white-blond hair is blowing stiffly in the wind. The butt of a Browning automatic sticks out from his waistband. "Welcome to Deepwater Two," he shouts. "You should have stayed home." I think that's what he says. The wind is too loud to make out the words. "Take them to the edge."

"Can I have the cop?" Spencer yells eagerly.

"Leave Zorn to me," Hammer shouts back. "He's mine. Dump the broad."

Spencer drags Angie to the rim of the helipad. She struggles to free herself, but he holds her tight. A man grabs me by my arm in case I try to do something heroic.

I briefly speculate about whether anyone could survive a fall into the ocean from this height. I decide not.

"Goodbye, Miss Flynn. Dump the bitch," Hammer calls out.

Spencer grabs Angie by both arms, preparing to fling her over the side.

Spencer then vanishes.

Angie crouches on the helipad platform, clutching one of the steel cables securing the helicopter.

In the lashing rain and the storm, Spencer is gone. I think I hear a scream as he drops to the ocean below. But maybe it's just the wind.

CHAPTER THIRTY-ONE

IN THE SPACE where Spencer was standing, there's now only Stryker and Angela.

Stryker grabs Angela by her arm and pulls her away from the edge of the helipad. The gunman standing behind me releases his grip on my arm. He steps forward to get a clear shot at Stryker. I hit the gunman hard with a kidney punch and he crumples to the deck. The pain in my right hand where Angela bit me surges through my arm up to my shoulder.

Hammer reaches for the Browning at his waist. I swing around and smash my elbow into Hammer's throat, crushing his larynx. Hammer staggers, gasping for breath. He drops, gagging, to his knees.

I snatch the Browning from his hand and point it at his head. The remaining functioning gunman on deck is paralyzed.

"Drop your weapons or your boss gets it," I yell. I doubt the gunman hears what I'm saying, but he gets the message. When he hesitates, I fire the Browning, and the round tears a hole in the gas tank of the Bell helicopter and aviation fuel gushes onto the helipad.

"If that stuff catches fire," Stryker yells, "we all done for."

"Then it's time we got out of Dodge," I yell back.

I kneel and yell into Hammer's ear. "I ought to dump you into the ocean to join your buddy."

Hammer is silent, his eyes wide with terror as he stares at the pooling aviation fuel moving toward us. Of course, Hammer can't talk just now, with his throat being crushed and all.

I take out my cigarette lighter and flick it. The flame struggles to stay alight in the wind and the rain.

"Call off your man," I order. "Now! Or I toss this lighter into the gas."

Hammer shrinks away from the fuel that's flowing from the helicopter gas tank. He looks terrified and waves his hands and arms frantically at the armed man to stand down and leave the helipad. The man disappears.

Hammer takes one fast look at me. Scared and furious. He scrambles to his feet and disappears through the door to the bridge.

"Turn that thing off," Stryker yells to me urgently. "You gonna kill us all."

I flip the lighter closed. Stryker grabs Angela by her arm. She stands cowering near the door to the interior of the rig.

"Come with us," I yell.

She struggles to free herself from Stryker's grip, but she can't pull away, and they stumble after me toward the top of the steps that lead to the platform at the base of the rig where Duke is waiting for us. We rush down the first flight of steps, keeping an eye out for Hammer and his gunman.

"Stop!" Stryker yells. In front of us, at the top of the next staircase, stand three armed security men.

One of the men guarding the steps takes a shot at us. In the wind and rain, it's a wild shot, but I know the next one will be better aimed. I fire the Browning at him. I also miss. The shooter gets the message and crouches down behind the iron scaffolding.

We're safe for a couple of minutes, but the armed guards block the staircase and our only exit from the rig. We can't get past them or down the steps to get to Duke and his boat. And I know we have only minutes before Hammer and his men emerge from the safety of the rig interior and come charging after us. We're caught between two armed groups intending to kill us.

"This way," Stryker shouts. "Follow me!"

Stryker and I rush Angie, protesting, to the deck just under the helipad. In front of us lie four massive objects painted a brilliant orange. Stryker reaches down and pulls Angie up onto the top of the object nearest us. He points to an open hatch. "In you go!"

"I'm not going in this thing. You can't make me."

Stryker lifts Angie by the shoulders, holds her squirming body over the hatch, and lowers her gently inside. "You next," he says to me.

I scuttle to the open hatch, swing myself over the edge, and drop inside. Stryker is right behind me and secures the hatch above us. He switches on a dim overhead light.

We're inside what seems to be an oblong metal container that's large enough to hold a dozen men. There are folding seats along the sides and above us is a translucent plastic canopy.

"Where the hell are we?" I ask.

"We inside an escape pod," Stryker answers.

"I don't like it here," Angie complains. "I have claustrophobia."

"They've found us," Stryker says. The sound of boots stepping heavily on the iron hull of our escape pod. Flashlight beams flickering through the heavy plastic canopy. Figures of men peer in at us. A wheel on the hatch begins to turn. "Grab the hatch wheel," Stryker calls to me. "Don't let them in!"

I catch the wheel on the inside of the hatch and feel it being turned from the outside, counterclockwise. I hold on tight and twist it back, clockwise. The pain in my right hand shoots through my shoulder.

"Don't let go," Stryker shouts. "If they get in, we all dead."

Pop, pop, pop. The sounds of rounds hitting the metal hull.

"How long will the canopy hold?"

"It's not bulletproof. Hang on," Stryker calls out. "We're in for a rough ride. Take a seat and harness your seat belts."

He reaches to the roof of our escape pod, grasps a heavy handle, and yanks it down hard.

"What's going on?" Angie demands in a voice close to tears. But she sits and straps herself in.

I feel the escape pod tremble and begin to move.

"I've released the pod from its mooring," Stryker yells. "In a moment, we'll slide down the escape chute and out over the ocean. We'll be suspended by a cable and lowered to the sea surface. After that, we on our own."

The escape pod shakes violently for several seconds and then there's total silence as the pod swings back and forth over the ocean.

"I think I'm going to be sick," Angie wails.

I'm feeling about the same.

"Hold on tight," Stryker calls out. "Gonna hit water."

The pod slams into the ocean, shaking us violently. Then we're bobbing in the heavy seas. Stryker dives for the control panel at one end of the craft. The controls seem to consist of an iron tiller, an ignition switch, and a compass. Stryker presses the ignition and starts an engine somewhere that I feel vibrating through the hull.

"We gotta get back to land," Stryker calls over the motor sound.

"Find Duke first," I call back.

We plow through the heavy waves, the escape pod rising and falling violently. Stryker motions for me to take his place at the tiller while he stands and peers through the canopy searching for Duke.

"I see the boat," Stryker calls out. "It's on fire. To our right."

I pull the tiller hard, changing direction.

"Hold steady," Stryker commands. "Tiller to left," he calls out.

"Angie, hold the tiller," I yell.

"I don't know how!"

"Do it, Angie! Now."

She releases her seat harness, scrambles across the floor, and grips the tiller in both hands.

I join Stryker to look for Duke. Against the glare of a burning boat, I see Duke's head bobbing in the water twenty feet to starboard. Everywhere is black night indistinguishable from the black sea.

"His boat's dead ahead," I shout. "Steady."

We creep forward. A large wave breaks over us and I see Duke's head again. He's clinging to some object and then disappears below the crest of the wave. Stryker opens the hatch, grabs a coil of rope, and climbs out. Buckets of water pour in around him. I climb out through the hatch and join Stryker on the top of the pod, holding on to a handgrip. The pod is rising and falling in the heavy seas. The iron surface under our feet is slippery and I'm half-blinded by the stinging spray in my face.

"I see him." Stryker points at a large wave that's coming at us. Duke's head rises just above the top of the wave. Stryker uncoils the rope and flings one end toward Duke, but it lands far to his right and out of reach. Stryker almost loses his balance as he hauls the rope back in. I grab Stryker by one arm while he flings the rope in the direction where we last saw Duke.

The rope tightens. Duke's got it. Stryker pulls at the rope. Duke is just within reach, and we both grab him by his arms and pull him onto the pod. He's drenched, and seawater flows from his head and mouth. But he's alive.

A heavy wave hits us, and all three of us are almost thrown into the boiling sea. Stryker and I grab handholds and keep a tight grip on Duke who, for a moment, swings out over the waves. We don't let go and, with a final effort, we haul Duke over the hatch and lower him into the pod. Stryker and I follow. Stryker quickly secures the hatch above us.

Duke looks around the interior of the pod as Stryker grabs the tiller and we all sit in miserable, cold, wet silence trying to catch our breaths. Angie shrinks away from us.

I hear the sounds of high-powered rifle rounds pinging the outside of the hull.

"If one of them rounds punctures the canopy, we'll be swamped," Stryker yells. "We got to get out of here. Fast."

"Does anyone know how to get back to the marina?" I ask.

"I'll manage," Duke says, taking a seat at the control panel and grasping the tiller. "As long as this compass ain't broke, I'll get us home." He wipes streaming water from his face, studies the compass, shifts the tiller, and moves the craft slowly away from the rig and his burning boat, and the men firing at us. The pod rocks violently as we're hit by heavy seas.

"What happened to your boat?" I ask.

"They fired tracer rounds into the gas tank, and it exploded."

Angie is seated on one of the seats, her legs drawn up beneath her and her arms held tightly around her body. "I want to go home," she whimpers.

"Does this escape pod work?" I ask. "I mean, can we make it go where we want?"

"Within limits," Stryker replies.

With Duke controlling navigation, we ride through the violent seas for a few moments.

"Can you go any faster?" Duke asks.

"It's got one speed—slow," Stryker answers.

I examine my right hand, which is still aching from Angela's bite. It's too soon to see whether it's infected, and I can't help but wonder whether Angie is rabid. While Duke tends to navigation, Stryker sits next to me.

"How is it you knew about this escape pod?" I ask.

"I tol' you, I worked the rigs. A rig can be a real firetrap. It's everyone's nightmare. We were trained on getting in and out of the pods. And how to run them in an emergency. I gotta say, I was scared outta my mind when you lit that lighter. I thought we was all done for."

"I want to go home," Angie says to us from her perch across the pod. "You can't keep me here."

I sit next to Angie. "How're you doing?"

"I'm just great. I'm cold and I'm wet and I'm hungry and scared. I want to go home."

Angie crosses her arms and shuts her eyes. Conversation over.

We plough through the heavy seas for what seems an eternity, numb and stiff from the cold and from being thrown around inside the iron craft. Angie eventually gives up her sulk attitude, and I can see she's crying.

"I'll talk to the girl," Stryker says and for the next hour, he sits next to her, speaking softly. Sometimes she nods and sometimes she even smiles. Mostly she just listens. I can't hear much of what Stryker is saying. Whatever Stryker's telling her seems to be having a soothing effect. The only other sound I hear is the sound of the craft's engines and the waves crashing against us.

CHAPTER THIRTY-TWO

IT'S ALMOST SIX in the morning when Duke finally pulls into the marina and guides our escape pod up to the pier. We climb out, stiff and cold and wet. The wind has died down, and the rain has stopped. I scan the area to be sure no one is waiting for us. I walk to the end of the pier with Hammer's Browning clutched in my left hand. The place is deserted.

"We need to get back to Washington as soon as possible," I tell Stryker.

"The first flight with connections out of Gulfport-Biloxi International to DC leaves at ten," Stryker tells me. "I used to take that flight when I worked the rigs."

"That gives you about four hours," Duke says. "If you hang out in those wet clothes, you'll catch pneumonia. This young lady is doing poorly." He looks at Angie, who stands dripping water and looking miserable. "You come to my place and my wife will fix you up with dry clothes and something to eat."

Duke and his elderly wife live in a small but neat house near the docks. She hustles poor Angela into some mysterious back room while Duke rummages through closets and wicker baskets and assembles a temporary wardrobe for Stryker and me. Finding clothes that fit a man who is five foot two for a man who is over six foot three is a challenge.

My right hand, where Angie bit it, is painful but does not appear to be infected. Mrs. Duke, if that's her name, gives me some ointment and that seems to help. We sit at a simple wooden table and eat a meal of fish and shrimp. Angie does not appear. We're told she's asleep. Somehow, while all this is going on, Duke's wife has managed to clean, dry, and press the clothes we wore. By the time we're ready to leave, we look human and almost respectable.

Stryker collects the rental car, and we wake Angie, who's in a bad mood. Stryker drives us to the airport. On the way, I have Stryker pull the car over to the side of the road, and I toss Hammer's Browning pistol into a swamp.

Before we catch the flight to DC, I send a text message to Chief Flynn's private number. *Special delivery arriving national airport, Gate 24 @ 12:22 p.m.*

I take the window seat, Angie's in the middle, and Stryker's on the aisle, so Angie can't escape and denounce us as lunatic killers to the cabin crew. She complains for the first ten minutes of the flight about having to be in the middle seat, which she claims makes her airsick. Stryker speaks to her gently, and eventually she settles down. The rest of the flight is uneventful, and I manage to get some sleep until the flight attendants instruct us passengers to return our seats to their upright positions.

We're in a descending glide path, and I see nothing unusual waiting for us at National Airport. It's not until we've touched down and are taxiing along the runway and about to turn into the access lane that I see the flashing lights of fire engines and police cars. As soon as we're clear of the active runway, the pilot, instead of taking us to our disembarkation slot, stops the aircraft. There's a period of almost ten minutes of silence from the aircrew. Then the pilot, using the soothing baritone voice male pilots adopt in such situations, informs us that there is a slight delay, but he will have us at our gate very soon.

A crew wheels portable steps up to the side of the aircraft, a member of the flight crew opens the aircraft door, and a crowd of people enter. There seems to be an urgent conversation with the pilot.

DC Police Chief Kelly Flynn, followed by three heavily armed men in SWAT team outfits, strides down the aisle until she stops at our row. Stryker has seen the chief and her entourage swarm the plane and has prudently left his seat and stepped to the rear of the aircraft.

Chief Flynn kneels in the aisle.

"I'm not going home . . ." Angie starts to say. She sort of cringes into her seat and points at me. "That man was mean."

"Darling." Flynn speaks softly. "I love you dearly, but if you make the slightest trouble or say one single word, I'm going to have Sergeant Crowley here"—she points to one of the three hulking figures standing behind her— "put you in handcuffs and remove you from this plane by force, if necessary. That would be embarrassing for everybody. Now get up and walk down the aisle with Sergeant Crowley like a proper young lady."

Angie silently unbuckles her seat belt and stands up, adjusts her skirt, and follows the sergeant off the plane, not looking at me. The passengers, of course, are watching open-mouthed at this circus. This has got to be more entertaining than the inflight movie.

Chief Flynn turns to me. "Don't tell me what happened, Zorn. I don't think I want to know."

Then mouths silently, "Thank you, Marko."

CHAPTER THIRTY-THREE

CARLA LOWRY IS waiting impatiently for me in the VIP lounge.

"Do you know how much trouble it was to get you in to see Digger Granger?" Carla asks.

"I've visited many inmates in federal prisons. There's usually no problem."

"Digger Granger is no ordinary prisoner. There have been attempts on his life while in lockup. He has a lot of enemies. I had to sweet-talk not only him and the warden but also the director of the Bureau of Prisons and my own bosses in the FBI. They are not happy with you being anywhere near Digger Granger. You have a reputation."

"But you did it, Carla. Once again, your charm won the day and left your opposition helpless."

"Don't ask me for another favor anytime soon. We're scheduled to see Digger during visiting hours the day after tomorrow. Remember. I'll be watching you."

"The timing is perfect. I have to make a quick trip out of town. I'll meet you when I get back, and we'll solve the famous theft of Vermeer's *The Concert.*"

I catch a flight connecting through Chicago O'Hare to Indianapolis International. I make no effort to cover my tracks this time. Angie is safe and I figure it's okay if someone wants to know I'm coming for them. It's past time my quarry knows I won't give up until one of us is dead, although they've probably figured that out by now.

I pick up a rental car and drive to Indianapolis. I reach the headquarters of Altavista Corporation late in the afternoon and park in a lot marked "For Visitors." I catch a circulating bus decorated with the Altavista logo in blue and green colors, which takes me to the main entrance of the Altavista complex. The large, brightly lit reception area is decorated in soothing pastel colors and gigantic video screens featuring happy people, glowing with good health, gamboling through lush, green meadows. A large sign over the reception desk announces, "Your Home for Good Health." I'm duly impressed and feel better already.

Half a dozen young men and women stand behind the long reception counter, smiling broadly. A pretty young woman asks, "What can I help you with, sir?"

She wears, as do all the other receptionists, an outfit of starched white linen, resembling a nurse's uniform, and a lime-green name tag informing me her name is Cassie. No last name. Next to it, she wears a badge that greets me with the words, also in bright green lettering, "Welcome to Altavista, the Home for Good Health and Good Living." I wonder whether the nice people at the reception counter have anything for my right hand, which still hurts.

If Cassie weren't so young and so anxious to please, I'd take her for a doctor, or some other kind of medical practitioner. I suppose that's the purpose of the white outfit she's wearing. You'd think we were in the waiting room of some hospital of the future. Of course, if we were, the first thing she would do is demand proof of insurance. She's obviously not a real doctor.

"My name is Marko Zorn. I would like to speak with Mr. Colin Stone."

Cassie's pretty blue eyes widen. She's probably never been asked that before. It probably wasn't included in her indoctrination course. Though startled, she doesn't lose her composure.

"Did you say, 'Mr. Colin Stone'? *The* Mr. Stone?" Her smile remains, but it's pasted on now.

"That's right. *The* Mr. Colin Stone. Would you let *the* Mr. Colin Stone know *the* Detective Zorn from Washington is here to see him? It's *the* Detective Zorn."

Cassie steps back from the reception desk and looks a bit helpless. Then she gathers her wits. "Alan, can you step over here for a moment?"

A tall young man approaches the desk. He wears the same phony medical outfit as the other receptionists, but he's a bit older than the others and has an air of authority.

"How can I help you, sir?" he asks, flashing me a broad smile.

"I'm here to see Colin Stone."

He raises his right eyebrow to indicate mild skepticism. How do people do that? It must take years of practice to learn how to raise just one eyebrow. Is it possible it's part of the Altavista training program?

"You're not on Mr. Stone's visitors list." The smile fades a bit.

"You didn't check the visitors list."

"It wasn't necessary. Mr. Stone doesn't have a visitors list." I can see he's about to say "no" and blow me off.

"Just tell him that Detective Marko Zorn from the Washington, DC Police Homicide division is here to see him. Personally. It's about murder."

"Nobody may see CEO Stone without the prior approval of our legal department."

"Where is this legal department located?"

"In San Francisco."

"Are you saying I'm supposed to go to San Francisco to get approval to come here?"

"That's correct, sir. Without legal's approval, you are not permitted to see CEO Stone."

"That's not what Max Poole told me."

That gets Alan's immediate attention. "Did you just say Maximilian Poole sent you?"

"Maybe it was Sabastian Poole. I can never tell which is which. Can you?"

This exchange was not included in Alan's orientation class. The other receptionists, including Cassie, have stopped talking to the people standing in line at the reception counter and are obviously straining to hear what we're saying.

"Maybe I should call Mr. Stone's office directly," Alan tells me, without much grace.

"Maybe you should do just that."

Alan steps away and disappears into a small office, where he talks urgently on the phone. His call does not take long, and he soon returns. "Mr. Stone will see you now. Sorry for the inconvenience." He doesn't sound sorry. "Come with me. I'll take you to his office."

Alan leads me into the campus of the Altavista Corporation. There are dozens of small buildings surrounded by a parklike atmosphere with trees, trimmed hedges, and meandering paths. There are fountains and, in the distance, a small lake on which several couples are paddling canoes. The weather is warm, and many employees are outside, sitting on the grass in the shade of the trees. It looks downright bucolic. The scene reminds me of a small New England college campus—one with a very good endowment. It just goes to show how deceptive appearances can be. This is not real. This is a stage set.

In the center of the campus is a single building fifty stories high. I figure that must be where my guy hangs out.

Alan is silent as he leads me along the sylvan paths. We're occasionally passed by men and women riding bicycles. Alan, I observe, walks several feet away from me, as if he were afraid I had some communicable disease or might try to jump him. When we're about halfway to the high-rise building, we're joined by two new men. They stay at least ten paces behind us but are careful to keep pace with us. They wear white uniforms with Coldcreek Security patches on their shoulders and they carry sidearms.

In front of the fifty-story building, which, I assume, is Altavista's headquarters, is a broad plaza surrounded by stone benches. We enter the building into a reception area. This is manned by more security guards. They don't have the warm smiles Cassie had at the first reception desk.

Alan speaks to one of the guards, then ushers me into a large elevator decorated with fancy wood paneling and gold trim. We're joined by the armed men who followed us across the campus. We rise, in total silence, to the fiftieth floor.

The elevator doors slide open, and I step into a luxurious reception area with French impressionist paintings on the walls. In front of me is a mahogany reception desk behind which sits a large man who glares at me.

"The Poole brothers told you to see the CEO?" The large man behind the desk looks bewildered. A little anxious.

"There's been a little problem back in Washington. About Harvey Young. He was burned alive in his car. Harvey was, until recently, an employee here at Altavista. The brothers thought if I had a word with the CEO, all this could be cleared up."

The security guys look ashen.

"Mr. Hammer also urged me to speak personally with the CEO. He can be very insistent. You know how he is. The director of Coldcreek Security. Like your boss?"

"You know Mr. Hammer?" The man at the reception desk is looking more anxious.

"He and I go way back."

"He never mentioned your name."

"He's just being modest."

"I'll check with CEO Stone, Mr. Zorn."

"It's Detective Zorn."

CHAPTER THIRTY-FOUR

"You should not have come."

Colin Stone stands before me. He's a small man, about seventy. He's wearing an expensive, tailored, light-gray suit and handmade western boots. Black with elaborate red and green stitching. The walls of the office behind him are painted a soothing gray. There's no desk in sight, no office equipment of any kind. No telephone or computer. To show how important he is. He has underlings to talk on the phone and to write things for him.

There are two long couches and half a dozen armchairs, all upholstered in soft, pearl-gray leather. The walls are decorated with large, abstract paintings. A six-foot-tall rabbit of polished stainless-steel stands in the middle of the room. At the far end is a wall of glass looking out onto an open terrace and, beyond that, the Altavista campus.

"That will be all," Colin Stone says softly. Alan slips silently away. Stone and I are now alone. "I've been expecting you, Detective." He speaks in a low, cultivated voice as we shake. "My security people tell me you're a policeman from Washington."

"You do not seem surprised to see me."

"I've been expecting you. Maybe not you personally. Maybe not today. But someday. In fact, I've been waiting for you, or somebody like you, for years. It's almost a relief to meet you face-to-face at last."

"You said I should not have come."

"Of course. It could prove fatal."

"To you or to me?"

He shrugs. "Either. Or both."

He indicates I should follow him into his office. Here there are a dozen large vases, filled with flowers, and the room is heavy with a pleasant fragrance.

"Will your art collection be included in the Pooles' gift to the nation?"

"Of course. Everything at Altavista belongs to the brothers."

"I'm not here to talk about art, Mr. Stone. I'm here to talk about murder."

"Of course you are. Forgive me. You're investigating, I believe, the tragic death of my old friend and colleague Harvey Young."

"I'm investigating the murder of Harvey Young."

"Murder. Quite right."

"I want to know the secret Harvey Young was going to reveal to the FDA."

"Then I suggest we step out onto the balcony to continue our conversation."

"Is that because your office is bugged?" I ask.

Stone shrugs and smiles slightly. He stops at one of the leather chairs to pick up a long, bright-red woolen scarf that he wraps around his neck. "I suffer from chronic throat problems. The result of smoking two packs of cigarettes a day. I wear this when I'm outside on the balcony. It can get a bit cold and windy. One must be careful with one's health. Don't you agree?"

Stone leads me across the office and out through the large glass sliding doors. I follow him onto the balcony that overlooks

the domain of the Altavista Corporation. My heart is pound-
ing. There's nothing but a low wall between me and doom fifty
floors below. I shudder and grip the wall hard. I try not to look
down.

"Are you all right, Detective?" Stone asks.

"I'm afraid of heights," I say.

"I used to suffer from acrophobia myself. I've learned to live
with it."

Stone stands at the edge of the balcony and leans over the parapet. He seems to gain strength from the height.

"You know you're taking a terrible risk," Stone says at last, turning
to me with a slight smile, "coming here to meet with me like this.
You have no backup. Mr. Hammer tells me you do not even carry
a gun. All I'd have to do is call for the security team and you might
suffer a terrible accident—like falling over the parapet here. If you're
not very careful, it's so easy to fall."

Damned if he doesn't have a twinkle in his eye.

"I'll take my chances, Mr. Stone."

"As you wish." Stone shrugs and adjusts his red scarf tightly
around his neck. "Tell me what happened to Harvey."

"He was burned to death."

Stone flinches. It's the first sign of emotion I'd seen in him. "Did
he suffer much?"

"I'm sure he suffered a great deal. Wasn't that the point?"

"The point?" he asks distractedly.

"You knew Dr. Young, I believe."

Stone takes his time before answering. "We were once very
close. Harvey and I were in college together. We created Altavista
together. He was best man at my wedding. I was best man at his.
Harvey married my sister. Did you know that?"

"So she told me."

"You've spoken with her? Of course, you must have, wouldn't you. How is she taking Harvey's death?"

"Very badly, as you'd expect."

"Naturally. I'm truly sorry. You should know, Martha and I haven't spoken in years. Harvey and I had a bitter argument. She took his side. It's all so stupid. After graduate school, Harvey and I set up a small biological research firm called Altavista. We developed a promising new drug. We called it Zemlon."

"Did something go wrong?"

"Maximilian and Sabastian Poole entered the picture. They wanted Zemlon, and they offered us a deal. I wanted to accept their offer. Harvey was against it. Maximilian and Sabastian always get what they want. They bought Altavista and, with it, Zemlon. It was not an easy transaction. Maximilian and Sabastian at the time didn't have the cash to close the deal. They ended up getting the financing from their sister, who was independently wealthy. They closed the deal and got me along with Zemlon. I was made CEO of Altavista."

"That sounds like a good deal for you."

Colin Stone makes a sound that's supposed to be a laugh. "It certainly was profitable. Of course, there were certain conditions attached."

"What became of Harvey Young?"

"Harvey stayed on here at Altavista to continue his drug research but ended up hating what he was doing. He hated what Altavista became. Under the rule of Sabastian and Maximilian Poole, everything changed."

"How did it change?"

"Altavista no longer did original, groundbreaking research looking for new, life-enhancing drugs. Instead, Altavista buys or steals research done by others. It feeds on the small companies like the one Altavista once was. We also get our basic research from university labs and even from the National Institutes of Health in Washington."

"Isn't that what all big pharmaceutical companies do these days?"

"Of course. But Altavista is no longer run by its scientists and researchers. Now it is run by its marketing division and by the lawyers."

Stone turns to look me directly in the eyes. "Why are you really here, Detective?"

"I'm here to make you a proposition."

"Go ahead."

"Withdraw your application to the Food and Drug Administration to market Neuropromine. Stop manufacturing the illegal by-product known as Speedball."

"And in return?"

"I'll see that you and the Poole brothers are not charged with the murders of Dr. Young and Dr. Alsop."

"I believe you met with Maximilian and Sabastian and made the same proposal to them. You heard what they said. No deal. The brothers were not happy with your visit."

"I wasn't so happy with the visit myself. They tried to kill me."

"What did you expect?"

"You're the CEO of Altavista. You can stop this criminal outrage yourself."

"Altavista is a subsidiary of Magma Capital Management. Magma Capital makes all strategic decisions."

"Is Duncan Forest, CEO of Magma Capital Management, the one in charge?"

He shrugs. "Sometimes."

"Was it Duncan Forest who decided to falsify the results of the Neuropromine tests? Is he the one who authorized the illegal sale of Speedball?"

Colin Stone turns to me. "Are you asking whether Duncan Forest is behind Altavista's production and sale of illegal drugs?"

"That's exactly what I'm asking."

"Then you've got the wrong end of the stick. Forest was against Neuropromine from day one. He is something of a fanatic when it comes to narcotic drugs. His son died of an overdose when the boy was in college. Forest tried to stop the Neuropromine program and the sale of Speedball as soon as he learned what we were up to. He was overruled."

"Who overruled him?"

Colin Stone shakes head.

"I'm serious about having you and the brothers prosecuted for murder. And whoever is running the show these days. I'll find out who it is."

"Sabastian and Maximilian will never allow that to happen. They have powerful friends in Washington."

"You know that Neuropromine is so addictive it will make addicts of millions of people. It will kill thousands. Doesn't that bother you?"

"Of course, it bothers me. When I learned what we were doing, I ordered all further production of Neuropromine discontinued, and I informed Sabastian and Maximilian about the dangers. I recommended we shelve Neuropromine and withdraw our application with the FDA. And stop the off-label sale of Speedball. Forest backed me up."

"Then why did you continue with the production of these dangerous drugs?"

"About two weeks ago, the Poole brothers sent Hammer here. Instead of closing down Neuropromine and Speedball, he ordered me to double the sales of Speedball and organize a major marketing campaign for Neuropromine. I told Hammer the FDA would never approve our application. He said he'd make sure the FDA did what it was told."

"So you went ahead with a major marketing campaign for Neuropromine despite the harm it will do?"

"Hammer can be very persuasive. He told me to prepare to market Neuropromine as planned and to suppress all negative test data. 'Bury it,' he said. 'Place all negative data in our confidential files.'"

"Did Hammer say why the sale of Speedball was to be increased?"

"It seems Maximilian suddenly needed a substantial amount of cash. It sounded as if he was about to make a significant art purchase. Hammer instructed me to transfer a large amount of cash to one of Maximilian's personal accounts."

"How much?"

"Ten million dollars."

"How did you do that?"

"I used accounts used by one of Altavista's companies, Bismarck Moving and Storage. I had the funds converted to cryptocurrency and transferred that to one of the brothers' charity trusts in a bank in Greece."

"You could do that?"

"I do it all the time. Not usually in such large amounts, but it's one of my many responsibilities. The charity trusts are normally flush with cash. They're the brothers' personal piggy banks. The sales of Speedball are intended to replenish the charitable trusts."

Stone takes a gold cigarette case from his jacket pocket but doesn't open it. "That was two weeks ago. We thought we were in the clear until the whistleblower showed up. Mr. Hammer learned someone within Altavista had inside information about Neuropromine and had contacted the FDA. By that time, we were already producing large quantities of Speedball for the illegal market. These drugs are never produced here in the US, of course. We use our plant just outside of San Cristobal in Mexico."

"The Mexican authorities allow that?"

"The Mexican authorities know nothing about the drug production. The plant produces fertilizer, and the product is shipped to the US and around the world as fertilizer."

"When did you learn about the whistleblower?"

"Hammer told me someone had gotten access to Altavista's main vault where we keep our most sensitive information. I knew right away who the whistleblower must be.

"I called Harvey to my office, and we stood right here on this balcony. It was the first time we'd talked face-to-face in over a year. He begged me to stop Neuropromine before thousands became addicted and died."

"What did you say?"

"I told him he didn't understand how large corporations do business. I accused Harvey of betraying our trust and told him I never wanted to see him again. He was out. Fired. I warned him to have no more contact with the FDA and not to interfere with Magma's business plans. I reminded him of what happens to people who do.

"But even as I was saying those terrible things to Harvey, I felt relief—a kind of contentment, almost. I knew in my heart that Harvey was right."

"Just quit. Denounce the Poole brothers. The way your former partner wanted to do."

"Harvey was the strong one. I never had his moral courage."

"You still have a choice. Your old friend and partner was brutally murdered. An FDA researcher, Dr. Alsop, was murdered. Just walk away."

He shakes his head. "I can't. The brothers own me."

"Report them to the FDA. To the FBI. You can make a deal. I can help you."

"It's too late for me. I'm too deeply involved in Altavista's illegal acts. I've signed off on a FDA application that misrepresent the results of our research. We hide data in our reports. We routinely do fraudulent pricing. Drug diversion. We've been caught a few times, most recently for Medicare and Medicaid fraud. The company had to pay big fines. But it's chicken feed compared to the billions in profit the Poole brothers earn from Zemlon and from Speedball. And what they expect to earn from Neuropromine. The Poole brothers long ago decided if these activities were revealed publicly, we could tough it out. They'd use their friends and allies in the medical community and in Congress to suppress any bad publicity. As we always do."

My worst suspicions about Big Pharma are proving true. I wonder whether I should clean out my medicine cabinet when I get home. And throw out all those bottles. God knows what's in those pills and capsules.

"Did you know all along what Altavista was doing?"

"Of course, I knew. It's my company. In theory. With Neuropromine we were creating the next big drug. The potential profits were huge."

"What makes Neuropromine so special?"

"You want to know our secret?"

"That's one of the reasons I'm here."

"We add sufentanil to the Zemlon formula. In trace amounts. And in stronger amounts to Speedball."

"I'm aware of sufentanil. Can you get it without a doctor's prescription?"

"Absolutely not. It's a very controversial drug. Because it's so powerful, it is hard to control its abuse. It leads to addiction and death. Sufentanil is so powerful and so dangerous it can't be used in the United States except under very special conditions."

"The DEA will eventually link the sale of the drugs that have been mixed with sufentanil to the Poole brothers."

"The Poole brothers have seen to it that they have clean hands and all illegal activities lead to me and to me alone. My name is on the paperwork."

"The brothers must receive income from the illegal drug sales. That can be traced."

"The brothers never see a dime of direct income. When they need cash, as they recently did for their art purchase, Mr. Hammer comes to me. I dip into one of the charitable trust accounts."

The mention of charitable trust accounts rings a bell but, for the moment, I can't connect the dots.

"And it's not just the scams," Colin Stone goes on. "It's all the deceit we use to sell our products. We let our friendly doctors, the ones who are high prescribers of analgesics, know that Neuropromine will be special and their patients will be very happy with the results. Until, of course, they die."

My doctor seems like such a nice man, I think. Can I trust his advice on curing a cold now?

"I've just organized a conference with hundreds of eminent doctors invited to discuss recent medical research. In reality, to get doctors to prescribe Neuropromine as soon as it's approved by the FDA. Our medical guests are provided with lavish accommodations and entertainment. I personally took some of the high prescribers to exclusive nightclubs that provide special services to gentlemen with unusual tastes."

I don't want to think about what "special services" and "unusual tastes" mean.

"I create patients' committees, ostensibly to advocate on behalf of patients, but actually, as front organizations to promote Neuropromine."

"Isn't that against the law?"

"Of course it's against the law. I'm in charge of scores of field reps trained to assure prescribing physicians that Neuropromine has been thoroughly tested and proven to be safe and nonaddictive. You'll never be able to link the Poole brothers to any of these illegal activities."

Colin Stone looks out over the parapet. "I pay bribes to doctors, medical groups, hospitals, to members of Congress, and journalists and publications. I even bribe law enforcement agencies." He looks at me closely as if I might be a possible candidate. "I arrange for kickbacks to health care providers. It's all in a day's work."

I'm feeling nauseous. Colin Stone recounts his story in the same tone as if he were describing allocating parking spaces for his employees. I sense no shame. No remorse. Nothing. He stands next to the parapet and a fifty-story fall to the ground below. A gentle push would be all it takes. But I can't do that. Besides, it's only a matter of time before Stone makes that trip with no help from me. I must be patient.

Colin Stone is silent for a moment. He tightens the scarf around his neck. "It's all over now, isn't it?"

"Yes, Mr. Stone, it's all over. Over for you and for Altavista. And it will soon be over for Magma Capital Management and for Maximilian and Sabastian Poole. I'll see to that. I promise you."

"You'll never convict the brothers. They're too careful. They have too many friends."

"Their friends won't be able to help them this time. I'm going to take Magma Capital down."

"I don't see how. The brothers spent decades putting together an elaborate system of hidden and interlocking companies. The system is so complex that nobody understands how it works. Even the brothers themselves have probably forgotten the details."

"There must be a weakness in the system somewhere."

"Right now, I'm the chief weakness in the system. I know how it works. I don't expect the brothers to allow that weakness to continue much longer."

"There must be some other vulnerability."

"If I had to name a single weak spot, it would be the Bank of Thessaloniki in Greece. Most of Magma's international financial transactions are funneled through secret accounts in that bank. Of course, all accounts are encrypted and protected by multiple layers of passwords. But if anyone could ever penetrate those accounts, they could be used to destroy Magma Capital. All it's criminal activities would be revealed."

Colin Stone takes a deep breath and adjusts the long red scarf. "It's time for you to go, Detective Zorn. At least for the next few hours, I have some little authority here at Altavista. Very soon the brothers will learn you've been here and they'll come after you. There will be nothing I can do to protect you."

He opens his gold cigarette case. "This was a gift from Harvey many years ago. A gift to me as his best man at his wedding." He takes out a cigarette. "My doctor tells me I should not smoke. It doesn't make much difference now, does it? Might you have a light?"

I take out my lighter. Colin Stone lights his cigarette from the flame and takes a deep drag.

"Before I go," I say, "I have one more question for you. You worked for the Poole brothers for years. You did their dirty work. But today, you betray them. What made you change your mind?"

"When Harvey came to see me and confirmed he was the whistleblower, he reminded me of the company he and I created many years ago. We were supposed to discover new drugs and medications to cure diseases and make people's lives better. His last words to me were: 'This wonderful company we created has now become the Whore of Babylon. Now you're no more than a pimp for the whore.' It was then I fully realized what I had become."

Stone turns away from me. He has nothing more to say. Our meeting is done.

Two armed security guards escort me from the executive office, down the elevator and out onto the campus. When I leave the Altavista building, I pass employees strolling along the broad plaza in front, chatting among themselves.

Suddenly the crowd is frozen in horror. Faces look up. I turn and watch as a man with a long red scarf streaming behind him plunges headfirst, fifty stories to the ground.

This time I can hear the scream.

CHAPTER THIRTY-FIVE

THERE'S A RECEPTION party waiting for me when I arrive at Reagan National Airport. Actually, there are two reception parties. Three men stand near a concession stand in the waiting room, scanning arriving passengers from Chicago. I don't recognize any of them, but I know they're Coldcreek Security. I know the type. They're ready to grab me as soon as I'm well inside the waiting area. There will be others I don't see yet, positioned near the exits to head me off if I make a break for it. If I do, they won't wait to hustle me out of the airport into some waiting van. I'm sure their orders are to dispatch me right there in the airport. They'll take their chances with airport security.

The ones at the concession stand start to move in on me. They're intercepted by my second reception party. Stryker and six heavily armed men who belong to Sister Grace's crew. They block the way, standing between the Coldcreek crew and me. Stryker wears a new porkpie hat.

The Coldcreek contingent hesitates. Stryker and his friends are not part of their game plan. The Coldcreek men stand paralyzed, whispering among themselves. One of them speaks into a radio-phone, I assume to get new orders. Stryker and his group close in and surround me. No one on either side moves and we're at a standoff. I just hope no one draws a gun.

"We can take them down," Stryker says to me softly as he stands at my side.

"Not now. I don't want a gunfight."

Stryker nods and I'm pretty sure we're out of trouble. At least for the moment. The Coldcreek men are mercenaries, employed by the hour. They're not paid enough to die today. Almost in unison, the Coldcreek men break ranks and move away. They head quickly for the exits while they keep a close watch on me and Stryker's team. In a few short minutes, the last one is gone.

"They won't go far," Stryker says. "They'll regroup and try again."

"Then let's get out of the airport. There are too many innocent people here who'll get in the way if there's a shoot-out."

"We've got wheels." Stryker leads me and his men through the concourse, down an elevator to the drop-off and pickup area, where a large SUV and a very old, beat-up Chevy station wagon await us. The wagon must date to the early sixties.

"Did you steal this car?" I ask.

Stryker looks offended. "We don' steal shit like this. It belongs to my brother-in-law. He bought it years ago an' keeps it in his garage. He waitin' till this model becomes a collector's item and the price goes way up. Then he gonna make a killing."

"Don't hold your breath. Your crew take the SUV. You and I take the wagon."

"Do you mind drivin'?" Stryker asks. "I don't know how to use a stick shift."

Stryker's crew gets into the SUV and heads off. Stryker and I climb into the wagon. I take the driver's seat and we head along the George Washington Memorial Parkway toward downtown

Washington. The wagon runs okay. Sort of. There are many strange noises and twinges that make me think the car hasn't been serviced in years.

As we cruise down the parkway along the banks of the Potomac River, I pull into the left lane. Traffic is light in both directions. Ahead, the Washington Monument rises above the city. We're in the clear until Stryker says, "We got company, partner. Behind us on our right."

In the rearview mirror, I see a white Dodge Durango coming at us at high speed, weaving in and out of traffic to catch up with us. I know for certain what'll happen next. They'll pull up alongside our car and open fire. They are almost certainly armed with heavy, rapid-fire weapons that'll tear our ancient wagon to shreds. Not to mention us.

"Hold on, Stryker! We're in for a bumpy ride."

I flick the Chevy station wagon steering wheel slightly to shift the car's balance to the right, jam the clutch down, and shift the gear into second. The Dodge is right on top of us, edging into the right lane, ready to overtake us.

I pull the wagon's steering wheel hard to the left and feel the wagon sway as we slide into a controlled skid. The car's suspension must be made of Miracle Whip. The wagon fishtails and makes a full 180-degree turn. We're now facing the opposite direction, heading back the way we came, toward the airport. In the wrong lane.

I jam the accelerator and pray I don't blow out the transmission. Behind me, I hear screaming breaks and honking horns. And, lost in the noise, probably a lot of angry cursing. Cars and trucks pull off the parkway to avoid collisions. The driver of the Dodge Durango, his face twisted in fury, has pulled past us, and flown off the parkway, moving too fast to stop, and is now rolling out of control over the grass toward the Potomac River.

"Do you see any collisions?" I ask.

"I don' see none. The dudes in the Dodge not so lucky. They in the river now. Hope they know how to swim."

I drive back toward the airport and then switch over toward Crystal City.

"What's that thing you did back there?" Stryker asks, half laughing. "How'd you move the car like that?"

"It's called a 'smuggler's turn'."

"Where'd you learn to do that? Turnin' the car 'round like that?"

"A misspent youth in the back roads of Maine."

As we take the highway toward Washington, we're passed by dozens of Virginia police cars and emergency vehicles going the other way, headed toward the scene of the monster traffic pileup I just created. It'll take them hours to untangle the mess. Not to mention hauling the Durango and its passengers out of the river.

"Go home, Stryker," I say, when we reach my house.

"I got to stay by you, partner. You still in deep trouble."

"I'm going to fix that trouble. Your job is done. Go somewhere safe and keep your head down. The opposition now knows your face and, probably, your identity. They'll come after you. And tell your cousin to get rid of this heap."

CHAPTER THIRTY-SIX

CARLA AND I are ushered into a small interview room by two armed prison guards. I've been in a lot of prisons in my time, including the federal maximum security prison in Colorado. It's usually voluntarily as a visitor. Sometimes not. No matter in what capacity, prisons give me the creeps. When I walk through that outer prison gate and hear the heavy locks close behind me, I can't wait to get out.

U.S. Penitentiary Lewisburg is a typical medium-security prison. You see one, you've seen them all. The same government-issue furniture and dull paint on the walls. The same official notices prohibiting spitting and assault on prison officers. Someone has tried to make the interview room less an institution of punishment by adding some artificial flowers and watercolor prints. The effort is a failure.

"We'll be right outside if there's any trouble," one of our guards announces. "Just give us a shout. We'll be monitoring your interview."

"The prisoner we're here to see is seventy-nine years old," Carla says. "I think between the two of us, we can handle him."

The guard shakes his head. "Don't be fooled. Watch his hands at all times. He's a mean son of a bitch. And he's quick."

There is one man in the room waiting for us, sitting in a large chair, a walker placed in front of him. His white hair is thin and scraggily. He studies us suspiciously as we approach.

"Who's this handsome young man you've brought along with you today, Carla?" the old man demands.

I step forward and stand in front of him. "My name is Marko. Marko Zorn."

"*The* Marko Zorn?"

"There's only one of me."

"God, I hope so," Carla murmurs behind me.

"I don't like cops."

"Am I supposed to be scared? You're in a federal prison, serving two life sentences."

"That's never stopped me before." He holds out a scrawny hand. "My name's William Granger. My friends call me Digger. Maybe you've heard of me. I'm a notorious felon." He smiles. "Carla told me that you want to talk to me. Why should I talk to you?"

"To help Carla and me solve a mystery."

"You mean the Gardner Museum thing? I got nothin' to say about that. You wasted your trip."

"You have nothing to lose, Digger," Carla says. "The statute of limitations has long since expired on the Gardner Museum theft. After all these years, nobody is going to be charged with a crime."

"So why do you care?"

"We want the stolen art found and returned to the museum."

"I told you a hundred times, Carla, I don't know nothing about that."

"And I told you, I don't believe you."

I hitch my chair close to Digger. "You once said to Carla that if you ever revealed the location of the Vermeer painting stolen from the museum, it would mean a death warrant for you. Are you still afraid somebody will get to you?"

The old man is suddenly caught up in a fit of hacking and coughing. He snatches a very soiled, red bandanna from his pocket and holds it to his mouth until the coughing subsides. When he catches his breath, he says, "It's more complicated than that."

"Who you are afraid of?" Carla asks.

"You heard Carla. We're here to help you. How long do you want to live under a death sentence like this?"

"I've lived under a death sentence for over thirty years. You get used to it. You don't understand. These guys are relentless."

"These guys? Which guys are that, Digger? Are we talking about the men who planned and financed the Gardner robbery?"

Digger shrugs impatiently and wipes his mouth with the bandanna.

"Two men who live free and comfortable lives while you rot away here in prison? It was two men, wasn't it? Tell us their names."

"What's in it for me?" Digger asks. "Except a bullet in the back of the head?"

"Carla will give you full protection. And you can become a public hero. You can prove to the world you were the big man."

Digger studies me intently. "How am I supposed to do that?"

"By revealing the secrets of the Gardner Museum robbery. By telling us where the stolen art is hidden. We can get a reporter from the *Boston Globe* here for an interview. Give him your first authentic, exclusive interview where you reveal all. There would be enormous public interest. I can almost guarantee you lots of coverage on social media. Maybe even a book contract. Maybe even a movie option."

Digger sits up straight, his eyes alight. "I don't know," he says.

"There have been many newspaper stories about Whitey Bulger. Even a movie. Why nothing about Digger?"

Digger spits on the floor.

"How come they make movies about Whitey," I ask, "but no movie about you?"

"I was the brains behind the Winter Hill Gang. I did all the planning and the hard work. The movies make Whitey out to be a really cool mobster. But he was nothing. You hear me? Nothing."

"Then tell us what happened," Carla says.

The old man clutches the handle of his walker. "You can arrange an interview? Not the *Globe*. It's got to be the *New York Times*."

"I can arrange that," I say.

"And a book contract."

"That depends on how complete your story is."

"Okay, as long as Carla guarantees me complete protection." He looks at Carla, who nods in agreement, looking pained. Digger coughs again and wipes his lips. "Back in August of 1988, I was part of the Winter Hill Gang. In those days, Whitey Bulger ran the outfit. Somebody, I don't know the name, approached Whitey and offered him a deal. This guy claimed he represented an interested party who wanted to arrange the theft of a certain painting from a museum in Boston. Whitey was never supposed to meet the principals. No one was—except for me, and that was just one time. It was a big operation that would involve a lot of time and planning, and cost money. Whitey and this middleman negotiated a deal and agreed on a payment of two million dollars for the job, including delivery of the painting. That was a lot of money back then. Whitey didn't know zip about stealing stuff from museums. His game back then was extortion. But I had some experience in property theft, so Whitey brought me in on the deal and told me to take over the project. I was to be paid $100,000 for the job."

Digger's face flushes with anger. "$100,000! For a job worth millions! Whitey didn't do anything. It was me. I did all the work. I took all the risks. I never got any credit." Digger spits on the floor. Wipes his mouth with his bandanna. "The papers used to make a big thing of Whitey Burger. The 'crime kingpin of Boston.' Later on, his name was in the papers almost every day. Not just his name. His picture!"

By now Digger is on his feet. He lifts his walker and slams it to the floor. "And not just the local rags. The *New York Times*!" Digger is overcome by his exertions. He falls back into his chair, gasping for breath.

"Calm down, Digger," Carla says.

Digger's not done yet. "Whitey was nothing but he gets all the credit." Digger stops to catch his breath. "They even made a movie about him. With Johnny Depp. Whitey was a fraud. They say he was a big-shot gangster. That's bullshit. It was me that pulled the Gardner deal off. Me. I want Leonardo DiCaprio to play me in the picture."

"Don't get ahead of yourself," I say.

"Did Whitey tell you the names of the principals?" Carla asks.

"I never was told their names. I don't think Whitey knew. And he didn't want to know."

"Did you ever see the principals?"

"I met them once. They wanted to see the face of the man who would carry out the robbery. I figured out later why they wanted to do this. But by then, it was too late. We agreed to meet at this museum in Boston.

"Whitey told me to go to the Dutch gallery in the Gardner Museum at two thirty in the afternoon on June 27 to meet the men financing the job. When I arrived, a couple of private security types checked me for weapons before letting me in. The gallery was empty, except for two men sitting on chairs."

"What did they look like?"

"How the hell do I know? It was thirty years ago. I barely remember what I had for breakfast this morning."

"How old were they?"

"Maybe forty. Older than me."

"Both?"

"They were twin brothers. One was wearing glasses. That one pointed his walking stick at the paintings. 'See that picture? The one with the group of people.' He pointed at a picture of three people standing around some kind of piano or something. They wore old-fashioned clothes. Know what I mean? The man with the stick said, 'I want that painting. I want to be sure you understand which one I must have.'"

"Did you identify yourself?" Carla asks.

Digger wipes his mouth. "Whitey warned me never to give them my real name. If they think you crossed them, cheated or betrayed them, they won't think twice about killing you and everyone in your family. At the end, they both got up at the same time and left the room without a word.

"It took me almost six months to plan and organize the heist. I had to get maps for the layout of the museum, get detailed plans for the security system. I had to recruit a couple of yo-yos to carry out the actual theft. Guys with no police record and no fingerprints on any file anywhere. They had to be completely clean with no Boston connections. I had to find a place to hide the paintings after the robbery. They had to be secured in a space where they would be protected from damage. I was told they had to be stored in very special conditions—exact temperatures and humidity. That kind of thing. I found a storage company in Quincy that met the requirements.

"On the night of the robbery, everything went like clockwork. I collected the paintings from the thieves. I paid them off and told them to get out of town. And never come back. I put the pictures in the storage facility in Quincy. End of story."

"What went wrong?" Carla asks.

"Money. I got greedy. The papers the next day reported this was the largest art robbery in US history. The art was worth over two hundred million dollars. And I was being paid peanuts. I'd done all the work and took all the risks. But I had an ace in the hole. Nobody knew where I hid the art. Not the robbers. Not Whitey. Not the principals.

"The principals threatened to kill me if I didn't tell them where I'd hidden the art. They didn't know who I was, so I figured I was safe.

"A few days later, the middleman was found floating in the Charles River. He'd been tortured before his throat was cut."

"They didn't suspect Whitey?" Carla asks.

"Whitey got out of town. The FBI eventually arrested him in California and brought him back east. He was charged and convicted for multiple murders. No one is safe from those brothers.

"But I thought I was still in the clear. They'd seen me that one time at the museum, but they didn't know my real identity. I kept my head down."

"What happened to change things?" I ask.

"I got arrested and charged with murder. That was very unfortunate. That got my picture in the papers. Something I'd managed to not do for years. One of the brothers must have seen my picture and recognized me, even after so much time. It wasn't even a good picture. They came after me. Or one of their guys did. He even found me in federal maximum-security prison a week or so later."

"This man who came to see you in prison, he said he represented the two brothers?" I ask.

"He made that clear. The brothers wanted their painting. He said if I didn't cooperate, I'd be dead. I told him I'd make a deal."

"What was the name of this man?" Carla asks.

"He didn't have a name."

"Did he have white-blond hair?" I ask.

"Who are you talking about, Marko?" Carla looks at me, angry. "Do you know this man?"

"Our paths have crossed."

"Two days later the same guy shows up in my cell. He said the principals were ready to deal."

"What was the deal this man offered?" I ask.

"He promised there would be no attempts on my life."

"And in return?"

"I was to tell him where I hid the painting. He said they'd even pay me a substantial amount of money as a kind of bonus. We agreed on ten million dollars if we could arrange the transfer quickly."

"I said I need to go through a middleman we both trust. We agreed on a New York art dealer we both had dealt with."

"I need a name," I say.

"Is that really necessary?"

"It's really necessary."

"Zoltan."

"Zoltan Adar?"

"You know him?" Carla looks at me suspiciously.

I don't answer.

"He deals in stolen art," Digger explains. "As soon as the money was safely in my account, I'd tell Zoltan where I'd hidden the paintings."

"Digger," Carla asks. "What are you going to do with the ten million dollars? You'll never leave this prison. I'll see to that. You'll be a wealthy man, but you'll never be able to enjoy it."

Digger sighs. "I wanted those damned brothers to pay for the aggravation they've caused me." Digger turns to me. "I may be safe for a little while longer." Digger looks at me intently. "But you're in real trouble. The word is you're on the brothers' shit list."

"Trust me, Digger, they're on mine, too."

"Forget it. They've got a billion-dollar company behind them. They've got powerful friends. There's nothing you can do to touch them."

"They have one major vulnerability."

"You'll never find their vulnerability."

"I already have. You just told me."

CHAPTER THIRTY-SEVEN

CARLA'S CAR STOPS in front my house. Ever since we boarded the FBI's Gulfstream passenger jet after we left Lewisburg Penitentiary, Carla's been on her phone trying to get some federal employees flayed alive for allowing Hammer to get close to Granger. I'm about to leave the car when she puts her phone away.

"You lied to Digger," she says indignantly. "You made up all that stuff about book contracts and a movie. Give me a break! You're shameless."

"He's a murderer. Do you care?"

Carla bites her lower lip while she thinks of something scathing to say to me. Then, to my utter surprise, she says, "Marko, please be careful."

"I'm always careful."

"This is different. You told Digger you were going after the two men behind the Gardner Museum robbery. Those two men are the Poole brothers."

"I know that."

"The bureau's been after the Poole brothers for years. Every law enforcement agency in the federal government has targeted them. We've never gotten close. They have too much money. They have too many powerful friends. They're very dangerous. If you try to take them on, they'll destroy you. I know you too well. You're an arrogant son of a bitch who thinks he can do anything. This time you're out of your league."

Carla stares at me intently. "Marko, I don't want to see you hurt. Don't be stupid. This time I won't be able to help you."

I climb out of the car. Carla pulls the door shut without looking at me.

I'm in front of my house. But I'm not alone. Parked at the end of the street is a police cruiser, and leaning against the front fender is my partner, Tyrone Clifford. My other partner.

He waves at me and strolls to where I'm waiting. "Have you been slumming? That car you came in looks like a Fed vehicle."

Tyrone is doing his job: trying to find out what I'm up to. I don't intend to make his job easier so I don't answer. Instead, I walk up the steps to my front door. Sitting on the top landing is a cardboard box. My name and address are printed on a label. There is no return address. Just a handwritten note:

"A bottle of Burgundy. In memory of our evening at Romano's. Ann." There are little hearts, written with a red felt marker, floating above my name.

It's heavier than I expected. "Can you give me a hand and open the door for me?"

"I don't have a key," Tyrone answers.

"It's a cyber lock. The number is nine-three-five-seven-eight."

Tyrone punches in the key code and pushes open the door. He follows me into my house. I go to the kitchen and place the box on the black granite kitchen countertop. Tyrone stands at the door, surveying the room.

"Thanks, Tyrone. I'm no longer an employee of the police department. I'm no longer your responsibility."

Tyrone shrugs. "I don't understand about you getting fired. You're one of the stars on the force. Why would the chief do that?" Tyrone hesitates, then turns and leaves. I grab a carving knife. One of those razor-sharp Japanese knives. I pick up the box and shake it gently, my ear pressed against the cover. I hear no sound of any metal but a little bell goes off in my head. No bomb. But there's something not quite right about the package. It doesn't feel like a bottle of wine.

The package has been sealed with heavy packing tape. I cut through the tape and cautiously pull open the thick cardboard cover.

Inside is filled with shredded newspapers.

The shredded newsprint moves furiously. And a snake's head emerges. I swear it's staring at me. With tiny menacing eyes. Its jaws wide open. The inside of the mouth is pitch black. Its fangs glisten. I jerk my hand from the carton and stumble away.

The snake slithers out of the box and onto the granite countertop, then over the edge and onto the kitchen floor. The damn thing is hunting me.

We're about ten feet apart, the snake coiled, its head raised, swaying. I'm in a crouch, clutching the carving knife. I know if I could get to it, I could destroy the snake with my knife. But my enemy moves with lightning speed.

It's coming at me, twisting and coiling. It looks to be about four feet long and is a mottled brown color. I grasp my knife tightly, preparing for a final encounter. Which will leave one of us dead.

There's a gunshot and the snake bursts into two pieces. The two halves twitch for a moment on the tile floor, then lie still. Tyrone stands at the kitchen door, holding a smoking Glock 26, standard-issue police automatic.

"I see it didn't get to you." Tyrone puts his weapon back in his shoulder holster.

"How do you know it didn't get to me?" I'm a bit irritated at what I feel is Tyrone's casual attitude toward my near existential fate.

"If it had struck you, you'd be dead by now. Or pretty close. That's a pit viper. Probably a black mamba. It's one of the deadliest poisonous snakes in the world. It's a juvenile but just the same, deadly. Do you have any heavy plastic bags?"

"In the cabinet next to the microwave." My mouth is dry. "That snake scared the hell out of me."

"The viper was probably just as scared of you as you were of it."

"I seriously doubt that."

"This is now an official murder investigation," Tyrone says. "I'm assigning a number to the incident. When I turn in my report, it will be assigned a case number."

"I know the rules."

"A member of the Homicide team will be given investigative responsibility."

"That will probably be you."

"More than likely. I hope that doesn't cause you any problems."

"Not at all." I examine the carton the snake came in without touching it. There are no indications of how and from where the carton was shipped. Just my address and the note from "Ann." The paper in the box is shredded newsprint.

"Do you know Ann?" Tyrone carefully places the remains of the pit viper into one of the plastic bags.

"A liaison from many years ago," I say. "She was an artist. Very avant-garde. She did 'happenings'. She went to New York and hasn't been heard from since."

"When did you last see this Ann?"

"The last time I saw her was the night before she left Washington. We had dinner together at Romano's."

"The people who sent you this gift must know about your relationship with the lady."

"I vaguely remember that evening. A lot of celebrities go there and there was a photographer from the *Washington Post*. It wouldn't have been hard to track down that picture and find our names. I am known to the managements at the restaurant."

Tyrone carefully wraps the carton in the second plastic bag. "Did you and Ann part on good terms?"

"Do you mean, do I think Ann sent me this snake as some kind of memento? No way. She was an avant-garde artist. She would never do hearts with a red marker. Our affair petered out. And she wasn't the type to carry grudges."

"Just the same, I'll have NYPD ask her a few questions. If you don't mind."

"Go for it."

"If it wasn't your old flame Ann, who do you think sent you this gift? Understand, this was attempted murder. Regardless of your status as a former homicide detective, this must now be investigated by the rules."

"I remember the rules. How come you know about snakes and all that?"

"I minored in zoology in college. I took a class in herpetology for extra credit." Tyrone writes out a description of the items in each plastic bag along with the date, time, and location in his police-issue notebook. "I'll turn these into the forensic lab. I don't expect to learn anything useful. Whoever sent you this present was careful."

Tyrone is standing at the kitchen door.

"Would you like a drink, Tyrone? You saved my life today. Good. That calls for a celebration."

"Thank you, Mr. Zorn. I don't drink."

"In which case, stop calling me 'Mr. Zorn.' My name is Marko."

I accompany Tyrone to the front door and watch him descend the steps.

"Okay, Poole brothers," I say to myself, "now it's personal."

Tyrone stops and turns back. "Did you say something, Mr. Zorn?"

"Nothing. Just thinking aloud."

CHAPTER THIRTY-EIGHT

SHOWTIME!

I lock my front door and check the central monitoring station, including CCTV cameras and motion sensors. Although I can't forget what Carla told me and I make a mental note to upgrade my security system.

I descend to my basement office, where I double bolt the door and check for serpents. I sit at my cluttered desk and start to destroy the Poole brothers and their empire.

"Good afternoon," a soft-spoken, sexy woman's voice greets me. "How may I help you?"

She's one of several thin, attractive assistants, always dressed in severe black, the gallery employs to lubricate potential customers. Offering a glass of sherry, or something stronger if "the gentleman prefers", sometimes with the hint of future sex.

"I want to speak with Mr. Ader," I announce.

"Mr. Ader is with a customer," she says sweetly. "May I be of assistance?"

"Tell Zoltan that Marko Zorn is calling."

"I'm sorry, but Mr. Ader cannot be disturbed." The honeyed tones have disappeared. There is no longer any hint of future romance.

"Tell Zoltan to ditch his customer. I have a question about a missing Vermeer painting and I won't wait."

I hear a faint intake of breath at the other end of the line. Then she says, "I'll see what I can do, Mr. Zorn."

In no more than two minutes, Zoltan Ader is on the line. "Marko, old friend! Cynthia tells me you're calling with a question about a Vermeer painting." There is a moment of silence. "I hear through the grapevine you've been making inquiries about *The Concert*. That was stolen decades ago. It's lost."

I've worked with Zoltan Ader and his Helicon Gallery on Fifty-Seventh Street in New York for a long time. He has helped me buy several of my favorite pieces. These were legitimate deals with authentic provenances. I also know that, for other, very select, clients, and for a price, he handles stolen art objects. He was very nearly caught last year trying to sell objects stolen from the Iraqi National Museum in Baghdad.

"*The Concert* is in the wind, Zoltan," I say.

"It was valued at over two hundred million in 1994 when a broker was last approached. The Vermeer is essentially unsellable. No one could ever exhibit it—not even a Russian oligarch or a Saudi prince. It's too well known to everyone in the art world. Who would pay a penny for a piece of art they could never exhibit?"

"A nearly blind man with lots of money might. Maybe you know of such a person. Were your clients Maximilian and Sabastian Poole?"

"I don't want to talk about them."

"You've done business with them in the past?"

"A few minor *objets d'art*. Everyone in the field knows them. They're major players. Just six weeks ago, I helped in a difficult exchange. Strictly legitimate. One of the brothers insisted on purchasing a suit of armor he'd seen years ago in a museum in Essen,

Germany. I managed to get it for the brothers. It was actually an inferior piece. A mix of different eras and styles. Mostly fourteenth century, but the helm was late fifteenth century. And it came with a double-handled broadsword. Totally inappropriate for that style of armor. It was a bitch to ship and reconstruct. The damn thing weighs a ton."

"What was your role in the Vermeer transfer?"

"Is this being recorded?"

"Of course not. On my honor, this is strictly private, between us."

"I was told where the art stolen from the Gardner Museum was hidden. As a man with an acute sense of public responsibility, I retrieved the art. I brought it here to my gallery for safekeeping."

"The art trove included Vermeer's *The Concert*?"

"I delivered that item to a person representing the buyer."

"And you kept the remaining stolen art for yourself."

"I never claimed I was a saint."

"No one has ever mistaken you for one. The man who picked up the Vermeer from you, did he have white-blond hair?"

There's a heavy sigh at the other end. "Yes."

"One last question. When did this person pick up the painting from you?"

"Ten days ago."

I cut off the connection.

I send a text message to Carla Lowry on her private cell, suggesting she organize a raid on a gallery on Fifty-Seventh Street in New York and look for the art stolen from the Gardner Museum. I ask her to say hello to Digger.

I go into the dark net for my next step. I do a deep dive into the cyber world in search of my usual contact. I hope he's around somewhere and is awake. I have no idea in which time zone he exists, or whether he's in a mood to respond. Sometimes he sulks and refuses to work with me. I'm not even sure if he's still alive. He's unpredictable that way.

After a nerve-wracking silence, he answers. "I'm out of the game. Find someone else. I'm retired."

He calls himself Warlock. I have no idea what his real name is. He uses a mechanism that disguises his voice so I don't know whether he's a man or woman or how old he might be. I've worked with Warlock a number of times. I think he's from Ukraine. Or maybe it's Iran. And he's probably linked somehow to the Russian Intelligence Service. I don't really want to invite the Russians to my party, but sometimes that just can't be helped.

"Why would you retire?"

"Too much competition. The scene is getting rough and danger-ous these days."

"It's only dangerous if they catch you."

"Given the risks, I'm very selective about what projects I accept. For old times' sake, I may consider coming out of retirement for you. One of my kids has just been accepted at Brown and tuition is steep. Just what is it you want done this time?"

"I need you to create serious problems for a certain company."

Warlock pauses. "Name the company."

"Magma Capital Management."

"What's your beef with them?"

"That's none of your business. Can you make the company crash?"

"You're not looking to close down the California power grid or anything naughty like that, right?"

"Certainly not. I just want to make life hell for this one corpo-ration and its owners. Can you do it?"

"That depends on how robust Magma Capital Management's security system is. First, I'd have to find an opening to penetrate

Magma's codes. Then I'd look for programming errors to give me access to their computer network and find an attack vector I can use to get through their security. One that hasn't been patched yet. I don't like doing that anymore. It takes a lot of time and effort and I'm too old for that kind of thing. What would you do if I got in?"

"Make Magma crash."

"You mean what your Pentagon calls D-5? Deny, degrade, disrupt, deceive, and destroy?"

"I like the sound of that. It's got a nice ring to it. Go for D-5."

"That'll cost you."

"The last time I hired you, you got what I wanted for ten thousand dollars."

"Times have changed. There are a lot more actors out there these days, including your National Security Agency and your Defense Department's Cyber Command. Not to mention, their Russian and Chinese and Israeli counterparts. These people gobble up everything in sight, leaving crumbs for the rest of us. They've totally fucked up the free market system."

"What would I get if you were able to breach Magma's security?"

"With luck, whatever you want—source codes, bugs, software glitches, log-in credentials, stolen emails, passwords, usernames. You name it."

"Can you shut down a bank?"

"A piece of cake. I'd just have to create a 'brick' that would deny access to whatever target you want and shut people out of their accounts."

"Go for the Bank of Thessaloniki."

"Do you have any suggestions for weak points in your Magma target I can start with? I need something to help me get initial access."

"There's been a recent transfer of ten million dollars from accounts associated with Poole Charity trust and transferred through Bismarck Moving and Storage Company with an office in Reston, Virginia. The funds were converted to cryptocurrency and from there were transferred through the Bank of Thessaloniki to a secret account."

"I can work with that. I'll need a deposit from you. That'll be $100,000 in crypto."

"$100,000 for a deposit? That's pretty steep."

"The final invoice may be for twice that."

"Once you're inside the system can't you just withdraw funds from the Bank of Thessaloniki and transfer them directly as payment to your own crypto account?"

"That doesn't seem very sportsmanlike. Charging the victim to break in."

"Just do it."

"Very well, but it goes against my better instincts."

"You don't have better instincts."

"I'll pretend I didn't hear that."

"And while you're at it, peel off an additional quarter million and have it deposited to my Malta account."

"That's hardly fair play."

"I'm not playing games."

"Magma Capital should be on the rocks by this afternoon."

CHAPTER THIRTY-NINE

DURING THE DAY, I check news alerts to see if anything shows up about Magma Capital Management, but find nothing significant. I check the *Times* and the *Post* online. The *Times* carries a small item about the death of Colin Stone, the CEO of Altavista, and quotes police sources in Indianapolis characterizing his death as a probable suicide. The story mentions rumors of serious financial problems with Altavista Corporation.

In the early afternoon, Warlock calls. "Good news and bad news. The good news is I've gained access to Magma Capital Management. Your tip about the transfer of ten million dollars through Bismarck Moving and Storage was a help. There are bugs in their antivirus program I was able to exploit and, with that, I now have remote code execution capability."

"What can you do with a remote code?"

"I can construct a Trojan horse and get in through the gates. Within an hour, I'll have complete access to Magma. That means I can make their systems do whatever I want."

"And the bad news?"

"It will cost a bit more than I quoted. I'll need $250,000. Do we have a deal?"

"We have a deal," I say. "Don't forget my share. I want $250,000 deposited to my personal account."

"You have a heart of stone. What do you want me to do with Magma Capital?"

"I want Magma Capital Management and all of its subsidiaries to crash and burn. Their entire system must go dark."

"What else?"

"Magma Capital is owned by two men—Maximilian and Sabastian Poole, who live in Washington. I want their personal accounts frozen."

"Not a problem."

"Cut off their access to their bank accounts. And the Internet. And all phone service."

"You really want to screw these guys, don't you?"

"You bet I do."

"That will be done within the hour."

We close communication, and I return to my kitchen and make myself a double espresso while monitoring the financial news coming in on the TV on my kitchen countertop.

During commercial breaks, I call Tyrone Clifford's cell. I expected him to be doing a follow-up investigation on my snake attack. But all I get is his answering system. I call back, using the official police line and am told Tyrone's away from his desk. I leave a message asking Tyrone to call me as soon as possible.

When I go back to the news, there is now chatter on MSNBC about possible financial problems with Altavista and Magma Capital Management. There's a rumor about some banking crisis in Greece that is interfering with international financial transactions. Magma Capital Management is not listed on the New York Stock Exchange, but Altavista shares are and sales have been suspended. Right on time.

I call Tyrone at two, and again at five. All I get is a voice mail. When I check with the squad room, I'm told he's out of the building and no one knows where he is or when he'll be back.

There's nothing more I can do but wait for Armageddon. I try to read a book but I'm too restless to sit still, so I double-check my security systems for the tenth time.

Magma Capital Management stories are beginning to percolate as some of their smaller subsidiaries make public statements that they're experiencing communications difficulties. One of these is Coldcreek Security, which announces it's discontinuing all security activities worldwide for Magma and its subsidiaries because all their assets have been frozen. By late evening, the Twitter world is aflame with rabid speculation about Magma Capital. Leland Taylor from the *Washington Post* phones three times. I don't take his calls.

My phone rings at nine thirty. The ID shows the caller is Tyrone Clifford.

"Tyrone, I've been trying to reach you all day."

"Sorry. I've been tied up."

"What's happening with the Young and Alsop murder investigations? And what have you learned about that damn snake you executed?"

"I need to talk to you about those. I'm parked in your driveway right now. Can you come out for a couple of minutes? I'll fill you in."

"Why don't you come into the house? I'll get you some coffee."

There's silence on the other end. "Actually, I'm in a bit of a hurry," Tyrone says. "I've got to get back to headquarters. Can you come out and talk to me in the car?"

That's a strange way to get briefed, I think. But what the hell. "Sure," I say. "I'll be right out."

A DC police cruiser is parked in my driveway. Tyrone is in the passenger seat of the cruiser and a man is next to him. I sense something off about this, but I'm impatient to hear what Tyrone has found out about the black mamba. I go down my front steps and around the large yew trees at the end of my drive.

And freeze.

Tyrone and the other man are now out of the cruiser, standing at the rear of the vehicle. The man with Tyrone is no police officer. Hammer is holding a Browning pistol inches from Tyrone's head. Tyrone's face is bruised around the mouth, and one of his eyes is swollen almost shut. He's groggy and having trouble standing straight.

"One false move, cupcake, and I blow your buddy's head off." Hammer speaks with a harsh, raspy voice. Something bad has happened to his trachea and epiglottis. I'm pretty sure I'm the bad thing that happened.

I hold my hands up in a sign of truce. "Tyrone's got nothing to do with you and me, Hammer. Let him go." My words, I know, are pointless. Hammer's not going to let anyone go.

Tyrone looks tense but not panicked. There's two of us and only one of the opposition. But Hammer has an automatic pistol and I know he's prepared to use it—even on my peaceful residential street. And if one of my neighbors should happen to pass by and look up at the wrong time? He'd kill my neighbor without hesitation. Or a curious child.

The odds don't look so good now.

"If I had my way," Hammer rasps, "I'd blow you both away right now. But the brothers insist on speaking with you. They stressed that I bring you back alive and intact.

"Now, this is the way it's going down. You stay where you are. If you move, you're dead. I'll just make my excuses to the brothers. Officer Clifford here will climb into the trunk. Then you and I will take a little drive. Clear? I want no misunderstanding on this."

Hammer grabs Tyrone's arm and drags him to the back of the cruiser. He pops open the trunk.

"No way I'm getting in there," Tyrone yells. His lips are swollen from the beating and he's having a hard time speaking clearly.

Hammer waves his gun at Tyrone.

"Hell no! I'm not doing it," Tyrone yells.

"Have it your way, sonny." Hammer slams Tyrone's head with the butt of the Browning. Hard.

Tyrone's knees buckle and he drops to the ground. I start to move toward him, but Hammer waves me away. Tyrone's left arm twitches. I breathe again. Tyrone's not dead, but I know he's been hurt.

"There was no need to do that," I say. "You didn't need to smash his head."

Hammer steps away from Tyrone's body. "Now you do it. You put your buddy in the trunk." Hammer speaks in a hoarse whisper.

"He needs medical attention."

"Who cares?"

"He's probably bleeding on the brain. He has a concussion. He needs to see a doctor."

Hammer moves away from Tyrone and stands ten feet from the cruiser. He stays safely out of my reach, but within easy range with his gun. He motions with the Browning toward the open trunk. I take Tyrone's limp body by the shoulders and haul him to his feet. Manipulating a limp body into a car trunk is always a challenge.

I'm disappointed not to find a twelve-gauge shotgun stored in the cruiser's trunk. All I see is a spare tire, some old city maps, a tire jack, and a Kevlar bulletproof body vest. The tire jack is heavy and

I consider for a moment throwing it at Hammer. But he's too far away and I'd almost certainly miss.

"Move it! We're in a hurry. The brothers are not patient."

I make Tyrone as comfortable as I can among the debris. He's breathing, but it's shallow. I don't know how long he's got.

"Now get into the driver's seat." Hammer slams the trunk shut.

Hammer stands behind me, his gun pointed at my head. He's close enough that he won't miss if he shoots, but he's too far away for me to reach him.

"Get in behind the steering wheel."

I do as he says. Hammer gets into the rear seat and holds his Browning pressed hard against the back of my head.

"The keys are in the ignition," Hammer says. "Start the vehicle and back out of the drive. Very slow. Nice and easy."

It's dark now and no one is out observing us at this hour. No one is walking their dog or grabbing a late smoke. Thank God.

"Go to Connecticut Avenue and drive north. No funny stuff. I don't have a sense of humor. Stay under the speed limit."

We drive like this for half an hour. Hammer is using standard evasion tactics and does not relieve the steady pressure of the gun at the back of my head. Once he's satisfied we're not being followed, he has me drive across town on Military Road to Sixteenth Street and we come to the gates to the Poole mansion.

This time there are no armed guards waiting. There's nobody here at all as I drive along the wide, leaf-strewn driveway toward the great house. All the Coldcreek Security guards have disappeared. They walked off work, I suppose, when told they wouldn't get paid. There's no point in getting killed for free.

As we approach, the mansion looks more forlorn and creepier than last time. I see no lights anywhere as we circle around the abandoned, leaf-filled fountain. This place is dead.

I park at the bottom of the front steps. Hammer gets out and stands a safe distance from the cruiser and from me. "Get out of the vehicle. Slowly. Open the trunk. Get your buddy out and bring him into the building."

I pop the trunk and reach in to get hold of Tyrone. I can see he's conscious now. He's still dizzy but can move on his own. He stands, a bit wobbly.

"You okay, Tyrone?" I ask.

"I've been better."

"Shut up, you two. No talking. Go up the steps and into the building."

Tyrone stumbles and I grab his arm to steady him. I help him up the front steps. I cautiously push the door open.

"You know the way, Detective," Hammer yells. "Go."

Tyrone and I step into the long, dark corridor. This time, there's no light at all. Hammer switches on his cell phone flashlight. I can see faint images of myself and Tyrone in the blotchy mirrors hanging on the wall. The corridor remains cluttered with trash. I bump into the Schwinn bike that leans against the wall. We both stumble and I grab Tyrone by the arm.

"When I say 'go'," I whisper to Tyrone, "drop to the floor and roll away as fast as you can. Drop and roll."

Hammer is too far away to hear what I said. I just hope Tyrone is not too punch-drunk to understand what I'm telling him to do.

"I said no talking," Hammer growls.

We move cautiously down the hall. Tyrone has regained his footing and balance a bit and manages to walk on his own. We hesitate at the door at the end of the corridor.

"Keep moving." Hammer is right behind us. I push open the door and Tyrone and I enter.

The vast room before me is dark, except for a little street light streaming through the French doors. I can make out the heaps of boxes and debris. I hear, just barely, shallow breathing from somewhere not far from me.

Hammer pokes me in the back with his gun. "Move it, sport." I step into the room.

To my right is the grand piano. Even in the semidarkness I can just make out Vermeer's *The Concert* lying on the piano lid.

"Don't dawdle." Hammer jabs me in the back and we move farther into the room.

None of us can see much. That gives me a chance. But darkness provides an advantage to the blind man in the dark, waiting for me. I see the dim glow of a lit cigarette and a figure seated in a wheelchair ten feet away.

"Good evening, Officer Zorn," an ancient voice croaks from out of the dark. That would be Sabastian. The guy with the shotgun.

"Why did you bring me here?"

"Are you responsible for the disaster that has happened to Magma Capital Management? Are you responsible for disrupting our companies?"

There's a hoarse laugh from another part of the room. That must be Maximilian. The odds are now three of them against the two of us. Not that Tyrone can be much help in his condition. "Our companies are in ruins," Maximilian says. "Our credit is frozen. We can't move our assets. Our most reliable and trusted employees have vanished. Our communications have been cut off. We have no Internet access. We don't have electric power. You, I believe, are responsible for all that. I demand you fix this disaster you made."

"When I was last here, I made you an offer. Stop selling Neuropromine and Speedball and I'd leave you alone. You refused my offer. That was stupid."

"If you don't tell us how to fix the mess you made, you will die."

I reconstruct the topology of the room from my last visit—the heaps of old newspapers, the mattress boxes, the grand piano, the man in armor, the narrow paths winding through the heaps of trash. I think I have Sabastian's location clearly fixed. If Maximilian hasn't moved from where he sat in his velour armchair last time, I have a general idea where he is as well. I'll have to get him to speak again in order to fix his location more precisely. That leaves Hammer, who's mobile.

Sabastian coughs a dry smoker's cough. I think I hear him suck a deep breath of oxygen from his canisters. I move, very slowly and in silence.

"We can make you a very rich man if you help us," Sabastian says.

"Sabastian, you're a damn fool." It's Maximilian. I know his position now for certain. "This policeman can't be bought."

"Anybody can be bought. We must salvage the company."

Now I've located them both. I just need to get rid of Hammer without putting Tyrone at risk.

"This man, Zorn, will never tell us what he has done," Maximilian shouts. "Not without inducement. Mr. Hammer, did you bring Detective Zorn's partner?"

"Affirmative, sir."

"Mr. Zorn, tell us what you did and how to fix it within the next five minutes. If we do not get a satisfactory explanation in that time, Mr. Hammer will have to kill your partner. Is that clear, Mr. Hammer?"

"Affirmative, sir."

"And then you may kill Zorn as well."

I crouch down, making myself as invisible as possible in the dim light, and move farther into the room, away from Hammer, careful not to bump into anything.

"Mr. Hammer," Maximilian calls out from the dark. "The police-man's on the move."

"Stop him, Mr. Hammer," Sabastian screams. There's a shot from somewhere in the dark. I see a muzzle flash. From the sound, I make the weapon to be a .38. This must be Sabastian who is only a few yards away. I think I hear the round strike a heavy carton, maybe six feet to my right. Now I've got two armed guys after me. Swell.

"Sabastian, stop shooting." It's Maximilian calling from across the room. "You'll kill the wrong man. Mr. Hammer, use your light. Find him."

Immediately the light beam of Hammer's cell phone sweeps the room. I catch sight of Maximilian in his armchair, then Sabastian in his wheelchair surrounded by oxygen canisters, holding a lit cigarette in one hand and a revolver in the other. Then the brothers, too, disappear as Hammer spots me and fires wildly. I duck behind a shoulder-high stack of *National Geographic* magazines.

"You've lost him," Sabastian whines. "I told you we should have killed the policeman when he was here last time."

I watch as the light beam sweeps around the room, searching for me. Hammer is now standing about ten feet from me, just on the other side of the man in armor. I move silently and crouch behind a waist-high heap of cardboard boxes containing newspapers.

There's a shot aimed at where I was a moment ago. This is a differ-ent gun, fired from where Maximilian sits in the armchair.

I edge toward the center of the room, careful not to run into the heaps of trash. I know I've got to keep moving. Hammer has a gun and I now know Sabastian and Maximilian are both armed and prepared to shoot—wildly.

"Mr. Hammer," Maximilian shouts, "the policeman is on the move again."

Damn, he has good hearing.

Somewhere a gun is fired. From where I'm crouching, I can't see the muzzle flash, but I sense it was fired from about ten feet away and to my right. That must be Sabastian again.

Maximilian makes a barking laugh.

I move quickly. There's another shot but I can't tell where it comes from.

"Mr. Hammer, he's near you. Shoot him," Maximilian screams.

"I don't know where he is, sir," Hammer yells back.

The bright light sweeps around the room. I've located Hammer but, before I can move, the light finds me.

"Shoot the damn policeman, Mr. Hammer," Sabastian screams.

There's a wild shot from somewhere. I keep moving. Hammer is having a hard time holding his cell phone and aiming his weapon accurately.

"Idiot!" Sabastian screams. "You've lost him. Don't let him get away!" I hear the creaking sound of the wheelchair moving.

Through a gap between two large cartons, I see a small flame. Sabastian's face appears, illuminated by a flaring match as he lights a cigarette.

Hammer aims the flashlight so it's shining directly at where I'm crouching.

I move quickly. There's another shot and I hear a round strike the case of the piano. The strings zing discordantly. I hope he hasn't shot a hole in the priceless Vermeer.

Hammer switches off his light. He must be afraid it will give away his location and I'll jump him. I hear a squeak as Sabastian moves his wheelchair. He must sense my location because he's moving toward me in the dark. There's a shot from across the room not far from the French windows. A round tears through a crate near my head. This has to be Maximilian. The damn fool is firing blind—literally. He's depending on his acute hearing to locate me. That means I now have three shooters in the room with me, shooting in the dark. It's the O.K. Corral and the Clanton Gang moving in on me.

Sabastian fires again. God knows what he's shooting at. The air is now filled with the smell of gunpowder.

"Stop shooting, Brother Sabastian!" This is Maximilian yelling. "We'll kill each other. Mr. Hammer, turn on your light."

Hammer's light switches on again and its beam for the moment is aimed at the ceiling. Hammer swings the light around the room, searching for me.

There's another volley of small-arms fire. Then a piercing groan from the far side of the room.

"Brother Sabastian, you fool!" Someone gasps.

Hammer swings the flashlight beam toward Maximilian. He's slumped in his velour armchair, his thin chest covered in blood. "Sabastian, you killed me," Maximilian groans.

I race through the room, weaving in and out among the heaps of junk and debris until I reach the man in armor. Hammer must sense my movement and follows me, crashing into boxes as he does.

"You can't escape," Sabastian yells, then he is caught in a fit of coughing. "He's near you, Mr. Hammer. Finish him off. Now!"

"What about Brother Maximilian?" Hammer demands. I can sense he's close to me—just beyond the man in armor.

"Forget Maximilian. Kill the policeman!"

Somebody fires. Two times. I hear the clang as the rounds strike the armor of the massive figure standing in front of me.

The light from Hammer's cell is moving in on me. Hammer's a few feet away now, on the other side of the iron man. I can see his shape coming toward me.

"I've got him, Mr. Poole," Hammer yells. He's almost on top of me. I reach out and feel the cold steel of the broadsword clutched in the iron gauntlet of the man in armor. I grab the handle and yank it free. It's heavy and I have to grip it with both hands and I almost lose my balance as I swing toward where I think Hammer is stepping around the knight in armor.

Hammer grunts as the sword strikes him somewhere in the upper chest area. I sense him stumble backward into the dark maze and hear the sound of metal striking the floor. I think he's dropped his gun and cell phone. He's now groping around in the dark trying to find them.

I don't think I cut Hammer when I hit him. The blade of the sword is not sharp. It was never intended to cut or stab. It was meant to hack and so hack I do. Hammer scrambles away to avoid the heavy blows from the sword.

He twists out from under the sword blows. Then he's on his feet, towering over me. He's holding something in his hand, but it's too dark to see what. Hammer swings and whatever it is he's holding hits me upside my shoulder. The object's large and hard and heavy. I stumble back and almost fall and lose my grip on the sword. I figure he's hit me with a heavy log from the fireplace.

I move back, almost tripping on the iron man's feet. Hammer swings again, but I parry the blow with my sword.

"Do you have him?" Sabastian wheezes from somewhere in the dark.

"Affirmative, sir."

"Stop dawdling, Mr. Hammer."

I regain my balance just in time to avoid being hit again by the log. I get a firm grip on my broadsword and swing at him again. He grunts loudly as I hit him, I think, in mid chest. My aim isn't good, but at this close range, I don't need accuracy. The sword is so heavy it would probably bring an ox to its knees.

I can just make out Hammer trying to get his breath as he crouches on the other side of the man in armor. I push at the iron man as hard as I can. For a second, it teeters on its base, then falls to the floor with a deafening, metallic crash. I hear Hammer scream, buried beneath the mass of chain mail and iron.

"Didn't anybody ever tell you?" I call out. "Never bring a gun to a sword fight."

I dash for the door to the room, crashing into cartons and piles of newspapers and junk on my way, not caring about the sounds I make.

"Go!" I yell as loud as I can. Did Tyrone hear me? Did he understand what he's supposed to do?

I stumble on the row of oxygen tanks and I'm almost on top of Sabastian in his wheelchair. He's clutching the shotgun in his shaking hand. Nothing will stop this guy, I think. Although it's too dark to aim the damn blunderbuss accurately, it can still do a lot of damage at such short range.

"That's as far as you go, policeman," Sabastian gasps.

I snatch up one of the steel oxygen canisters, ready to throw it at Sabastian. The damn fool shoots and the round hits the canister. I feel the canister jolt violently in my hands as the slugs tear through the steel. There's the sound of compressed oxygen escaping from the hole the slug made.

I pull my lighter from my pocket and flick it alight. In the dim flair, I can see Sabastian's pinched face sucking on his oxygen tube.

"Drop your gun, Sabastian, or I toss the lighter into the room."

Sabastian is not so gone he doesn't understand what that would do to us. He lowers his shotgun.

"Tyrone," I call.

"Right behind you," Tyrone gasps.

I grab Tyrone's arm and we make a dash for the door to the corridor. As we pass the piano, I reach out with my one free hand and snatch the painting. I hope I have the right picture. In the dark, I can't tell. There are two wild shotgun shots fired at us from behind. Then I feel a hot blast as I slam the door to the great room closed behind us.

I hear and feel the sound of seventy years of accumulated newspapers and trash and rubbish going up in flames, ignited by Sabastian's shotgun muzzle flash, accelerated by the pure oxygen in the room.

Tyrone is stumbling so I push—almost carry him—to the front door, holding the painting under my arm. We're barely out on the steps when the door to the large room that I just closed behind us explodes in flame. Tyrone and I stumble down the front steps and dive into the dead garden beyond. Flames are pouring from the windows on the ground floor, and I can feel the heat on my back as we race along the driveway. By the time we get to the front gates, the entire mansion is in flames.

Tyrone leans against one of the gate pillars while I dial 911. "Ambulance needed. Police officer badly injured. And send a fire engine. There's a house on fire." I give the street address. Not that the fire brigade will do any good.

Tyrone and I stumble across the street and stand in somebody's front lawn, watching the Poole mansion go up in flames.

"Emergency medical crew is on the way," I say to Tyrone.

"What's that you're carrying?" he asks, pointing to the painting in my hand.

"Just a souvenir." It's too dark to see what I've got. I hear distant sirens. We watch to see whether anybody comes out of the burning mansion. What's the point? No one is going to escape that inferno.

Ten minutes later, a fleet of fire trucks and ambulances arrives. While the emergency medical personnel take care of Tyrone, I move out of their way to give them room. The fire trucks drive through the iron gates and disgorge the first responders who rush toward the mansion, now engulfed in flames, dragging fire hoses. The air is by now filled with ash and smoke that stings my eyes.

A few minutes later, a figure in full fire department rig approaches me. It's DC Fire Department Chief Collins, the same person who was in charge of the car fire investigation I spoke with at the first crime scene.

"Are you here to investigate a murder?" she asks me.

"There's been no murder here, as far as I know. It's just a terrible accident."

"Let's hope so." Chief Collins examines my face closely. "You aren't by any chance a firebug, are you? You know, a guy who likes fires. Someone who likes fires so much he sometimes sets fires."

"Me? No way. Personally, I'm afraid of fires."

"I'm glad to hear that. In the future, if there's a suspicious fire, I don't want to see you anywhere around the neighborhood."

CHAPTER FORTY

ONCE INSIDE MY HOUSE, I turn on my central monitoring system and retreat to my basement office. Using plastic gloves, I lay the canvas on my desk. I have it! I got the right one.

It had been removed from its frame but is still on its original stretchers.

My eyes water a little as I gaze at the exquisite object spread out before me. I sit for I don't know how long just looking at it. I want coffee, but the thought of spilling coffee on a painting estimated to be worth more than two hundred million dollars makes me hesitate. That's all I'd need to wrap up a perfect day. To ruin a priceless piece of art.

The painting is small, almost a miniature, and depicts a young woman seated at a harpsichord. Meanwhile, a second woman is singing, and a man, his back to the viewer, is playing a lute. A viola da gamba lies on the floor near the group. Bright sunlight floods the room, from a window to the viewer's upper left. As usual in Vermeer's work, there's a sharp contrast between the bright areas lit by sunlight and the shadows. This contrast is reflected in the black and white marble floor. The room seems to be large, unlike many of Vermeer's interiors, which are often small and intimate. This is the home of a wealthy family.

I switch on a bright desk light and examine the canvas closely. There are some small signs of damage, all recent and probably from the period it was in the hands of the thieves. I see some signs of older damage that has been professionally repaired, probably dating back to when it was on display at the Gardner Museum. The varnish needs cleaning. It's a bit cloudy with dirt and the normal effects of age. When cleaned or replaced, the bright spots, such as the skirt and sleeve of the girl at the harpsichord and the white marble on the floor, would pop. But the canvas is in good condition, considering what it has been through over the last thirty or so years.

I can't deny I feel a powerful urge. There's nothing to prevent me from just keeping this exquisite object for myself. Nobody has a clue about its fate. Even if it were traced to the home of Sabastian and Maximillian Poole, it would be assumed it was destroyed in the conflagration. It could never be traced to me.

The painting has been in my home. I've viewed it alone. I've touched it. That's more than most people ever have, or ever will have. But it deserves to be seen by everyone, and should not be hidden away in my safe to be taken out and admired by me alone on special occasions.

I don't know how long I sit at my basement desk, admiring the painting. Struggling with my conscience. Maybe the transfer can wait until tomorrow. Another day or two won't make any difference to the world. Or maybe even the next day. It's almost dawn before my conscience wins out.

I put in a call and send for a courier I know and trust. I wrap the painting in several layers of heavy cardboard. On the outside I write "Carla Lowry, FBI, 935 Pennsylvania Avenue, NW. EXTREMELY FRAGILE. To be delivered to Carla Lowry in person."

I give no sign of the sender or a return address. She'll know.

Once I've placed the package into the hands of my courier, I return to my sanctum and place a call.

"Harlon Vine, Drug Enforcement Administration," a voice answers.

"Good morning, Harlon. Marko Zorn calling. Sorry to bother you so early in the morning, but I have information you must have. You told me that your agency thought Speedball is manufactured in a facility abroad. Have your agents in Mexico check out a fertilizer plant outside of San Cristobal. I don't have a name, but it's a subsidiary of Magma Capital Management. It won't be hard to find. The plant has a sideline producing illegal drugs, including Speedball. Call the Mexican authorities and have them shut down the plant."

"I'll get on it right away. Marko, where'd you get this information?"

"Sorry. Gotta go. I've got another call coming in."

It's Leland Taylor. "Are you watching the news, Marko?"

"I haven't even had my coffee."

"Turn your TV on. There's a major story about Magma Capital Management breaking in Chicago." He hangs up and I turn on the TV. The story is on every channel.

A crowd of reporters are milling around on the street, shouting questions. Standing in front of a set of massive double doors of an office building is Rebecca Poole with several men in dark suits hovering behind her. It's downtown Chicago. It looks like somewhere on State Street, near the river.

Ms. Poole holds up her hand in a call for silence. "There is nothing more I can tell you about the tragic deaths of my uncles, Sabastian and Maximilian Poole, besides that they perished in a fire last night in Washington, DC. Local authorities there are investigating the event. All questions must be directed to them."

More questions are hurled at her.

"The problems that have affected Magma Capital Management in the last few hours are being looked into. Our IT team is investigating the intrusion and have concluded it was an act of deliberate cyber sabotage. I can guarantee it will all be set right within days. The finances of Magma Capital are sound. I have no comment on the story that several millions of dollars from Magma Capital's reserves have been stolen from a bank in Greece. The appropriate authorities are looking into that. I assure you Magma Capital Management will be back in business by the end of the week.

"The breakdown in the financial system has nothing to do with the wild, unsubstantiated rumors that one of our subsidiaries is involved in the production of a dangerous narcotic drug. I have personally directed that the product in question be taken off the market.

"The welfare of our customers is the highest priority for all our companies. Mr. Forest, the CEO of Magma Capital Management, has resigned this morning at my request. He will be replaced by somebody in whom I have full confidence. I owe that to the memories of my two beloved uncles. They were my family. They raised me as if I were their own child. I will not tolerate the names of these beautiful men to be sullied by unfounded rumors."

Like their own child? Yeah, right, I think.

There is another pause while Ms. Poole listens to a shouted question. "If the rumor is true that a member of the Washington, DC police department was at the scene of this tragic event last night, I will personally see that individual is tracked down and punished. I am directing Coldcreek Security to investigate the claim."

She looks intently into one of the cameras. Is she looking at me?

Another shouted question. "Yes, I have heard reports that the body of a third man was found by the DC fire department. I can confirm that the man's name was Hammer. We believe he was an agent of Duncan Forest. Hammer has a long criminal record and may have been in the house to harm my uncles."

I sit up straight. What's going on here? The name Hammer has never been disclosed publicly. Not even in confidential police files. How in hell does she know about Hammer? There's only one way. If he worked for her. Rebecca Poole turns away from the crowd of newsmen and disappears through the double doors, followed by her entourage.

I sit breathless and stare for a long minute at the TV screen, which is now showing newspersons commenting on what just happened.

I realize I've just been conned. By a real professional. Rebecca Poole has been lying to me all along—probably from the moment we first met. This is a long con and I'm the mark. This woman who I took to be a guileless ingénue has just taken me for a ride. Big-time.

She told me she despised her two uncles and now I'm supposed to believe they were beloved members of her family. If she was lying about that, what else was she lying about? Colin Stone said the illegal transfer of funds was done through the Pooles' charity trusts. Who runs the Pooles' charity trusts? Rebecca Poole.

Rebecca is a graduate of Bryn Mawr. What has education come to these days? What do they teach their girls? How to construct a bomb using ingredients from your home kitchen? The proper knife to use for an assassination? How to run an international drug cartel? Poisonous snakes of the world?

Rebecca Poole is telling the truth about one thing, though: she will find out I was involved in her uncles' deaths, and when she does, she'll come after me.

Come and get me, lady. I'll be waiting for you.

I decide I need fresh air to clear my head. I go out into my front yard. Many of my neighbors are walking their dogs or are out with children this morning. Some wave at me cheerfully.

Standing at the foot of the steps is Stryker.

"Good morning, Stryker. Come on in. Have some coffee."

"Thank you, Detective. I've got to hurry. I promised Prophet Divine I'd go to church for choir practice."

"Congratulations. I'm happy to hear you have mended your ways."

"I never said that. I thought you should know that Dr. Love has disappeared. He didn't show up at his usual places. His backup enforcers are gone. Sister Grace says to thank you. Looks like Speed-ball is off the streets."

"Don't celebrate yet, Stryker. The source may be closed down for now, but there's a lot of poison in the pipeline. Sorry to say, you'll still have problems for a while. There will be new distributors and new dealers selling new drugs with new names very soon."

"Sister Grace knows how to take care of street dealers. As long as they don' have heavy backup like Speedball had. We can manage on our own." A police cruiser pulls up in front of my house. "Gotta get to church, Mr. Zorn."

"Before you go, I have a question for you. What is your name?"

"You know my name, Detective. It's Stryker."

"I mean your real name. The name your mama gave you."

Stryker looks uncomfortable. After a moment of silence, he says. "Roosevelt. Roosevelt Davis. It was a pleasure working with you."

I'm cautious about the police cruiser and its occupant that are pulling up as Stryker disappears. I consider returning into my house and taking refuge in my fortress. But I'm too late. The passenger door opens and Police Chief Kelly Flynn steps into the street. She's dressed in jeans and a loose blouse decorated with a floral print. She consults with the uniformed police driver who then drives off. Flynn walks up my front steps, waving at me.

"I've just come from George Washington University Hospital," she tells me. "I visited with Tyrone. The doctors tell me he was badly beaten and suffered a major head injury, but he'll be okay. He'll be on medical leave for some time, though. I'll see about getting you a replacement."

"Don't be in a hurry."

"I listened to Rebecca Poole's press conference on the radio coming here. Do you know her?"

"We've met a couple of times."

"What's your assessment of her?"

"She serves good wine."

"Do you think she was involved in the marketing of Speedball?"

"Ms. Poole was deeply involved. I'm now convinced she's been running the whole show at Altavista Corporation. I couldn't prove any of that in court but I have no doubt."

"Do you think she knows what happened at the Poole mansion last night? And your involvement? Whatever that was."

"I'm pretty sure she'll find out."

"That means she's not finished with you."

"Once she gets Magma Capital Management on its feet again and reconstructs the organization, including her security network, she'll come for me."

"If you ever need my help . . ."

"I can take care of myself."

Chief Flynn looks dubious. "Did what happened last night have anything to do with the abduction of my daughter? Or the financial collapse of Magma Capital Management?"

"I don't think you really want to know the details."

"According to the DC fire department, last night's fire was a terrible accident, and yet one of the victims died of a gunshot, one was crushed beneath a suit of armor, and one was blown up."

"Must have been quite a party."

"The entire house was one enormous firetrap. The fire marshal is surprised it didn't go up in flames years ago. Some good news. The FBI has informed me the missing paintings from the Gardner Museum robbery have been recovered."

"How is Angie?" I ask, hoping to change the subject.

"She doesn't seem to have suffered any trauma from her experience on the oil rig. She's young and she's tough. I've packed Angie off to stay with her father in Austin. Until she gets over her current obsessions."

"I didn't know she had obsessions."

"She told me she's in love with you."

"I'm certain it's not serious."

"Do you remember what Lady Caroline Lamb said when she first met Lord Byron? She described him as 'Mad, bad, and dangerous to know.'"

"And you think that description fits me?"

"Like a glove."

"You think I'm Lord Byron?"

"Worse. Lord Byron was never involved with a criminal drug syndicate or the destruction of stately mansions."

"As I recall the story, Lady Caroline promptly went to bed with Lord Byron soon after they met."

"Some women don't have the sense of a flea. I'm keeping Angie far away from you."

"Thank you, ma'am."

"I came here today to tell you that I will reinstate you in the Washington Metropolitan Police Force, effective tomorrow. Frank

Townsend will have your shield and paperwork ready for you. And your service weapon. Please don't lose it this time. And you can drop the ma'am. Call me Kelly. At least when we're not in the office."

"Kelly it is, then."

"But it's much too fine a day to talk shop, don't you think?" Flynn studies a twig on one of my azalea bushes. "You told me you drive a motorcycle, Marko."

"When I have good company."

"What kind of bike do you drive?"

"A Harley Road Glide touring bike."

"Outstanding. It sounds like a real beast."

"It is."

"I let my driver go and I'll need a ride home. I don't suppose your bike has a bitch seat?"

"Of course it does. I like company when I go places. Would you like to see the bike?"

"I'm counting on it."

I take the chief to the parking garage beneath my house. She studies a row of seven motorcycle helmets hanging on hooks, each a different color. She takes a bright, shiny red helmet. I take my usual black one and I wheel the Harley out onto the street.

"Get on," I say. "Let's see if this thing works."

I climb onto the bike and start the engine. Chief Flynn straps on her helmet. She slips onto the passenger seat behind me and wraps her arms around my waist.

"Am I holding you too tight?" she asks.

"Just right," I say.

"Where are we going?" she asks.

"Let's see where this takes us."

NOTE FROM THE PUBLISHER

We trust that you enjoyed *Firetrap*, the third novel in the Marko Zorn Series.

While the other two novels stand on their own and can be read in any order, the publication sequence is as follows:

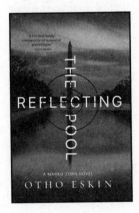

The Reflecting Pool (Book 1)

Washington, D.C. politics at its most savage and brutal—with Marko Zorn in the crosshairs of the White House and competing D.C. gangs.

"In *The Reflecting Pool*, Eskin has created the best crime hero this side of Michael Connelly's Harry Bosch."

—Jon Land,
USA Today best-selling author

Head Shot (Book 2)

D.C. homicide detective Marko Zorn is assigned to protect the beautiful visiting prime minister of Montenegro when they are targeted by the most lethal and elusive assassin on the planet.

"An authentically nail-biting thriller—I could not turn the pages fast enough. *Head Shot* is instantly cinematic—and completely entertaining!"

—Hank Phillippi Ryan,
USA Today best-selling author

We hope that you will read the Marko Zorn Series and will look forward to more to come.

If you liked *Firetrap*, we would be very appreciative if you would consider leaving a review. As you probably already know, book reviews are important to authors and they are very grateful when a reader makes the special effort to write a review, however brief.

For more information, please visit the author's website:
www.othoeskin.com

Happy Reading,
Oceanview Publishing
Your Home for Mystery, Thriller, and Suspense